Y0-AER-189

NOVELS BY ELLERY QUEEN

The Roman Hat Mystery
The French Powder Mystery
The Dutch Shoe Mystery
The Greek Coffin Mystery
The Egyptian Cross Mystery
The American Gun Mystery
The Siamese Twin Mystery
The Chinese Orange Mystery
The Spanish Cape Mystery
Halfway House
The Door Between
The Devil to Pay
The Four of Hearts
The Dragon's Teeth
Calamity Town
There Was an Old Woman
The Murderer Is a Fox
Ten Days' Wonder
Cat of Many Tails
Double, Double
The Origin of Evil
The King Is Dead
The Scarlet Letters
The Glass Village
Inspector Queen's Own Case
The Finishing Stroke
The Player on the Other Side

BOOKS OF SHORT STORIES BY ELLERY QUEEN

The Adventures of Ellery Queen
The *New* Adventures of Ellery Queen
The Case Book of Ellery Queen
Calendar of Crime
Q.B.I.:
Queen's Bureau of Investigation

EDITED BY ELLERY QUEEN

Challenge to the Reader
101 Years' Entertainment
Sporting Blood
The Female of the Species
The Misadventures of Sherlock Holmes
Rogues' Gallery
Best Stories from *EQMM*
To the Queen's Taste
The Queen's Awards, 1946
Murder by Experts
The Queen's Awards, 1947
Twentieth Century Detective Stories
The Queen's Awards, 1948
The Queen's Awards, 1949
The Queen's Awards, 5th Series
The Literature of Crime
The Queen's Awards, 6th Series
The Queen's Awards, 7th Series
The Queen's Awards, 8th Series
Ellery Queen's Awards: 9th Series
Ellery Queen's Awards: 10th Series
Ellery Queen's Awards: 11th Series
Ellery Queen's Awards: 12th Series
Ellery Queen's 13th Mystery Annual
Ellery Queen's 14th Mystery Annual
Ellery Queen's 1960 Anthology
Ellery Queen's 15th Mystery Annual
Ellery Queen's 1961 Anthology
Ellery Queen's 16th Mystery Annual
Ellery Queen's 1962 Anthology
The Quintessence of Queen
To Be Read Before Midnight
(17th Mystery Annual)
Ellery Queen's 1963 Anthology
Ellery Queen's Mystery Magazine (23rd Year)

CRITICAL WORKS BY ELLERY QUEEN

The Detective Short Story
Queen's Quorum
In the Queens' Parlor

UNDER THE PSEUDONYM OF BARNABY ROSS

The Tragedy of X
The Tragedy of Y
The Tragedy of Z
Drury Lane's Last Case

The Player on the Other Side

The PLAYER *on the*

———————————

OTHER SIDE

Ellery Queen

RANDOM HOUSE New York

FIRST PRINTING

 Published in New York by Random House, Inc., and simultaneously in Toronto, Canada, by Random House of Canada, Limited.

Library of Congress Catalog Card Number: 63–13552

MANUFACTURED IN THE UNITED STATES OF AMERICA

To Lee

Contents

PART ONE

Irregular Opening

Emily York's House
Percival York's House
York Park
Robert York's House
Myra York's House

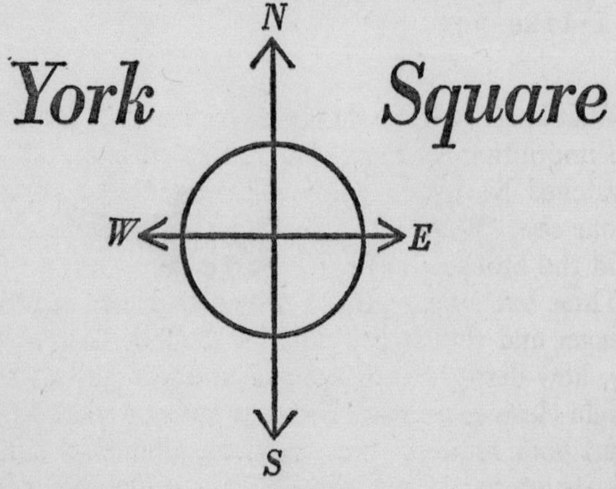
York
Square
N
W
E
S

1. Y's Gambit

He had written:

Dear Walt:

You know who I am.

You do not know that you know.

You shall.

I write this to let you know that I know who you really are. I know the skill of your hands. I know the quality of your obedience. I know where you come from and what you are doing. I know what you think. I know what you want. I know your great destiny.

I like you.

Y

Walt knelt with the sun on his back and the hard sharp bronze letters imprinting his knees, TH on the left knee, RK on the right. He watched his hands, whose skill was known—was known!—to someone else. (*Who?*) . . . Watched his hands trimming the grass around the bronze plaque.

Three left fingers pressed the shorn blades gently away while the finger and thumb felt out the shallow, narrow channel; and deftly, how deftly, the right hand wielded the turf hook, making a margin clean as a moon. Did anyone know that Walt had made the turf hook himself?—would anyone admire its right-hand bevel below, its left-hand bevel above? Who would applaud the creation —who but the creator? And wasn't that enough?

It had been enough. Walt shifted gingerly from the toothed

serifs of the memorial plaque and set his knees carefully under IN LIVING MEMORY, with the small OF between them. It had been enough just knowing he was doing his job perfectly. So perfectly, in fact, that in the York matrix of four strange castles and a private park he existed like an invisible mend.

It may be that Walt had numbly wished to be known and noticed; he could not recall such a wish, but he must have wished it. For years he had been contained and content within his own quiet excellence, patient as a pupa. But now . . .

"*. . . I know who you really are. I like you.*"

It was troubling.

Had Walt ever read Bernard Shaw (he had not), he might have been pleased with the line, "When you have learned something, my dear, it often feels at first as if you had lost something." It would have given flesh to this queer unsettled feeling, together with the comfort that he was not alone in feeling it. He had not truly known how desperate his need had been to have someone say to him, *I like you.*

Only now that it was said, he did not know what to do with it.

A shadow crossed his clever hands. Walt did not look up. There was no necessity. To look up would have been to see Robert York—black homburg, suit hard and gray as iron, waistcoat like an old mint coin, blank gray cravat—wearing his morning face below the rimless glasses, a face drum-tight as an empty bed in a barracks.

"Good morning, Walt," said Robert York correctly.

"Morning, Mr. Robert." It was (as always if the encounter took place just here) seven minutes before ten o'clock.

York Square must never have had a youth; its little formal tapestry of a private park, its grizzled guardian corners of little castles, each with its watchful tower, surely looked old and out of place and time even when the masons laid down their trowels. And what York Square was in stone, Robert York was in the flesh. Imagine him a child if you could, and still you saw only a dwindled Robert York as he stood, in black homburg and iron-gray, with a gray cravat above an antique waistcoat (and spats before May 15th), the unrimmed glasses making him eyeless in the morning sun on his drum-skin face. Compelling Robert York to live in one of York Square's four castles was like compelling a man to be a biped; commanding that he uphold the York tradition was like commanding that the grass in the little park grow green. They were all alike—he, the park, the castles, York Square—punctilious, outmoded, predictable. Neatly Walt worked on the grassy borders of the plaque as, neatly and to the dot, Robert York took his morning stroll about the park.

Walt trimmed the grass along the right side of the bronze. Not all the Yorks were like that, of course.

Miss Myra.

Miss Myra was younger than Robert, which made her forty-four. She had a secret, unmentioned by the other Yorks. Easily remarked by anyone who got close enough to see the twitching lip-corner, the gentle unfocused eyes. She had also a secretary-companion, a kind and lovely girl named Ann Drew, who was walking with her now on the far side of the little park. Ann Drew provided an arm under Miss Myra's, guided at the same time she supported the older woman, taking slow synchronizing strides to Miss Myra's quick small uncertain ones.

Miss Myra held one of the girl's hands tightly in both of hers, and every ten steps or so she smiled a sort of "I did it!" smile, and Ann Drew cooed little acknowledgments into her ear. As much as he liked anyone, Walt liked these two, Miss Myra and the girl. The girl was kind in a special way; when you spoke to her, she seemed to stop thinking of whatever she had been thinking and listened to you altogether. No one else ever did that, Walt was sure. And Miss Myra York—she was, oh, harmless, and it didn't really matter that she was ill.

Walt watched the pair for a moment. He did not wave. He never waved, or passed the time of day, or nodded or did anything of that sort.

He bent to his work again, deftly trimming the turf around the imbedded plaque. When he was finished, and the crumbs of earth were swept and scattered, he stepped back to look.

IN LIVING MEMORY
OF
NATHANIEL YORK, JR.
BORN APRIL 20, 1924

And I, thought Walt, and I . . .

"Walt?"

He was startled, but there was that about him which made it impossible to show what he felt, an instant and utter reflex of stillness to counteract all outward evidence of surprise, fear, anything. Walt turned woodenly. Emily York had come up behind him.

The Yorks were alike only in that no York was like any other York. Emily York was younger than Myra and looked older. She was square and sturdy-backed, with a salt friz of thinning hair, bulby blue eyes, a militant mouth and hard-working hands. Compelled like her cousins to live in a castle, Emily recorded a permanent protest against such trumpery by taking as her own the smallest of the maids' rooms and decorating it with all the elaboration of a Trappist cell. She insisted upon living on what she earned, which was no more than most social workers on the fourth-floor-walk-up level earned, and a good deal less than some. Where the other Yorks employed help—Robert a secretary-assistant, Myra a companion, Percival a sleep-out housekeeper whom he shared with Robert—Emily took pride in her ability to do for herself. Having to fix things, however, defeated her; she was about as mechanically inclined as a tuberose.

"Very nice, Walt," approved Miss Emily, nodding at the manicured plaque. "You do take care of this place as if it were your own."

Walt nodded back his total agreement to this.

"My garbage can," said Miss Emily. "It doesn't quite close. I have to pile three World Almanacs and a dictionary on the lid to hold it down. So then of course I have to lift them off each time I step on the little you-know thing."

"Yes, Miss Emily."

"It should close tight, you know. Flies?"

"Yes, Miss Emily."

"And germs." Miss Emily paused. "If I could fix it myself, Walt, I certainly would."

Walt put his hand in his left trousers pocket and grasped his passkeys. "Yes, Miss Emily."

"Well," said Emily York. "Thank you, Walt."

Without expression, he watched her walk briskly toward the nearest subway entrance. Then in his deliberate way he gathered up his tools and went to fix Miss Emily's step-on garbage can.

He had written:

Dear Walt:

You have been so much alone, you do not always know the good you do, how good it is. Nor the fine things, how fine they are. I know (do you?) that you have never said "Sir" to any man. I know about you that "good enough" is never good enough, and that you put as much care into fixing a garbage can as another might into setting a jewel.

Are such excellence and care too good for the jobs you must do? No, because you could not do any job another way. Should you be doing some other job? Yes, you should. And you shall.

You have been patient for a long time. You are right to have been so patient. You know (don't you?), and I know, that your destiny holds great things for you, that you are about to play a role of great importance, to begin at last your larger and more glorious life.

Men do not make their destinies, men fulfill them. The course is set for you, but you must travel it, you must be obedient. (But you already are; it is part of your splendid nature.)

A great trust will shortly be placed in your hands. You will accept it. You will carry it out. For what you are about to do, the world will be a better place. This I assure you.

Since my first letter three days ago I have watched you carefully. Every minute I become more pleased that I chose you for my instrument. I will write again soon, with exact instructions for the first of the great tasks which I have planned for you.

Meanwhile, let no one know that your destiny has come to you, and so be sure to destroy this and all other letters from me. Do this, and you shall please

Y

Like the other, the letter was written on ordinary school note-paper, with faint blue horizontal lines. It was flawlessly typed, undated, and without a return address. It had arrived in a plain envelope inscribed, simply:

WALT
York Square
New York, N. Y.

2. *Positions*

"How's yours?" young Ann Drew asked.

Young Tom Archer shrugged. He had serious dark eyes and a dark serious voice, and a warm way about him. "Happy when he thinks of his Boscawen, sad when he thinks of his phony two-penoe." He laughed. "And how's *yours*?"

"She doesn't change," said the girl; and "Whatever *are* you talking about? What's a Boscawen? What's a penoe?"

"A Boscawen," said Tom Archer loftily, "is a provisional postage stamp issued in 1846 by the postmaster of Boscawen, New Hampshire. It's dull blue, and it says on it 'paid five cents,' but it's worth enough to pay your salary and probably some of mine for the next year. And Sir Robert of York owns one."

"And he's happy about it. He ought to be! What's the one he's sad about, the penoe something?"

Archer laughed. He had good teeth to laugh by; in this last-of-spring twilight they glowed like the loom of foggy lights. "The so-called 'penoe' is a blue 1848 stamp from the island of Mauritius, of two-pence denomination, showing the head of Queen Victoria. An error was not caught in one of the engraver's plates, and the word 'pence' was spelled with an *o* instead of a *c*. A number of printings of the error were made that year, in slightly differing shades of blue and on different thicknesses and shades of paper. They're all valuable—especially good copies—but the most valuable is the earliest impression, which is a sort of indigo-blue on thick yellowish paper. Worth more than the Boscawen."

"Do go on," said young Ann, successfully sounding fascinated.

"I had no intention of stopping," said young Archer. "Well, a couple of years ago Robert of York was hot on the trail of one of the earliest penoes, and sure enough he caught up with it. It was an especially fine copy, it was authenticated six ways from sundown, and he paid through the nose for it. And then—it's much too long a story—it developed that he'd been sold a beautiful forgery. He wasn't the only one fooled—a lot of reputable people were embarrassed. Of course he got his money back, but he didn't *want* his money back—he wanted a genuine, fine-to-superb earliest-impression penoe. He still does."

"Why?"

"Why?" Archer repeated severely. "Because everybody has an impossible dream, even people with umpty-eleven million dollars hanging over them ready to drop. What Sir Robert wants is one each of the world's ten most valuable postage stamps. He has six. Of course, he'll never get them all."

"Why not?"

"Because one of them is the rarest stamp in the world, the famous British Guiana Number 13, and Mr. York isn't likely to get his hot little paws on that baby—there's only one copy extant."

"My, you know so *much*," Miss Drew breathed.

"No, I don't," said Mr. Archer with extreme candor, although his teeth glowed again. "Mr. York, now: say what you like about that funny little guy, *he* knows. He really does. All I have is a sticky mind, and after hanging around the likes of him for nearly two years some of what he knows has stuck."

"Is that what you always wanted to be," Miss Drew asked innocently, "a sticky-minded hang-arounder of an expert philatelist?"

"Aha," said Archer. "Looking for the keystone of Archer, eh?"

"Oh, dear. I didn't mean—"

"You did mean, and don't deny it. And don't apologize, either. It's honest, normal curiosity, and if there's anything York Square can use more of it's something normal. Two years ago I was only too eager to be paid to hang around anybody who knew anything. I was one of those perennial school kids. Went from college to postgrad work, got my master's, then started on a doctorate."

"I didn't know *that*," the girl said.

"I don't advertise it because I didn't get it, and I probably never will. As I was girding myself for the Ph.D., the Army—bless it—reached out and nabbed me."

"Bless the *Army?*" she asked, for he had said it without rancor or irony.

"On two counts," Tom Archer responded. "One: those old jokes about brain surgeons being assigned to drive tanks are rapidly becoming just that—old jokes. The Army really does make an effort nowadays to find out what you're good for and at. When they came to screen me, I just wouldn't go through the meshes. Classification: Useless." He laughed. "Really. Pure academic background, philosophy major of a kind they couldn't even use in Public Relations or Intelligence. If not for the Army I might never have found that out. I might have gone on and on taking p.g. and extension courses for the rest of my pedantic life."

"And blessing number two?"

"The Army taught me how Classification Useless can get along. Do what you're told, no more and no less, never volunteer, and the Army takes care of you in every possible way, without letting reality come in contact with you.

"And as with the Army," Philosopher Archer went on, "so with capital L-i-f-e. The perennial schoolboy who pursues degree after degree as ends in themselves is living in the same dream-world."

"But he hasn't the Army to feed him," Ann Drew pointed out.

"I had an uncle who left me an income. It wasn't enough to eat well on, but it kept me from rooting in garbage cans, and as for the rest—well, I just kept getting those fellowships."

"Well," she said.

"So there you are. I mean, there *I* am. Learned I was useless, learned that a school is an army, and that they're both unbroken eggs. And the yolk is on me."

"Oh, dear," said the girl.

"And now you'll be saying to yourself that becoming secretary, assistant and philatelic clerk to a Robert York isn't functioning in the real world, either."

"I suppose I will. Yes, I will."

"The difference," said Tom Archer, "is that now I know it. B.A.—Before the Army—I didn't."

"But if now you know it," murmured Ann Drew. "—I shouldn't ask this, but you brought it up—why don't you go out and function in the world?"

"I probably will, and sooner than I think. I could teach—I don't want to, but I could. There's a school out West where you learn to run power shovels—I might do that. I don't know. The right thing will come along. This has been fascinating," the young man said suddenly. "I talk too much. Now let's talk about you."

"No."

"No?"

"It . . . wouldn't be fascinating," Ann Drew said.

"Let's try. You've been here about five months taking care of poor old Myra York—"

"Who's pretty happy in spite of your adjectives."

He tilted his head. "I thought we'd agreed it's best to live in the real world?"

"Not for Myra York it isn't," said Ann Drew.

"Clever," said Tom Archer. "Oh, clever. I want to talk about you and you deftly switch the conversation to someone else. All right, I'll talk about you all by myself. You're stacked. You're intelligent. You're *very* pretty. You were discovered somewhere, somehow, by our social-conscious, welfare-type York, Miss Emily. Which makes you some sort of waif."

"I don't like this," the girl said with an uncertain smile.

"Some of my best friends are waifs. Waives."

"I don't know that I like *you*, either."

"Oh, look," Archer said, swiftly and warmly. "Please don't not like me. Please don't even try to not like me—" He stopped, cocking his head in his quick, odd way. "You don't understand me at all, do you?"

She looked at him. "I do," she said reluctantly. "I had a father very like you once."

"That bodes well," he grinned. "Dr. Freud says—" But he was able to see, even in the dim light, that this was no time for a witticism. "I'm sorry," he said. "What happened?"

"He died," said the girl.

There was a long pause, as if she had an invisible book to leaf through. Finally she murmured, "Daddy was brilliant and . . . unworldly and impractical and . . . well, he just couldn't cope. I did everything to—I mean, I took care of him as best I could. After he died and there wasn't anyone but myself to take care of"—her pause this time seemed full of silent syllables, because it ended just as if she had not stopped speaking at all—"Miss Emily found me and brought me here."

"You like it here," Archer said.

She looked over at Percival York's house, then quickly around at the identical others. "I like the money I'm near. I mean, handed-down money. I like the feeling that nothing here ever has to change, nothing that starts from any . . . under-the-skin need." She shook herself, or shuddered. "I'm sorry. I didn't mean to say any of that. It sounds envious."

"I'm glad," he said seriously, so seriously that she could know for the first time that he really *was* serious. "These people—poor Miss Myra, do-gooding Miss Emily—and she does do good, I'm not denying it—Sir Robert and his little bits of expensive paper, and that *Percival*"—he said the name as its own cuss-word, without adjectives—"they're all laboratory specimens of the genus 'have.' The tendency of the like of us have-nots *is* to envy them, and why shouldn't we? It's hard to feel that they deserve what they've got, when you know and I know that they don't and we do."

She laughed as she had not been able to do when he was being not-serious. "That almost makes sense. Oh, dear!"

The last two words were evoked by the taxicab that pulled up before Percival York's little castle. From it alighted Percival, who after paying the driver assisted a blonde concoction to the sidewalk. The cab moved off and they had a wonderful glimpse, in the darkling light, of female calves taxing the tensile strength of the suffering nylon, of heels too high for the furtive speed urged on their wearer by Percival, of a black synthetic coat too glossily superb to be the Persian lamb to which it pretended—all surmounted by a piled-up confection of hair that looked as if it has been spun out of a cotton-candy machine.

"He has," murmured Ann Drew with a surprising touch of tartness, "and you have not, although you deserve it. Do you feel deserving of *everything* he has?"

"My modesty," replied Tom Archer, gazing with a slight shudder after the platinum blonde who was just being shooed into Percival's castle by its chatelain, "my modesty prevents me from being sure I deserve *that* part of it. Ann Drew, you're being catty."

"Yes," Ann Drew said. "Refreshing, isn't it?—*Eeeeeeee!*"

Her fingers all but met through his sleeve and the flesh of his forearm.

"God," Archer whispered. "How long has *he* been there?"

"Who? Where?" Her soft, shocked tone commanded the exact softness and shock from him. "Why, it's . . ." And Archer barked: "Walt! What the devil are you doing there?"

"Mr. Robert sent me looking for you," said Walt in his pale voice.

"Did you have to come creeping up like that?"

Walt stood in a pool of shadow close by the memorial plaque. "I wasn't creeping, Mr. Archer."

"Did Mr. York say what he wanted?"

"He only said to find you—he's got a Seebeck."

"He's got a Seebeck," groaned Archer. "Go tell him I'll be right there."

Only then did the girl release his arm; she fumbled in her handbag. "Walt. Wait."

Walt waited.

"I was at the post office just as it closed and they gave me this for you." She handed him a letter.

Walt took it silently in both hands and, holding it so, walked away from them, across the street toward Robert York's castle. He had an odd walk—not exactly a shuffle, for it was silent, nor a shamble, for it was very contained, but a sort of sliding along, as if the lower part of his body were on tracks.

"Creep," muttered Archer.

"How long *was* he there?"

"No telling."

"Probably not long at all." She was breathing as if breathing were something she had overlooked for a time. "And he *isn't* a creep."

"He looks like one."

"Don't you know why?"

"He just looks it," said Archer defensively.

"It's his eyes," said the girl. "They're almost perfectly round, didn't you ever notice? That's what creates the illusion of stupidity."

"It's no illusion. His brains are all in his wrists, and his nerves all run to his hands. I never yet saw that zombie angry or scared or worried or anything at all." Tom Archer said rather tenderly, "Do we have to talk about Walt?"

"All right," Ann Drew said. "What's a Seebeck?"

"Oh, Lord, the Seebeck! I haven't time now to tell you the whole dismal story—Sir Robert awaits. Take note of this, by the way, my girl—this is an historic occasion. You know, don't you, that the Naval Observatory calls him up to find out what time it is? And that the stars in their courses check with him before they shift their Dopplers?"

"I know he has very regular habits," she said cautiously.

"Agreed—when working time comes, we work, when quitting time comes, we quit. Now hear this: This is the very first, the number-one original time, Robert York has ever yelled for me after hours! It really *must* be a Seebeck." And Tom Archer waved his hand cheerfully, and he too set off across the street to Robert York's castle.

Ann Drew stood watching him. Then, very slowly, she shook her head. Perhaps it was wonderment.

3. Exchanges

Oh, another, oh, a new one.

Clutching the letter close (oh, there's something in it this time, extra pages and . . . and *a card*) he hurried to Robert York's house to deliver Tom Archer's message. It was with great reluctance that he removed one caressing hand from the envelope to get his keys out (Mr. Robert's door was always locked, as was Miss Emily's; Mr. Percival's and Miss Myra's, never). He let himself in, slid along to the library door and knocked.

"Archer? Come in, damn it!" At the incredible words from the unbelievable voice (for Robert York, though capable of waspishness, never swore and never shouted) Walt swung the door open.

"No, Mr. Robert, it's me. Mr. Archer says he'll be right here."

"Well, I should hope so," snapped York.

Silently Walt padded through the house, through the second of the kitchen's two rear doors, through the breezeway to the garage, then between the superannuated Buick and Percival York's rakish, ruined Ryan (by special arrangement; Percival's garage had gone up in smoke as the result of an innocent neighborhood delinquency and Percival had never found the loose capital to rebuild it), up the back stairs and, after unlocking it, through the door of his own quarters. He locked the door behind him, turned on the light . . . and was greeted by the dry rattlesnake buzz of the annunciator.

Walt turned his round eyes on it, his face giving no expression to the indignation he felt. All Walt wanted was to read his precious new letter, and here was Percival York summoning him from all the way diagonally across the Square. If he toyed with the idea of ignoring the buzzer, it was for a microsecond; he murmured, surprisingly, something about "I know the quality of your obedience" and went to the writing table, took out his keys, unlocked the middle drawer, deposited the letter far back in the drawer, carefully locked it, went to the door, canceled the annunciator, unlocked the door, passed through it and locked it behind him, went down the stairs and out through the garage's rear door (which he also locked behind him) and, taking the driveway, rounded Robert York's castle and cut across the little private park to Percival York's castle.

He went around to the rear and entered through the kitchen. The refrigerator door was open and an empty ice-cube tray lay on the floor in a grayish puddle, its crippled separator lying over by the door where it had been thrown or kicked. Walt picked up tray and separator, set them on the table and went down the hall to what was, in this castle of the four, a living room, though in Robert's it was a library, in Emily's a deserted cavern, and in Myra's something like an old curiosity shop.

As Walt touched the doorknob, there was an undignified scuttling inside. The door swung open on a tableau consisting centrally of a love seat, with Percival York at the instant of rebounding from the curved back at one end and, at the other end, an overfleshed blonde girl with one too many buttons undone, and a face like a molded-by-the-thousands kissing-crying-wetting doll crowned with cotton-candy hair.

"Walt, God," spat Percival. To the girl he said, "It's only the handyman." To Walt again, "Mrs. Schultzer, or Scheisser, or whatever her disgusting name is, defrosted the refrigerator and there's no blasted ice."

"Mrs. Schriver," Walt said.

"About that I don't give a damn. Just get some ice."

"Mr. Robert has ice."

"Tell him," said Percival York, wrinkling a gray nose on which the first red ruts and runnels of its ultimate condition were beginning to show, "tell him," Percival said, with rummily underlined irony, "tell him I'll return it, every cube, plus six per-bloody-cent." Percival York's eyes, like salamanders looking out of sacks, sought and found the girl and demanded tribute, which she delivered in a hoarse immediate cackle.

Walt returned to the kitchen. He checked the refrigerator setting, picked up the ice-cube separator, effortlessly straightened it, sighted down its length, straightened it a tiny bit more, then rinsed separator and tray. From a closet beside the refrigerator he took a string mop and blotted up the puddle on the floor. He opened the back door, hung the damp mop on the railing outside, returned to the kitchen, washed his hands and dried them on a paper towel (with which he whisked up the few splatters on the sink edges before he threw it away), took the ice tray he had repaired and another from the refrigerator, canted the latter's contents carefully into the drain (so it would not splash) and went out, shutting the door quietly behind him.

He recrossed the park and went around to the kitchen door of Robert York's house, which now he had to unlock. He rinsed the ice-cube trays he was carrying and filled them at the cold-water tap and set them on the table. He removed two trays from Robert York's refrigerator and replaced them with the two from Percival's. Then, just as he eased the refrigerator door shut, he was arrested by the sound of angry voices from the front of the house.

"I didn't hire you to make childish mistakes!" (Mr. Robert, more angry than Walt had ever known him before.)

"I don't concede that it is a mistake, and if it is I wouldn't call it childish!" (Mr. Archer, who had never talked back to Mr. Robert before.)

"Any fool could see that gum fluoresce! You've gone and saddled me with a lot of damned Seebeck reprints!"

"Those are not Seebecks! I have Borjian's word on it!"

"Borjian! Borjian! Don't stand there and give me Borjian! Borjian once sold me a forged—"

"—a forged penoe," and Tom Archer's voice cut in by shouting as loudly as he could. "I know the whole miserable story by heart, including the fact that Borjian returned your money and that plenty of other stamp-wise people were fooled, too!"

"Now you listen to me—"

"You listen to me! I won't have you bawling me out like a naughty kid over a measly forty bucks' worth of stamps!"

"It isn't the forty dollars!" (Mr. Robert was shouting as loudly as *he* could now.) "It's the idea of a *mistake!* If you can make a little mistake you can make a big mistake, and I will not tolerate *any* mistakes!"

"And *I* will not tolerate" (now Mr. Archer was mimicking Mr. Robert to his face, and he was doing it rather well) "being spoken to in this fashion! Tomorrow morning I will take those goddamn Salvadors down to Jenks & Donahue, and I will have those goddamn Salvadors put under the parallel-beam microscope, and I will pay for the inspection out of my own pocket, and I will come back here and accept your apology when you find out they're really genuine!"

"You'll come back here with proof that they are Seebeck reprints and I will accept your resignation!"

"Give me those stamps. We'll damn well see. Good *night!*"

The library door slammed thunderously. Someone hard-heeled up the stairs, obviously Mr. Archer. Mr. Archer's door overhead, though it was much farther away, slammed even louder.

Walt did not quite shrug or raise his brows; there was a flicker of tension in the controlling muscles and that was all. He picked up the two trays of ice cubes, took them out on the back porch, set them on the railing, softly closed and locked the door, picked up the trays again, retraced his steps to Mr. Percival's kitchen, found a double-walled pewter bowl on a shelf, released the ice cubes at the sink, placed them in the bowl and carried the bowl up the hall.

Mr. Percival, having heard the musical decanting of the ice cubes, stepped out of his living room into the hall, pulling the door to modestly. Mr. Percival was in his stockinged feet and he was holding his unbuttoned shirt together with one hand. "Where did you go for that ice," he rasped, taking the bowl, "Little America?"

"No, Mr. Percival. I got them out of Mr. Robert's refrigerator."

"Arrgh," said Mr. Percival. He slithered back into his living room, kicking the door shut with his heel.

Walt about-faced and passed through Mr. Percival's kitchen and out. The hot eagerness deep within him, to sprint across the park and up to his room, he contained. He wanted more than anything to tear open this new letter, plunge himself into its promised "*. . . exact instructions for the first of the great tasks which I have planned for you.*" But he had been chosen because of what he was; and what he was was deliberate, meticulous, careful and obedient—above all, obedient. He bore the pain of the waiting proudly, like a Christian martyr, as he paced off the way back to his room. For, "*Let no one know that your destiny has come to you.*"

The short heavy man had a cigar. The short thin one had acne. They were in the office too early for the phones to start ringing, but the short heavy man liked it that way, so that was the way it was. He lay back in the swivel chair, with his feet on the desk and his cigar aimed at the ceiling, and he dozed.

The short thin man made a happy sound, a short thin hum.

The man with the cigar moved only his eyeballs, which somehow managed to be both deep-set and protruding. "What you got?"

"Well, it don't pay off at Hialeah," said the thin one detachedly. He dropped his pencil, gathered up some yellow sheets, stacked them, then spread them again and picked up the pencil. "Or at no other regular track. But it sure whips a harness meet if you go all the way through."

"A system? You?"

"On'y on paper. I don't put down a deuce myself, not me."

"You're like a bartender. Don't make like a customer."

"On'y on paper, I told you."

"It's the same thing, you're tasting. Quit before you get hooked."

"Yeah, but listen," the thin man said eagerly. "You bet any favorite, see, but on'y if his post position is number one or two, and on'y if the odds is three to two or less. Otherwise you bet the favorite to place and the challenger to win. And then every race you get your longest long shot and lay on a couple of deuces, and that's it. They won't hit all the time, but they'll pay the freight and maybe the rent."

"System," said the man through his cigar; it sounded like spitting.

"All right, system! But I done this sixty-six times in a row and from $6.50 I'm up to $208.70."

"On paper."

"On'y thing is, you got to work from late odds and wear your spike shoes, get to that window last man in the place. You got to *be* there. You got to watch that tote board like it's a dirty movie."

"Now you listen to me," the cigar-smoker began, and then alarm replaced his severe amusement. "What's all that?"

All that was a sudden commotion in the outer office. It burst in on them in the forms of a grim, straight-backed maiden lady with a salty frizzle of hair showing from her bonnet and a black-jowled giant whose high tenor voice grew progressively higher as he tried to expostulate with the lady and explain to the cigar-smoker at the same time.

The cigar-smoker held up one hand. The giant stopped, and the lady began.

"My name is Emily York and you've been taking bets from my cousin Percival."

The man at the desk slowly took down his feet and rolled the cigar to the side of his mouth. "Percival what?"

"Percival York, as you know very well."

"We don't know any Percival York around here."

The acne with the system put in a word: "The sign on the door says Investment Counselors. You got the wrong place, lady."

"Percival York receives his income quarterly—January, April,

July and October," continued Miss Emily York. "His bills to date are already greater than his income for the entire year. The Raceway opens tomorrow, I believe, so that any bet he loses he will not be able to pay. And, of course, any bet he wins you lose."

"We ain't making book and we don't know no Percival York," said the acne.

"Shut up," said the cigar. "Lady, what do you want?"

"Don't take any bets from Percival York. And you'd better get in touch with every other horse parlor you know and pass the word along."

"Say," the acne said suddenly, "I think this dame—"

"Shut up," said the cigar. "You his wife, lady?"

"Good heavens, no," snapped Emily York. "I'm his cousin."

"You know what can happen to nosy cousins, lady?"

"Psst," the acne said hurriedly.

An interested glint came into Miss Emily's eye. "Are you threatening me?"

"Psst!" repeated the acne.

The black-jowled giant squeaked, "Boss, you want I should—?"

"Because if you are, I think you ought to know that I'm a well-known social worker and that from time to time I call the station in the precinct in which I happen to be working and tell the desk sergeant where I'm going and that if I don't phone back in twenty minutes he's to send two large detectives for me."

"You can get out," said the man at the desk. But he said it to the black-jowled giant, who precipitately obeyed. "Lady, you mean before you came up here you called the cops?"

"Indeed I did," said Miss Emily York.

"Jesus," said the man at the desk respectfully.

"That's what I been trying to tell you," the acne said, waving his arms. "She's the one closed up Rosalie's place. Single-handed!"

"Well," said the other man. "It's a good thing we're not in *that* kind of business. What's the harm, lady? A few bets now and then—"

"I'm not intending to close you up, if that's what you're worried about," said Emily York.

"Oh?" he said.

"At least, not just now."

"Oh," he said.

"Because at the moment I have a use for you. You can reach more horse parlors than I can."

"You really want this Percy oddballed—I mean blackballed?" asked the short heavy man at the desk. He was now smoking in quick short puffs.

"Percival. Don't you?"

"Me?"

"He already owes you nearly twenty-eight hundred dollars. If he can't bet he can't lose, and if he doesn't lose he might scrape up enough to pay you what he owes. Come, now! You're not a gambling man. The people who call you up on those telephones are gambling men, but you're not."

"That's what I been saying," the man said feebly.

She glanced at her wrist. "I must make my telephone call."

He rose in a hurry. "Well, thank you for coming in, Miss York. Not that I know anyone by that name myself, but I don't mind passing the word along to oblige a lady. In case I find somebody to pass it to—"

But Emily York was already on her way out. The black-jowled one put in his head and cooed anxiously, "Boss, you want I should—?"

"*Get out!*" said the short heavy man with venom.

The door slammed shut.

Slowly the acne said, "That fishy-eyed son of a bitch York."

"Get on the phone! That old bag's got a slice of the same income Percy's got. Any time he can't settle his bills the lien goes on the principal. This is the Yorks of York Square, stupid."

"Heavy sugar," mourned the short thin man.

"You'll find out how heavy if they hit you with it! Start phoning, will you?"

Meanwhile, Emily York was turning briskly into a cathedral-like establishment not far away, the famous name of which was lettered in heavy bronze castings prominently small in the windows; the floor of which was pelted in cilia like the interior of a royal digestive tract; and whose price tags more often than not included the word "The": *Forty Dollars The Pair* and *Four Hundred Dollars The Set.*

The place smelled male, not the metal-and-soap maleness of a locker room nor the malt-and-sawdust maleness of an old-time corner saloon, but the leather-and-oiled-wood maleness of a city club, as finished and self-consistent as the ash of a fine cigar. At sight of the skirted figure stalking him, the sole visible attendant took refuge behind a showcase; surely a giraffe, were it a male one, would have startled him less.

Emily York marched up to him, demanded and got the manager, and without preamble stated, "Mr. Percival York buys his clothes here. He charges them. If he continues to charge, his income will fall short of his obligations. If he ceases to charge, he may be able to cover his current account. It is easy to see how both your store and Mr. York can benefit." After that she fully identified herself, explained the matter all over again and departed, leaving the costly cavern in hushed consternation and the very carpet-pile puzzled as to the disposal of her spoor.

Next on her list (she had a list) was a quite different kind and manner of establishment—a liquor store every bit as discriminating as the second car of a subway local. She identified the manager only because he had, on his wrinkled gray cotton jacket, the word in scarlet script over the pocket. He was a sparse-haired man with one frank cataract and wet lips displaying dark brown teeth.

Miss York asked to open an account, and when she was bluntly told that state law forbade it she demanded to know why Percival York was so honored. She quoted to the brown-toothed manager the exact balance due, pointed publicly at his framed license, and promised him faithfully that the delivery to Percival York, for anything other than cash, of anything in stock down to and including cooking sherry would mean that both his store and he would learn something about locks. As a parting shot she suggested a revision, in his invoices to her drinking cousin, of special prices he had been charging. (It was a shot in the dark that cut nearly forty per cent off Percival's next bill, a fact Percival himself was never to appreciate.)

Having thus obeyed, with all her heart and to the best of her belief, the ancient edict that charity should begin at home, Miss Emily York boarded a crosstown bus and went to her regular work at the settlement house.

4. Maneuvering

He had written:

Dear Walt:

You are the one.

Are there men anywhere, in any walk of life, who are as controlled as you are, as dignified?

Yes, a few. Some, born to the purple, have their high code inborn. Some rise to the top openly by their own worth. And some, perhaps the worthiest of all, remain bound by their honor and their sacred duty.

These are the trodden, but not downtrodden. These are the lowly, but never the low.

The true measure of the size of a man is his anger. Does this mean that the violent man, the assertive and pugnacious man, is thereby the larger man? No, even though this is how most men behave. "Don't tread on me." A good motto — for a snake.

I can look into the hearts of all men. And I tell you this about them: Those who are quick in their furies are furious at themselves. This is because, and only because, they are not sure who they are, what it is that lives under their skins. They are afraid, afraid.

Not so the man who knows what he is. Righteousness is within him, it cannot be affected by anything outside him. A brave man is not afraid to appear humble. He knows what he is. He need not prove he is brave, just as a tall man need not prove he is tall. Bravery, righteousness, are sufficient unto themselves.

This is the true and inner meaning of the

words "The meek shall inherit the earth." The meek are the righteous who need never reveal their inner might to other men.

You are a righteous man. You are beyond fear. Have faith in me and I shall guard you and keep you and make you master. There is no thing I cannot do. There is no force I cannot control. Your faith in me must be absolute, for absolute is my confidence in you.

You know who I am. Do not speak my name. Do not be afraid to know me.

Now you may take the first small step toward your destiny.

With this letter I give you a white card cut in a special shape. You are to conceal this card where no one can find it.

Go then to Scholz's Toy Store on Fifth Avenue. It is a very large toy store and many people go in and out. Do nothing to attract attention to yourself, in any way. Move quietly among the people until you find yourself in the last aisle, which runs front to back by the north wall.

Halfway up the aisle you will see toy typewriters, printing presses, rubber stamp kits and the like. Move along until you see, on the wall shelves, a stack of boxes, blue with red and gold letters, marked PRINTS CHARMING. The price for one of these is $1.49 plus sales tax.

Have your money ready. Point and murmur. Do not speak up. Do not ask for it at all until the moment you have the clerk's attention. Make your purchase quickly, have it wrapped plainly, leave quietly. Step aside, make way, wait.

Do all you can to stay clear of others without calling attention to yourself.

Walk to Third Avenue and turn right. You will see a supermarket near the corner. You are not known there. Go in and buy enough groceries to require a large paper bag, but not enough to fill it. Slip your package from Scholz's into the unfilled part. From then on you are simply a man going home with a bag of groceries.

Go home. Lock yourself in your room. Lower the blinds. Open the box and take out the toy printing set. Remove the letter J — there are capital letters only in this set — and open the ink pad.

Press the J on the ink pad and practice stamping it on scrap paper until you get a good clear impression every time.

IMPORTANT: Be sure to gather up each scrap of practice paper afterward and destroy it.

Now take the enclosed card. Place it on the table in the following position:

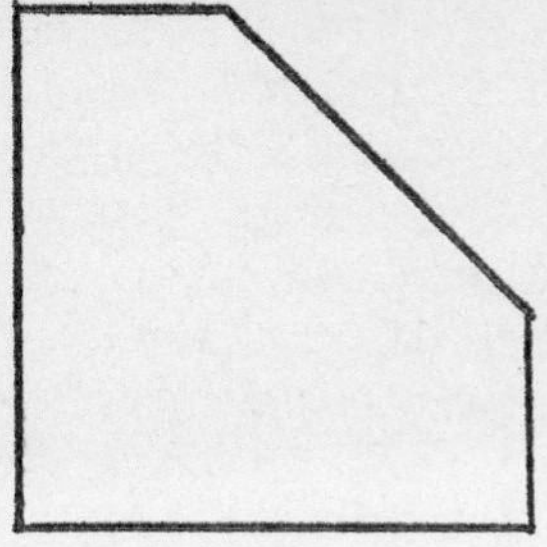

Now very carefully ink the letter J and very carefully stamp it on the card, so:

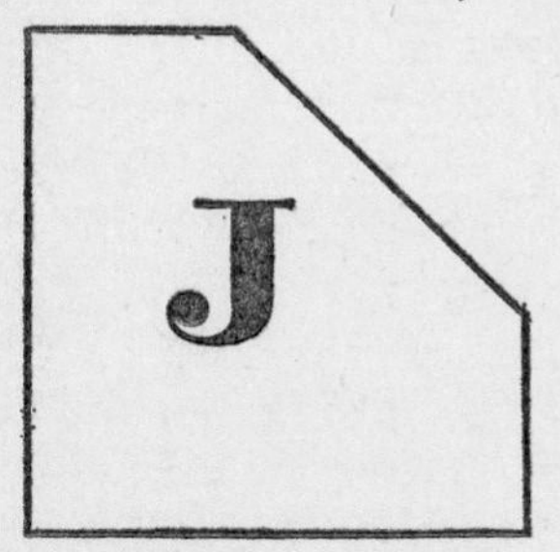

Let the J dry When it is dry, put the card. in a plain white envelope, seal the envelope and write on it in <u>plain</u> capital letters:

ROBERT YORK
YORK SQUARE
NEW YORK, N. Y.

Stick a 5¢ stamp on the envelope, place it

securely in an inside pocket. If you can get it into the mailbox at Surrey Street before 9:30, do that. If later, you must take it to the Church Street post office. Drop it into the mailbox outside. Do not hurry. Do not linger.

Carry out the instructions in this letter well, and the later, larger duties will be easy for you.

I know the past. I know the future. I predict: in a very few hours, a few days at most, when you turn your hand, they shall tremble.

Dispose of this letter as you have the others.

I am (but you know who I am!),
Y

5. Interplay

"I brought the mail."

Tom Archer's dealings with Robert York had been correct, dignified and beyond criticism. Work on the records of Robert York's philatelic holdings proceeded smoothly, and at lunchtime the day before, they had agreed with the politeness of duelists that the end was at last in sight and soon they could begin the final cataloguing. Work had also been done on the family accounts—that part of the accounts, of course, in which the four Yorks were concerned in common, not individually. Robert York, as eldest of the cousins, and as by nature the logical representative of the founding Yorks, had charge of this work by general consent. Tom Archer, as Robert's secretary, helped with the accounting and was privy to these particular matters—wages for the help, upkeep and maintenance of houses and park, prorating of part-time wages as in the case of Mrs. Schriver, the housekeeper who slept out and "did" for Percival as well as for Robert; and such trivia.

The waiting stiffness between the two men had doubtless contributed to their efficiency. Tom Archer (because he was at root a man of peace) and Robert York (whose self-righteousness had as one of its prime articles an insistence on fair play) were, each in his own way, ashamed of the outbreak of temper over the alleged Seebecks. And each, unknown to the other, had his special reason for wishing to preserve their relationship. In a way, then, this particular mail was a pity, for it could not fail to upset their precarious equilibrium.

Tom Archer set the mail down before his employer, and a sense of fatefulness flashed through him: *This will change things a bit!* But first, from his breast pocket he took a manila envelope, drew out its contents, and placed them on the envelope and the envelope on the small heap of mail.

"There!"

Robert York pursed his very thin lips. "What's this?"

"The analysis from Jenks & Donahue." Archer extruded a forefinger and slightly separated the sheets in Robert York's hand. "And here are the stamps."

"Hmp," said Robert York, and he began to read.

"Oh!" he said, after a second.

"Oh . . ." he said, after a minute.

Then he looked up, his skin tighter than usual, his barely bluish lips puckered with the bitter taste of crow.

"I said that if this report proved the stamps genuine, I should owe you an apology. You have it."

"Thank you."

"Mr. Archer, I meant what I said when I made your resignation contingent upon this." He tapped the report.

"I am quite aware of that, sir."

"Had it proved that you made a mistake, I should have insisted upon it. Since it's I who was mistaken I feel I must offer, rather than demand, the same thing."

"I don't understand, Mr. York."

"Then I shall explain," said Robert York stiffly. "It may well be that after what has happened you will no longer wish to be associated with me. If that is the case, I shall certainly understand it; and to do what I can to right the injustice, I shall give you the finest possible recommendation."

"Mr. York," Archer began.

"And perhaps a little more than the usual, ah, notice. In fact, if you'd like to stay on here while you look for something else—" He stopped to open the left-hand top desk drawer, frowning, then suddenly smiled a wan, pathetic smile, for even as he reached into the drawer, Archer had spun to the cabinet behind him, opened it, plucked a stack of tissues from a box and placed them on the desk beside the mail—all in the time it took Robert York to restore his reaching hand to the *status quo ante*.

York took two tissues, folded them once and blew his nose hard. "Mr. Archer, thank you. You're—you've been a good chap." It was as if Mahomet had gone to the mountain.

"Mr. York," said Tom Archer, at sea level, "I should never have spoken to you as I did, and it won't happen again. As for leaving you, I'd rather stay on."

"Indeed? Yes. Well." Robert York's museum features hardly reflected the gratification he felt; but his hand, as if by its own volition, folded another two tissues and brought them to his nose for another sharp, brief blow.

Touched, Tom Archer said gently, "Shall we get on with the mail?"

"The mail. Oh, yes." The eldest York removed his unrimmed glasses, whisked a Sight Saver from his top drawer, polished both lenses, restored the glasses to his eyes, dropped the Sight Saver and the four used tissues in his wastebasket, picked up the envelope on top of the heap, turned it over, put it down. "Mr. Archer—I don't quite know how to say this—would you sit down?"

Archer looked surprised and sat down in a facing chair. Robert York brought his cupped hand to his mouth and coughed delicately, twice. Then he leaned back in his swivel chair and surveyed his ceiling with intensity, as if searching for something.

"As you perhaps know," he began, "I at all times prefer to avoid the, ah—the emotional approach to things. I have never understood emotions very well. I like things to, ah—come out even. I mean to say, right-wrong, good-bad, yes-no. That sort of thing. Can you understand that?"

Tom Archer, heroically suppressing a quotation from Hegel which sprang to his lips, said instead, "Yes, indeed."

"I lost my temper with you over the Salvadors," Robert York went on, heroically also, "for the curious reason, I think, that I had had some words with my cousin Percival earlier in the day. It must be that the, ah—vessel of one's emotions has a limited capacity, that it fills up stealthily, as it were, and then—a few insignificant drops more, and it overflows. Is that possible, Mr. Archer?"

"It's not only possible," Mr. Archer assured him, "it unfortunately happens all the time."

"Yet it rather relieves me. Yes, it relieves me. You see, my cousin—" His precise voice became less precise, blurred, then faded away as in a bad overseas connection.

After a moment Tom Archer stirred. "Maybe, Mr. York, you really don't want to talk about it."

York started. "I beg your pardon?" Archer said it again. "Oh, but I do, Archer, I think I do. And now I feel that I may. That is, I find myself trustful of you after—well, you know what I mean."

"I believe so, sir."

"At any rate, my cousin asked me for money. Demanded it, really. I refused. To refuse a loan to a blood-relative who is coming into several million dollars shortly must strike you as very strange, Archer; but I felt that I must. As a matter of principle. My distaste for Percival's squandering and dissolute ways was quite secondary.

"You see," Robert York continued at a faster, warmer pace, "I have always deemed it my duty to carry out the spirit as well as the letter of Nathaniel York, Senior's will, and I have more or less assumed the burden of seeing that my cousins do likewise. Uncle Nathaniel's bequests to us were contingent upon our living in the four houses for a specified number of years, and I have confidently interpreted this—recalling our uncle's impeccable life and his pride in the family traditions—as far more than a mere matter of residence. As I have repeatedly told Percival—the latest occasion, in fact, was the other day—a York occupying a York house in York Square assumes the moral obligation and perhaps even the legal obligation to do so with honor and propriety. I went so far this last time as to suggest to Percival that I might have to take the matter up with the courts, that his unseemly mode of life might actually be an implicit breach of Uncle Nathaniel's will that would disqualify him from his portion of the principal inheritance."

"And what did Mr. Percival say to that?" Archer murmured, although he was reasonably sure of what Mr. Percival had said to that.

"A great many unpleasant things expressed in the most unbridled language," said Robert York uncomfortably. "Also, he laughed in my face. I suppose he was right about the legal aspects, and I knew it—probably that's why I was rather more emphatic in my refusal of his request than I should otherwise have been."

The admission apparently cost him something. He reached for a fresh tissue and patted his brow.

"Knowing Percival," Robert York went on, not without a brightening of tone, "I feel certain that I could, ah—readjust the resulting coldness between us even now by advancing him the money. But if I did that, you see, Archer, Percival would construe it as weakness of character, and then I should never be free of his demands. And I *am* free now, Archer—I assure you of that. The, ah—terms in which I couched my refusal, much as they distressed me then and now, had at least one virtue: I'm quite sure he won't ask again."

"Frankly," Tom Archer said, "I think the end in this case heartily justifies the means. I know how you shrink from being unfair to anyone, but this wasn't unfairness, Mr. York—you were actually doing Mr. Percival a favor to refuse him."

"You think so, Archer? You really think so? I must say I'm very glad to hear you say it. Yes! Well, then . . ."

"The mail, sir?"

"Of course! The mail."

And Robert York, with as nearly cheerful an expression as his Madame Tussaud face could perform, picked up the topmost envelope of the little heap of letters, accepted the letter opener that Tom Archer had for some moments been holding in readiness, slit the letter, returned the letter opener to Archer and withdrew from the envelope an oddly shaped card with the letter J stamped on it.

6. Y's Gambit Declined

"You'd think," snapped Emily York, "that he could do without his silly old nap just this *once*."

Ann Drew said soothingly, "He's a man of very regular habits."

"I admire regularity and I certainly approve of his. But there *are* times." She uttered the phrase with the completeness of a sentence.

Ann rose. "Excuse me a moment, Miss York. I'll go up and get Miss Myra."

"It isn't as if I had unlimited time, like certain others around here," said Emily, glaring at her nickel-plated wristwatch. "I'm due at the League Conference by half-past eight."

"I'm sure this won't take very long," Ann said from the door.

"Unwed mothers," added Emily, evidently assuming that the two words were pregnant enough with priority and haste to require no elaboration.

Ann Drew turned away then, so whether she smiled or not Emily York was not to know.

After a while the doorbell rang. Emily bounded to her feet, computing instantly that her cousin Myra and Ann Drew were still upstairs, thus presenting her with an opportunity to try to do what another might flabbily pass on as beyond accomplishment. She strode on her sensible heels to the front door and swished it open.

"Good *evening*, Percival." She had been right.

Percival York bared his teeth and pushed past her into the sitting room. He slung his expensive homburg onto a commode, turning and collapsing in continuous motion until he came to rest on a love seat, at the two extremities of his spine. He rolled a yellowing eyeball across the opposite wall, or rather at the clutter that obscured it: the East Indian whatnot stand, all spools and mother-of-pearl inlay; the faded print of Gainsborough's "Blue Boy"; the Albany, New York, version of an Arabian prayer rug;

the modernistic japanned shadow-box bearing an unsplendid specimen of *Euphorbia splendens*, or crown of thorns, and another and nameless succulent, both somehow achieving sadness without (like some sad house plants) bravery; and in the corner, on a massively ugly pedestal of some quasi-mahogany, the marble head of a laughing girl of extraordinary beauty. "This place," said Percival York, "always reminds me of a novel by Dickens."

Emily had seated herself straitly in a straight-backed chair, as if to admonish his sprawl, but at Percival's growl she inclined her body forward, ever ready to encourage the wastrel in cultural conversation.

"Oh, really? That's very interesting, Percival. Which Dickens novel does it remind you of?"

"*The Old Curiosity Shop*," said Percival, and the cultural conversation expired without a struggle. "I wish we'd have these bloody blood-is-thicker-than-water sessions somewhere else, the way we used to."

"You know perfectly well how confused poor Myra gets if she has to go out," said Emily coldly.

"I know how confused poor Myra gets when she *doesn't* go out. At my place, now," Percival added, apparently more to be offensive than to express an immediate need, "we could at least have a drink."

Emily set herself for the argument she knew was futile. "Unless my nose deceives me," she began. But then she shrugged. There would be other opportunities. "Here's Myra."

"Who's going to be here?" It came as a cooing, rather than speech. On Ann Drew's arm, Myra York had sidled in and was looking tremulously about with soft-focused eyes.

"It's all right, Myra dear," said Emily crisply, reciting the ritual assurance. "Just the four of us. And Ann, of course, and that nice young Mr. Archer."

"Don't worry, Myra," Percival drawled, "the ol' beau hasn't shown his face yet."

Myra York blanched. Ann Drew frowned. Emily barked his name. Percival scowled at them all and slumped further, sardonically watching Myra expel two large matched tears. "I really," she cooed, "don't know what you mean."

"There, now," said Ann Drew, dabbing at her with a handkerchief; and Emily straightened up to a little more than straight, a cobra-like movement, and hissed, "Percival, you are a—"

"Su-u-ure I am," Percival York drawled, looking at last quite pleased, as if he had accomplished something and was rather proud of it.

The doorbell rang again, and Myra York uttered a little shriek and sprang upright. Ann Drew quickly put an arm around her shoulders. "It's all *right,*" she breathed, "it's all right."

"It's just Robert," said Emily, "and I suppose Mr. Archer." She glanced at Ann Drew, all occupied with Myra, distraught; Percival, supine; and she visibly computed that preoccupation plus insolent non-co-operation equaled another trip to the door for Emily. She rose and went out.

"It's just Robert," Ann echoed to Myra's papery ear, "and I suppose Mr. Archer." She half pressed, half lowered Myra York back into her place on the divan.

"It's just Robert," mocked Percival, "fresh from his 7:31 P.M. beauty nap, a lost cause if ever I saw one. Right, Annie?"

"I'd like you to call me Miss Drew, please," said Ann.

"Okay, Annie, anything you say. Now watch," he said, leering at her. "Robert'll walk in, give *you* a hello, and call the roll of *us.* Then he'll sit down and cough twice. Twice, mind you." He rocked back until his nape thumped the back of the love seat, to stare again at the place where the wall met the ceiling.

"What is it, dear?" Myra murmured.

"Nothing," said Ann, which was not true. For sitting so close to Percival's tusked leer, she had shuddered.

"I do think, Robert, you could have gone without your forty winks this *once.* We've all been waiting." Emily entered with Robert, while young Archer stepped along behind them in an oddly oriental manner. This was the resultant of several divergent forces, one being his position of male secretary, which made him certainly not family and yet not a servant, either. Another was the pulsing anticipation Tom Archer always felt when he entered a room containing Ann Drew. A third was his reluctance to enter this room at all, for he had an inkling of some of the events scheduled. The sum totaled a bland, stooped carriage and the impression that he would bow rapidly from the waist at the slightest excuse.

"Good evening," Robert York said to Ann, ignoring Emily's scolding; and immediately, taking a brief bearing on each of the others, "Myra . . . Percival . . ." and indicating the straight chair to which Emily was headed, so that his greeting was also a command to sit-so-we-can-get-started, ". . . Emily." Then he sat down in a hideous brocaded Morris chair and coughed, twice.

Percival leered, in triumph this time, at Ann, who looked away. Robert held out a hand and young Archer placed an attaché case in it. "This," said Robert, opening the case, taking out a ledger, opening it at a broad orange bookmark and placing it on his knees, "this should not take very long." He thereupon covered the ledger pages with his forearm and spoke over them. "But before we begin, I should like to say—"

Percival groaned.

"—a few words. First of all, on the matter of Mr. Thomas Archer here. Mr. Archer has recently proved, beyond the scintilla of a doubt, that he is a young man of resource and integrity. Not that such proof is or ever has been necessary. Nevertheless, I now find it possible to delegate to him certain of my family duties and responsibilities which have kept me from pursuing my personal affairs as freely as I have wished. Actually, the delegation of these duties is a *fait accompli*. I am merely making it official.

"You have been aware for some time that Mr. Archer is thoroughly conversant with our mutual affairs, from these household details"—he tapped the ledger—"to the supervising of our investments and accounts. He will continue as heretofore, with one change."

Robert York drew a folded blue-backed paper from his pocket and agitated it. "This is a power of attorney, permitting Mr. Archer to act for me—that is, for us—in three areas: matters of maintenance of our houses and common property; the supervision of our investments and other paper holdings; and finally" (his deeply grave tone made this finality one of cosmic importance) "Mr. Archer will begin on the climax of my many years' work in philately—the remounting in uniform volumes, and the complete cataloguing, of my stamp collections."

He passed the paper to the astonished Archer. "But, Mr. York," Archer protested.

"Not a word, Archer. It's the right thing to do and I've done it."

"Let me see that!" Percival rocked forward and snatched the paper from Archer. He scowled through it and then gave the embarrassed Archer a long, calculating look. Percival opened his mouth, closed it again and handed the legal document back.

"Emily?" said Robert York.

The social worker took the paper and read it swiftly. "Of course I don't pretend to understand this sort of thing," she said. "But since it does, you know, specify—I mean, it sets out exactly—" She stopped to frown slightly. "I mean to say, it isn't a *general* power, is it? So I suppose it's all right." Then, as if what she had said sounded like an objection, she nodded to Archer. "Quite all right, Mr. Archer."

Archer (charmingly, to judge by Ann Drew's face) blushed and delivered a little grateful bow.

"For someone who knows nothing about this sort of thing, my dear Emily," said Robert York rather dryly, "you understand very well." He coughed, this time once. "So much for that. Now, there is one other matter—"

"You didn't show it to Myra," Percival said nastily.

"Yes? Yes?" Myra York looked to right, left, above, below, quickly, alertly. All quite meaningless.

"I thought," snapped Emily to the family skeleton, "you were in a hurry to finish this!"

"Not at all, Cuddles," grinned Percival. "It's just that I didn't want to come. But now that we're here, let's do it right, shall we?"

"It's all right, Myra," Robert York said hastily. "Just a legal thing. You may see it if you'd like."

Myra looked intelligent. "If it's all right," she said brightly, "then it's all right."

Robert York glared at his cousin Percival. "Leaving that, then, I shall bring up one other matter before proceeding with our ordinary business." From behind his display handkerchief he pulled a monarch-sized envelope, the cheap flat-finished kind obtainable everywhere. From it he took a five-sided card. "Which one of you is responsible for this nonsense?"

There was a moment of puzzled silence. Then Emily demanded curiously, "What on earth *is* it?"

Severe-lipped, Robert York handed her the card.

"J," said Emily, "hmm," and turned it over twice.

Robert extended his hand for it, but Percival had it first. "Hmm!" said Percival through flared nostrils.

Myra, her woolly attention caught by the traveling scrap of cardboard, asked, "What *is* it? What *is* it?" worriedly. Ann Drew leaned over and took it from Percival and handed it to her.

"What *is* it?" Myra said, exactly as before.

"Nothing, dear, nothing really," said Ann.

"I disagree, Miss Drew," said Robert York. "Indeed, I must once more ask—demand!: Which of you is responsible for this?"

"Not me," said Percival, so instantly that Robert turned on him a stare of profound suspicion.

"Heavens, Robert," Emily said. "It's just somebody's idea of a joke."

"I fail to see anything humorous in it," said Robert. "Can you, Archer?"

Archer started from his hungry appraisal of Ann Drew. "Well, sir, in line with your bisect theory, it might be some kind of advertising teaser was what I thought."

Robert snorted. "Did any of you get one of these foul things?" There was a general denial. "Then why should *I* be the only one to get one?"

"You did mention the bisect thing, Mr. York," Archer murmured.

"Well, I've changed my mind, Archer," said Robert testily. "Anyway, it would hardly interest my cousins."

"If it would explain your childish concern about this, Robert," said Emily brusquely, "*I'd* like to hear it."

There was at that moment a thump on the door in the north wall, opposite the hall entrance. Myra York shot to her feet, Ann Drew rising with her. "Someone's in there!" quavered Myra.

Archer strode to the door and snatched it open, while Ann shushed and "There, dear!"-ed, patted and stroked her.

Walt stood revealed. He did not recoil as the door was flung aside. His round eyes seemed as encompassing as an owl's, and his small full moist mouth was not pursed and did not tremble. He looked about the roomful of faces—angry, startled, puzzled, frightened faces—and when he came to Ann Drew he said dully, "It's fixed, miss."

"Thank you, Walt." Ann's clear soft voice cut across the moment's confusion. "The kitchen sink," she explained. "It's been slow."

"I found this in the trap," Walt said. He held out a small object. Archer, who was nearest him, took it. "A ring."

"Walt found your ring, dear," said Ann to Myra York. To Emily, who was wearing her how-can-other-people-be-so-careless look, the girl was moved to explain, "It isn't a valuable one at all, just costume jewelry. Here, dear," and she took the ring from Archer and gave it to Myra.

"While you're here, Walt," said Robert York, "tell me something. Did you ever get anything like this in the mail?" He leaned toward Walt with the card. Walt stepped into the room and took the card without expression. Also without response.

"Well? Well?" said Robert. "Have you or have you not received a card like this in the mail?"

"With a J on it?" Walt inquired.

"With *anything* on it!"

"No, Mr. Robert."

"Have you any idea what it might mean?"

"No, Mr. Robert." Walt handed the card back.

"Very well, then," said Robert York, and produced one of the imperious motions of the hand so characteristic of him—gestures he himself seemed quite unaware of. Walt apparently took it as a dismissal, for he blinked his round eyes once and backed through the door, closing it after him.

"Well?" Emily demanded. "What *is* the 'bisect thing'?"

Robert York twitched his head in irritation, and Tom Archer said, "It was just a thought of Mr. York's. In 1847 the U. S. issued a ten-cent black stamp. In those days, when a post office ran out of—say—its supply of five-centers, it wasn't unusual for a postmaster to make some out of his supply of ten-cent denominations simply by cutting them in half and selling the halves. Some exist on cover that were bisected vertically, others horizontally, and still others diagonally—that is, cut from an upper corner to the lower corner opposite.

"Well, there's long been a rumor among philatelists about a

supposed error among the 1847 black diagonal bisects. The story goes that some postmaster, instead of cutting diagonally from corner to corner, carelessly snipped a smaller triangular piece off the top corner of the stamps, so that what was left was actually five-sided—shaped something like this card. Since one of these, if it were found on cover, would be very rare—in fact, unique as far as we know—it would also be immensely valuable. Mr. York thought that maybe some stamp hunter's found such a piece and is taking this means of working up Mr. York's interest in it."

"Well," said Emily York, "that's just silly enough to explain it."

"All but the J," said Percival, adding a heh-heh sound.

Robert was scarlet. He snatched the card and flicked it, a tiny gesture expressing immensities of aggravation. "The J could be the fellow's initial, or—or something like that! Anyway, I *said* I'd changed my mind!" He dropped card and envelope into the open attaché case beside his chair. The scarlet remained, and when he spoke his voice held all the wistful anger of a simple-minded, clumsy-fingered man in a world of swift thinkers and capable hands. "I don't understand it. I don't like things I can't understand!"

"Then forget it, Robert," said Emily impatiently. "I'm late. Can't we push on? Is there anything important on the agenda?"

"Yes-by-God-there-is." It was an ugly snarl, Percival's. His glance impaled his cousin Robert. "I'm going to say this exactly once, and you'd better take it to heart: You keep messing up my charge accounts, Robert, and I'll-squash-you-by-God-like-a-by-God-roach!"

Robert York looked at Percival York wide-eyed, his yellow-pink skin turning yellow-gray. He glanced, startled, from face to face (Is it possible he's talking to *me?*), and finally back to Percival. (He *is* talking to me!) "I don't know what you mean, Percival."

"Don't add lying to your other talents, you double-crossing, two-faced, sneaky-hearted little would-be Napoleon," said Percival. "You know perfectly well you put her up to it."

"Her?" said Robert, again taking inventory of the familiar faces. (Emily's was a firm pink, but in his bewilderment Robert was color-blind.)

"Just don't you meddle in my private concerns again, that's all I'm going to tell you. Just don't, Robert. I warn you. I can do more kinds of damage than your rabbity little brain can imagine, and if this happens once more—*anything goes.*"

"But I don't know what you mean," was all the agitated Robert could find to say.

Percival showed his unlovely teeth in a wolfish grin, and he rose so suddenly that Robert shrank back. But all Percival did was to snatch up his homburg and stride from the room.

"But, Percival, what about—?" Robert mutely lifted the ledger from his lap.

Percival's reply was to *blam!* the front door.

Myra York clung hard to Ann Drew's hands. "Who was *that?*"

"Shh, dear. It's all right," Ann whispered.

Robert, surprisingly, said, "I'm sorry. I'm terribly sorry."

"It isn't your fault," said Archer, as consoling in his way as the girl was in hers.

"It most certainly is not," said Emily definitely. She seemed about to say more, but she hesitated and was lost.

"We'll get on, then," Robert said, wetting his lips—apparently to no purpose, for he had to do it again. "Now. We have a bill here for, ah—yes!—lawn fertilizer for the park. This of course will come from the general fund. And . . . I have a notation of breakage of a gold-trimmed meat platter from the Nathaniel York, Senior Collection. Although it was broken in Myra's house by the housekeeper, it really belonged to all of us. So replacement cost should perhaps come from the general fund—"

"It was a horrible thing," snapped Emily, back on safe ground. "Good riddance."

"Or on the other hand," continued Robert, "should it come out of the woman's wages? Archer, what was the inventory value of the platter?"

"A hundred and eighty dollars, sir."

"She really doesn't break very much," said Ann Drew timidly.

"Good riddance," Emily said again. "Write it off, Robert."

Robert looked from face to face, then made a mark in the ledger. "Very well. But naturally this must not continue. Now, ah . . . yes . . . Walt reports a broken curbstone in front of Percival's house. Percival really ought to be here to discuss this," he added fretfully. "Why on earth do you suppose—?"

"Forget it *and* him," Emily said hastily. "Please, Robert, get on with it. It's *late*."

So Robert York got on with it—the prorating of a tax charge; the distribution of an insurance refund; the recurrent argument over whether the Family or the Help, who were paid on the first of each month, should stand the loss of the extra day in thirty-one-day months—a standing controversy between Emily York, who was staunch for the rights of Labor, and Robert York, who was just as sturdy a defender of the prerogatives of the Employer, with the invariable result of "Tabled Until Our Next Meeting."

These meetings, they all realized, were more a fussy ritual than a necessity; their business could easily have been taken care of by one delegated person, with perhaps an occasional telephone call to one or more of the others. But so it had been decided when they took up their several residences in York Square (at the strange behest of the dead Nathaniel, Senior) and so it would be until death again intervened in their lives.

Robert York, still reacting to his cousin Percival's mysterious outbreak, concentrated on the petty agenda almost gratefully. Emily stuck with it because it was a Duty, and Duties were her life. Archer, full of his new responsibilities, bent to the task sincerely. Myra York paid close attention to an invisible something in a middle distance of Space and Time, and Ann Drew paid close attention to Tom Archer. Until at last it was done, the last entry posted in the ledger, the last item noted on the list of checks to be drawn, signed and mailed out in the morning; and at last, at last, the fixing of the date for the next meeting (always the second business day after the first day of the next month, a formula which invariably confused everyone but Robert). And then they went their ways: Emily to her unwed mothers; Myra to her bed; Ann to an innocent rendezvous with Archer after putting Myra there; and Robert to his study and the ever-engrossing plans for the grand cataloguing of his stamp collections.

No one, of course, checked up on Myra York after she was tucked in. Ann Drew and Tom Archer unaccountably missed one another. It happened that Robert did not get to work on his cataloguing plans after all. Emily was much later than she had planned in reaching her meeting. And no one knew just what Percival was up to (but then no one ever did).

It was just one of those days.

7. *Attack*

He sat alone in a hotel room. The bed had not been slept in, the two thin towels were untouched. On a cheap portable typewriter, working slowly and carefully, pausing only to adjust the machine to align exactly with the ruled lines on the tablet paper he was using, without ever an error, and with the even touch possible only to two-fingered typists of long practice, he was writing:

...and you will spend the morning trimming the ivy on the tower of Robert York's castle. When it is time for lunch, you will leave your shears on the tower and come down. You will go out by the front door this time, so that you may pass the door of his study.

You will stop just long enough to be certain — be absolutely certain — that your watch corresponds to his mantel clock, to the second. If anyone is about, pass on through and check it later in the day.

Under no circumstances overlook this detail — it is vital to my plan and to your glorious future.

At 7:20 make your way back quietly up to the tower. If you are seen and questioned either going up or coming down, say that you are going for your pruning shears.

At 7:31 o'clock you are to count the stone blocks on the north edge of the parapet, Number 1 being the first one to the right of the concrete coping at the corner.

At 7:33 you are to be in position with your hands on the 7th block. You will find the concrete cap cracked and the mortar cleaned away all around this block.

Precisely at 7:34 you are to push the block as hard as you can, so that it falls off the tower.

You will then quietly pick up your shears and, without hurrying, you will return by way of the kitchen and the garage corridor to the garage.

Place the shears on their hook as you go in, pick up the socket wrench from the bench, go round to the right side of Percival York's Ryan sports car, lie down on the mechanic's dolly you will find ready for you, roll under the car, and begin to drain the oil from the crankcase.

Ignore any sounds or voices you may hear unless and until you are called. If you are called, wait until you are called twice before answering. Then and thereafter you are to know nothing about the tower, the stone, or anything else connected with these orders. Stand firm, volunteer nothing and, above all, be yourself.

Be yourself, My Dear Walt. Be yourself, for by so doing you please me in my choice. Watch yourself being yourself, and share with me my pride in you, and recognize, as I have recognized, how infallibly I have chosen.

No one — no one at all — could do what you have done. No one will ever do what you will do. To qualify for that, a man would have to be you — and only you can be that. Be yourself, My Dear Walt.

Have you asked yourself why I call you, with these capital letters, My Dear Walt? — why I have not done so before, and whether there is some special meaning to it?

I assure you there is, and I promise you I shall make this revelation in my next writing.

And that will be after you have performed this service for me — for us.

Dispose of this letter as you have the others.

Y

8. Self-Block

The time came (yet again) when Inspector Richard Queen of New York City police headquarters had altogether and finally *enough*—up to here and brimming over. He recognized the signs. From long practice he knew how to contain what could be contained and how to sluice off the rest silently. But he knew also that when frustrated fatherhood reached the floodline, it would crest and overflow because of one extra drop—without warning, with a roar.

That time came one evening when, having let himself into the Queen apartment, the Inspector found no Ellery to greet him with a smile (or a frown) and/or a tingling highball to wash away the back-tooth grit of Centre Street.

The old man felt an almost audible *pop!* of disappointment. He kicked the foyer door to with his heel and put away his keys, frosted head and sparrow face cocked to listen; for the next most welcome thing, queerly enough, would be to find himself alone at this hour—meaning that Ellery had found something outside himself to interest and occupy him. The rattle of newsprint from Ellery's study ended that, and Level Two of anticipation went the way of the first.

Level Three was the wishful-thinking one, belonging as it did to the dream-of-glory family—of warty frogs turning into genuine handsome princes, of six-cent stock certificates suddenly quoted at $785. Anticipation on this third level, as it applied to Ellery's current plight, would have the voice of his typewriter soaring out of this world (away from Centre Street, or a private case, or an item in the newspaper) . . . high, high out of this world into the interplanetary spaces of Pure Mind . . . the voice bespeaking a new idea, a new twist, an Original. A sealed-room answer, perhaps, which no one had thought of before. A murderer with motive as deviously obscure as his logic was brilliantly clear to the all-seeing Ellery in the tale. Or the story might be The One, the ultimate case, the book for the books, satisfying on all counts, to all critics, to the author himself—and, of course, to the Inspector. For Level Three was a split level, whose impossible creation would bring joy even to an old man who knew how impossible it was.

But . . . listening to the inhabited silence, smelling the bitterness of coffee too long warming in the pot and of air blue-fogged by too much tobacco in a room dead-still with failure, Inspector Queen felt the bottom go out of his Level Three and the silly disappointment invade his shoulders, which it bowed.

The old gentleman crossed his living room to the son's study doorway and stood there looking in at the long limp ingrown figure at the desk—slumping as it had slumped yesterday, and the day (and week) before, and as it would likely slump tomorrow, at that mute, reproachful typewriter. Then Ellery turned his silvery eyes (tarnished now) from the newspaper, his head not moving, his spine remaining slack and hopeless, and in a voice as warm as ever (but tired as ever, too) said, "Hello, Dad. Anything happen downtown today?" And this was simply another way of saying, Because nothing happened up here today . . . as usual.

Anything happen? the Inspector thought. Oh, yes. A 183-ticket scofflaw happened. A bakery-truck driver allowed his eleven-year-old son to watch him blow off the mother's head with a 12-gauge shotgun; *that* happened. And two good officers were in critical condition, beaten up by what looked like the total population of the slum block in which they were picking up a pusher; there's a human-interest problem for you. And then there was the mysterious case of the teen-ager, a little girl really, who had already found out so much about life that she drank an incredible quantity of gasoline and was being rushed to the hospital when the ambulance struck a taxicab, killing both drivers, the taxi fare, the intern—everyone involved but the terrified kid, who would survive. And the thirty-year man the Inspector had known since the days when the police stables had dirt floors and smelled of honest horse instead of carbolic acid—a Captain now—*he* was caught today with his hand in the till; and what would you do with that, my son?

"Nothing," the old man said to his son.

"Rats," Ellery said. "I was hoping . . ."

This was the interchange, spoken and unspoken, this was the moment when the Inspector's containment could contain no more and the sluice spilled over, not silently.

"Well, what do you know," Inspector Queen said in a loud voice. "You were *hoping*," and the sluice-gate opened and out it poured, in a snarling rush. "You were hoping I'd bring you a present, little boy? Some nice chewy chocolate-covered goodie hot off Centre Street?"

Ellery took his feet down and swung about to look. An unbelievable pugnacity in his father's stance, weight shifted forward not quite to the balls of the feet, heels not quite raised . . .

"Hey," Ellery said, jumping up.

"So you *can* get off your backside! What did you do all day?"

Ellery said, "I—"

"What else did you use that typewriter for besides something to lean your elbows on?"

Ellery said again, "I—"

"How many cups of coffee did you drink today? How many packs of lung-buster did you smoke? Do you know how this room stinks? Ever hear of opening a window? It looks like one of those test chambers at Air Pollution Control in here! What's got into you, Ellery?"

"Well," Ellery began, "I—"

"Do you know I used to look forward to coming home at night? Just what do you think you're doing, anyway? Waiting for me to bring you home a story?"

Ellery said, "Wow," and chuckled. "That's pretty good, Dad. For a moment there I thought you were serious."

"*Serious?*" the Inspector hissed. He crumpled his topcoat and flung it across the room, at the same time charging up to the other side of Ellery's desk and leaning so far over with his chin stuck out that Ellery could see every aspen hair in his gray brush mustache. "I'll tell you how serious I am, Mr. Queen! I—want—you—the hell out of here!"

"What?" Ellery said feebly.

"Get out! *Go* somewhere, *do* something! You say you're a writer? Okay! Imagine something a living human being would do —anything at all!—and then just go out and pretend you're it. And pretty soon, Ellery, or so help me I'll have you embalmed!"

With which the waters of paternal anxiety fell off to a trickle, and the Inspector went over and retrieved his coat and stumped out of Ellery's study, muttering to himself. All of this Ellery watched with the round eyes and parted lips of an adenoidal idiot; and then he rubbed his unshaven cheeks and sat down again, looking intelligent.

So it was that (yet again) Inspector Richard Queen of police headquarters found himself, topcoat over his arm, keys in hand, standing in the doorway to his son's study, peering through the old blue fog at Ellery's recumbent length and bristling cheeks, chest at low tide, barely rising and falling. He seemed to be asleep.

The Inspector sighed. For him another working day had passed; for Ellery . . . "Still slaving away, son?" the old man said. There was even a sort of laughter in it.

But from this point everything was different.

Ellery's eyelids flew open, he sprang from his chair, he darted around the desk, he cried, "Dad, I've got it!"

The old man stepped back a pace, as if what his son had got might be contagious. "You have?"

Ellery followed him up, poking at him with a long, torn forefinger. "You were right the other night, Dad, but you were wrong, too. And I was wrong on *all* counts. I thought I had to wait for something to happen before I could write. Occupational blindness. All I had to do was figure out *why* I couldn't write. And I figured it out today!"

"You did?" the Inspector said cautiously.

"My trouble," Ellery chortled, snatching his father's hat off, grabbing his topcoat, tossing them both over his shoulder, forcing the old man down into the overstuffed chair near the fireplace, "my trouble is that I have a contemporary mind. That's all, Dad. That's absolutely all that's been wrong!"

"It is?"

"Certainly! I've always had a contemporary mind. I mean I've always written about the case I was working on at the time, or the one that was bothering you downtown—something *real,* in the here and now. But the times change, my old one," Ellery went on, striding up and down, rubbing his palms together like a Boy Scout making fire, kicking the rug, flinging himself onto the sofa, springing up again and darting to the study to pick up the Inspector's coat and hat, "and the more the times change the *faster* they change. Did you know that? Hah? Ellery's Law? Hell, they change so fast between one book and the next—what am I saying? between one day and the next!—that you don't even see it happen. Get my point, Dad? Do I convey anything to you?"

"No," said his father.

"Well, look!" cried Ellery. "What's happening to elevator operators?"

"What?" said his father. "Who?"

"Elevator operators. I'll tell you what's happening to them. They're *disappearing,* that's what—automated out of existence. Take the theater. Can you recognize a play any more? Ten-second scenes. Speeches consisting entirely of nouns and adjectives—no verbs. Actors moving scenery, and stagehands acting. Some of the cast in the audience. No curtain. No footlights. No *anything* of yesterday's theater. Everything's different, unexpected, purposely mystifying—not mystifying like a puzzle to be solved, but mystifying long after you're home in bed wondering what it was all about —and *meant* to be that way. My God, take this coat." Ellery whisked and twirled the Inspector's topcoat about, looking for the label. "Here! Dacron and orlon mixture with a nylon lining. This is coal, water and air you're wearing, Dad—I'll bet you thought it came from a sheep!" Ellery laugh-roared with the wonder of it, hurling the topcoat and hat across the living room into the foyer. "No, no, stay where you are, Dad—I'll mix 'em!"

"What?" croaked the Inspector.

"The drinks." Ellery scudded into the kitchen. The Inspector leaned back warily, keeping one eye open. He came upright to the alert when Ellery rushed back past him to the bar in the corner. "Yes, sir, that's what's been wrong with me, the contemporary mind," said Ellery briskly, snatching the stainless-steel ice mallet from its niche and striking his thumb smartly with it. "Damn." He aimed more carefully at the canvas-wrapped ice cubes. "Look. I don't want to sound mystic or anything, Dad, but sometimes I used to get the feeling I was a kind of natural counterpoise—"

"A what?"

"Well, that I existed because a certain kind of criminal existed. That I did what *I* did because he did what *he* did. He was"—Ellery probed finely—"he was the player on the other side."

"Other side." The Inspector wet his lips as he watched Ellery's hands at the bar.

"Yes. Well, that's it. I haven't been able to write any more because the player on the other side doesn't exist any more." He squinted at the small print on the bitters bottle. "The times have outdated him—swept him away, and me with him. I mean the old me. See what I mean?"

"Come *on*," the Inspector said.

"Right away, Dad. Because, you see, you constituted authorities have come up with just too much wizardry—a speck of dust, and you know the murderer's height, weight, prep school and breeding habits. Police science today specializes in making the unusual usual—instant communications, electronic bugs, consulting head-doctors, non-criminal fingerprint files . . ." He brought his father the long-awaited drink, which the knurled fingers seized greedily and conveyed mouthward with a snort of almost passion. "Why, even the TV writers, for all the hoke and hooey they shovel out, deal in dosimeters and polygraphs and other miracles of the lab, and sometimes they even use 'em right." Ellery fell back on the sofa, waved his glass. "So what chance does little-old-the-likes-of-me have, with my old-fashioned wonders? There's no wonderment left in the real world any longer. Or rather, everything is so wonderful the wonder's gone out of it. I can't outthink a solid-state binary computer; I can't outplay an electronic chess opponent—it'll beat me every time. Skoal."

He drank, and the old man drank again, keeping his eyes anxiously on his son's face while he did so.

Ellery banged his glass down on the coffee table. "So! Now that I know why I dried up, I know what to do about it."

"You do?"

"I do."

"And what's that?"

"I'm taking no more cases—mine, yours, anybody's. I'm through investigating crimes. What I write from now on is going to come out of here"—he tapped his temple—"entirely. Something new, something different. I don't know what yet, but it'll come."

"No more cases," his father said after a contemplative time.

"No more cases."

"Too bad."

Ellery pursued a fugitive thought.

After a while he looked up. His father was staring at him in the most peculiar way. In spite of himself, Ellery began to feel his way back along the past quarter-hour, like a man crossing a muddy stream on invisible stepping stones.

"Too bad?" Ellery said. "Dad, did you say 'too bad'?"

"That's what I said."

"Yes, and before that all you said was 'He did?' . . . 'You were?' . . . 'You do?' . . . 'What?'—"

"I did?" the Inspector said sheepishly.

Ellery chewed on his lower lip for a moment. "Dad."

"Hmm?"

"What is it?"

"What is what?"

Ellery exploded. "*Balls* of fire! The other night you chewed me out for waiting for a case to happen so I could start writing again. You know why you dumped your ill-temper on me? Because you were feeling guilty over not having a case to bring home to me! Tonight, when I announce I'm giving up case work as a basis for my novels, you start acting bashful and coy. Remember me, Dad? I'm the child of your loins and I'm starving! What nourishment have you brought me from downtown?"

Inexplicably, each began to laugh. Their laughter did not last long, but it sufficed. Where that laughter came from, words could not reach.

The Inspector shifted his wiry body a little and reached into a side pocket. "Fellow got himself slaughtered the other night. Person or persons as yet unknown. In fact, everything as yet unknown."

"So?"

"So. This came in the mail for him just before he was clobbered." The Inspector produced something from the pocket he had been exploring and rose and went over to the coffee table and dropped his find before Ellery.

Ellery leaned forward at the waist. His eyebrows drew ever so lightly toward each other as he studied what the Inspector had produced for his inspection.

It was a five-sided white card of peculiar proportions, with a capital J stamped on it in what seemed to be black stamping-pad ink.

The Inspector said, "That was the first one."

9. Y's Gambit Accepted

"Never saw anything like it," Inspector Queen was saying. "That house, I mean. It's laid out like a surgeon's tray. Chair in a corner had to be checked with a draftsman's triangle for exact placement. Big picture mathematically centered on the wall, with two little pictures the same size flanking it exactly the same distance away. Just so much floor could show at each end of the carpet. Whole house is like that except the secretary's room—I don't mean his room's grubby, just that it looks as if someone lives there, which the rest of the house doesn't. You'll see for yourself, Ellery."

Ellery made no commitment. He was staring at the card.

"But he—the lord and master of all this . . . this exactitude—he was the godawfulest mess you ever saw, *I* ever saw," the old man went on. "I've seen accident cases spread out over half a block didn't look as messy as that patio. I s'pose that's what gave me the feeling right off that this case is going to be a wrongo—your kind of wrongo, Ellery. He was lying on a steel-framed chaise on the patio just outside his impeccable dining room. Except for his head, I mean. That was scattered to hell and gone. Someone'd shoved a two-hundred-pound granite block off the top of the tower forty feet above him . . . onto his head."

"This is Robert York you're talking about," Ellery said suddenly. "Of York Square."

"How did you know that? Oh, the papers. Yump," the Inspector said, "it's the Robert York case, all right."

"May I handle the card?"

"Yes."

Ellery picked up the white card, turned it over, turned it back. "What's this J?"

"You tell me, son. There isn't a John, Jack, Jim, Joan or Jehoshaphat in all of York Square. Or a Johnson, Jackson or Jimson, either."

Ellery replaced the card on the coffee table and began to hypnotize it. "Go on. It couldn't have been an accident?"

"Not unless somebody accidentally chipped away all the mortar around the stone, accidentally cracked it loose with a pinch bar and then accidentally swept up all the stone dust. Velie got up there like lightning, and I wasn't far behind. Nobody'd have had time to do that thorough a clean-up job after the push-off. So it had to have been done beforehand—maybe days before, weeks. And that makes it premeditated murder."

"How was the granite block tipped off the tower?"

"By a good hard push. That stone wasn't teetering in the balance up there, Ellery. It was a solid block with a dead-flat seat under it. Even without the mortar it would have stayed put during a hundred years of hurricanes."

"So all the block-buster had to do was wait until York happened to be directly underneath—?"

"That's the beauty part. This Robert York 'happened' to be directly underneath on every mild evening from May fifteenth to October first at half-past seven, give or take ten seconds—you heard me, ten *seconds*—and there he'd stay until half-past eight on the dot. Rainy or chilly evenings he'd lie down on the settee in his study. But he always napped exactly one hour after dinner."

"Which, of course, everyone in the place knew?"

"And more people outside it than I care to think about trying to track down. He liked to brag about the to-the-second regularity of his habits. And how he could fall asleep on a dime and wake himself up the same way."

"Built-in alarm clock." Ellery nodded. "Who had access to the tower, Dad?"

"Everybody," grunted the old man. "There's an outside door that opens directly to the tower stairs, also an inside door in the downstairs hall that runs between the front rooms and the kitchen."

"Doors kept locked?"

"Only the outside door, but the lock is an old relic you could undo with your front teeth without leaving a mark."

"Who was in the house at the time the granite block fell?"

"Nobody. The handyman was in the garage, changing the oil in one of the cars."

"Didn't he hear or see anything?"

"He says no. Could be, too. The garage is pretty far from the terrace, and the block was—well—cushioned some when it landed."

Ellery made a face. "Who cooked York's dinner?"

"Housekeeper, a sleep-out name of Mrs. Schriver. She always had his meal ready at a quarter of seven, he was always finished at five after. Then she'd carry the dishes out to the kitchen and go home."

"Didn't wash them before leaving? Oh, of course. Don't disturb the master at his nap."

"Right."

Ellery pulled at his lower lip until it stretched like a Ubangi's. "Think of asking anyone how sound a sleeper he was?"

"Didn't I. Consensus is that you couldn't have waked York with a fire hose till he chose to wake himself."

Ellery frowned. "Then what's this nonsense about the housekeeper's not doing the dishes because it would disturb His Majesty's nap?"

"I asked her. She says it's a habit she got into when she went to work there three years ago and first found out about Robert York's after-dinner snooze. She just never bothered to change her routine."

"Big strong woman, is she?"

The Inspector showed his dentures in what might have been laughter. "*Little* strong woman."

Ellery communed with some invisible entity in midair. Suddenly he said, "What about this handyman?"

"Walt? Oh, he's a dandy little suspect. Up on the tower that day, too, trimming the ivy. Says even if the mortar under the block had been loosened by that time he'd likely not have noticed. I can believe that, by the way. The cracks are thin and deep-set; you can hardly see the mortar on or under the other blocks. Sure, Walt could have done the whole job, then skinned on down and out to the garage. But so could everybody else. Everybody."

"Ugh," Ellery said mildly. "All right—who found the headless paragon?"

"His secretary. Young guy named Thomas Archer. Archer is remounting York's stamp collections or something—been putting in a lot of night work."

"Did Archer have dinner with York?"

"No. He used to all the time, but Mrs. Schriver tells me he's eaten most of his meals out lately."

"Out where?"

"That night? At Myra York's house—the one in the southeast corner of the Square."

"How come?"

"Myra has a paid companion, a girl named Ann Drew, who's apparently stirred young Archer's blood. He had dinner with the girl in Myra York's kitchen. Myra was upstairs in bed, sick."

"So the girl alibis this Archer fellow?"

"They alibi each *other*," said the old man with a grimace, "which I hate. By the way, if this Drew number doesn't bubble *your* blood a little, son—"

Ellery interrupted. "And the other denizens of York Square?"

"Well, Cousin Emily claims she was alone in her house writing letters. Cousin Percival says he was alone in *his* house washing down a hangover so he'd feel up to building another one."

"And that accounts for the lot? Including the help?"

The old man nodded grimly. "That's it. Any one of 'em could have done it."

"Including the man from Dubuque," Ellery said thoughtfully.

"Theoretically, sure. But I don't think this was the work of a passing stranger. Strangers don't get to hang around York Square for days—or even hours—ahead of time chipping out mortar on one of the towers."

Ellery stared down at the inked J on the card. "The newspaper accounts say that Robert York's death means an extra million or so to each of his cousins when the whole bundle comes due. When is that, by the way?"

"According to the will, in about six months. Equal shares to all surviving heirs at the time the estate is distributed."

"The old tontine foolishness," Ellery said in disgust. "This is Nathaniel York, Senior's will you're talking about?"

"Yes. Robert's will left everything *he* has to the joint estate, too. It doesn't amount to much—I mean, compared to the sheer mass of the principal estate—although of course to you and me it would be a fortune."

They were silent for a while.

"Emily York's some sort of ascetic, isn't she?" Ellery murmured, looking up. "And Myra's an invalid? I can't see either of them going out of her way to jack up the big pot by cutting down on the number of heirs. Which would seem to leave Percival."

The Inspector's face took on a look of deep yearning. "Just between you and me, son, I'd like for it to come out that way. There's a walking, talking pimple if ever I saw one!"

"So I gather. But what would even a no-goodnik like Percival, who'll soon have three million dollars to spend, want with a fourth?"

"Are you kidding?"

"Enough to commit murder for, I mean."

"Oh, stop, Ellery. Next you'll be saying that babies really are delivered by storks. Besides which, I haven't counted out the lady cousins by a long shot."

"You think Emily or Myra could have pushed over two hundred pounds of stone?"

"They could have paid some muscle to do the pushing, couldn't they?—after chipping away the mortar themselves."

"Any indication of that?"

"Give me a chance, will you?" the Inspector grumbled. "But talking about motive. Take this Emily. Sure *is* an ascetic—a millionaire ascetic, the most fanatical kind. She uses only two rooms of that castle of hers, works for a settlement house, lives mostly on her settlement-house pay, and donates the bulk of her income from the estate *to* the settlement house. And she's got big plans for when she comes into her share of the millions, I understand, plans involving her work. She's a funny old gal, and if something happened to threaten the distribution of those millions in any way —I wouldn't put *anything* past her."

"And Myra?" Ellery asked.

The old man said slowly, "She looks harmless—*looks* harmless. Maybe she's what she seems to be. But . . . I don't know. Myra's some kind of nut. Trouble is, I can't figure out what kind. Vague. Unpredictable . . ." He shook his head. "You'll see, Ellery."

"Now I haven't said—" began Ellery.

"Oh. Sure. Excuse me," his father said. "*If* you'll join me in this head-breaker, you'll see."

Ellery grunted and subsided. "Is there anyone else who might feel better off in a Robert Yorkless world?"

The old man shrugged. "Far as I can tell, nobody loved him, nobody hated him. Young Archer, his secretary, tells me Robert always tried to be absolutely fair. According to Robert's lights, of course, which I gather very few people but Archer appreciated."

"Oh, so? How come? What about this Archer?"

"Bright, on the bookish side. We're interested in him because of that stamp collection of Robert York's he's remounting and recataloguing. He's been told by Emily and Percival to go on with the stamp work, because of course it goes to the joint estate along with Robert's other personal property—"

"Hold it." Ellery had sat up abruptly. "I must have been thinking of something else when you mentioned stamp collections a while back. Robert York—sure! His philatelic holdings are supposed to be quite remarkable. He was one of the best-known collectors in New York. That means this Tom Archer has his hands on some mighty negotiable valuables—"

"Sure has," grinned the Inspector. "He could tuck one measly little stamp in an old envelope and walk off with eight, ten grand. That's why we're watching him. Though it isn't likely he'd try it. You can bet that a man who kept an inventory of his collar buttons —that's right, our Robert still used collar buttons!—wouldn't leave his rare stamps around like old confetti. His executors—a bank, by the way—have a list of every last stamp Robert ever bought or sold, and it's up to date."

"Check," Ellery said, shrugging. "Does Archer get anything out of Robert York's death?"

"Not as far as I know. He got a raise in pay only a week or so ago, when Robert gave him power of attorney to handle the nuts-and-bolts details of running York Square—with the others' consent, of course. In fact, Emily and Percival—and technically Myra—want Archer to keep on in that capacity. He seems capable enough, and happy in his job."

"How happy?"

"You mean about the murder of Robert? No, that seems to have shaken Archer up. I'd say he came closer to *liking* Robert than anybody else we've talked to."

"Watch him, then," said Ellery. "Who's left? Oh, the handyman—Walt. What about him?"

"Speaks when he's spoken to, can do anything in the way of manual work, couldn't possibly be as dumb as he looks and acts. Takes care of everything around the place except what the housekeeper does."

"And the housekeeper? What's her name—Mrs. Schriver?"

Inspector Queen shook his head. "A housekeeper. Helps Myra York's companion—Ann Drew—with heavy cleaning once a week, straightens up Percival's place twice a week, used to cook and clean for Robert every day. Neither Mrs. Schriver nor Walt stands to gain so much as a second-hand salami by Robert's death—or anyone else's, far as I can make out."

"Leaving the girl."

"Ah, the girl," the old man said with a wistful nod. "Wait till you see that girl, Ellery—"

"You're not going to get to me that way," Ellery said, snorting. Again he stared down at the J-card. Suddenly he looked up. "Wait a minute! I'm really rusty. When you showed me this card . . . Did you or didn't you say something about its being the first one?"

"Hm?" said the Inspector. "Oh! That's right."

Ellery was glaring at him. "You mean there's been a *second* card?"

"Didn't I mention that?" the old man asked innocently. He dug into the other pocket, pulled out another five-sided white card, laid it delicately before his son.

It, too, bore a letter of the alphabet.

An H.

PART TWO

Middle Game

10. *Attack Continued*

He had sat alone in the cheap hotel room watching slit-eyed and lipless the steady pistons of his index fingers laying word after careful word down on the pale blue lines of the copy paper.

He had written, in part:

...to tell you, as I promised, why I write My Dear Walt. Each word I write means something, and when I write those words they mean something precious and special.

"My" means you are mine, my creature and my property. You of all people will glory in this, for you understand how mighty are the meek, and that they shall inherit the earth. Let the tall grasses hold up their arrogant heads for the scythe to take. Be little and brown and unnoticed, and you will be alive under the sun's eye when they, the tall ones, have been bundled away.

And "Dear" means, above all, "chosen," for I speak like this to no other living soul. It means "valued." It means "trusted." And most of all it means "invulnerable," for no one can harm you under my protection.

Last and greatest..."Walt." "Walt" means you, My Dear Walt, you, unique, gifted with grace-in-obedience, fated to command while invisible — dispenser of life and of death.

Now there is a small quiet thing to be done perfectly, and so I call upon you.

In the envelope with this letter you will find a second card. As before, you will practice with the printing set until you are sure of a clear impression.

You will then print the letter H exactly like this:

being sure that the diagonal side of the card is at the lower right. You will note that the H in your printing set has a crossbar that is above the center of the letter. Be very careful to print it as you see it in my drawing; for if you were to print it upside down, with the crossbar low, it would be wrong and unworthy of you.

When you have done this, seal the card in a plain envelope as before, and address it (in the same neat plain capital letters you used the first time) to:

EMILY YORK
YORK SQUARE
NEW YORK, N. Y.

Put a stamp on it. Destroy any traces of your work on your table, hands or anywhere in your room. Dispose of this letter and envelope as you did the last time.

Then go out and mail the new letter, following my original instructions.

I feel your gratitude, My Dear Walt. I know how grateful you are to me for having chosen you.

I am pleased with you.

Y

11. Development

"One thing is clear," said Ellery, poking the two white cards with a troubled fingertip. "This one with the J is the shape of Robert York's corner of York Square, the southwest corner; and Robert got the J-card and was killed. And this one with the H must represent the *north*west corner, Emily's, because Emily got the H-card—"

"My dear son, do I need you to tell me that?" the old man asked wearily. "And if it's protection for Emily you're worried about, I doubled the foot patrol for the entire neighborhood, and I have a prowl car hitting the Square itself every twenty minutes, day and night."

"I hope that's enough."

"You'd like me to put somebody inside? Then you figure out a way. Emily York has an exaggerated idea of what would happen to her with a man in the house. Absolutely put her foot down."

"Virgin territory, eh?" Ellery shook his head, frowning. "There's another thing that would bother me if I were you. The attempt on her life may be planned to take place not in the Square or in her house but somewhere else."

"You think I should have her tailed," Inspector Queen said dryly.

"I most certainly do."

"Well, so do I!" the Inspector snapped. "I had Hesse tailing her when she left for work yesterday morning. You know what?—Hesse can't get over it yet—she spotted him in three minutes and gave him the slip! Seems Emily thought he might be 'after' her. When I told Miss Eagle-Eye that Hesse is a detective assigned to protect her, you know what she said to me? 'I'm not taking chances on *anybody*.' She's a holy terror, that woman. We'll do our best, but you know how tough it is to guard somebody who won't co-operate."

Ellery looked unhappy. "I suppose you drew a blank on fingerprints?"

"Blank? The J-card has *everybody's* prints on it. Seems the late Robert passed it around at the last monthly powwow of the tribe, where they sweat out who owes how much for the garbagemen tips. He even let the housekeeper and the handyman handle it."

"Paper, card, envelope, type, ink, et cetera?" Ellery murmured.

"No sweat. You could duplicate the paper, envelope and card within spitting distance of the Square—or in any five-and-dime or stationery store in the U.S.A. Lab doesn't hold out much hope about the block-letter address. The rubber-stamp type and ink come from a kid's toy printing set called Prints Charming that's been a standard item for years. It's sold by the thousands all over town."

"Great," muttered Ellery. "And the H-card mailing?"

"Emily York's prints, of course. And a Miss Sullivan's. And a couple of smudged partials that may or may not belong to somebody else. And Ann Drew's—in her case just on the envelope. Don't look so happy. The girl happened to bring the Square's mail up from the Church Street post office. Dropped that particular envelope off at Emily's house, and Emily took it to work with her."

"A Miss Sullivan," said Ellery. "Who's Miss Sullivan?"

"Ah," sighed the Inspector. "I was coming to that."

It was Miss Sullivan (Inspector Queen informed Ellery) who had told him of Emily York's plans for the settlement-house development. Miss Sullivan ran the place, a converted brownstone, its grand past barely hinted at by the time-chipped interior, condemned for life to the seething street the city had long since abandoned to its fate.

"I can't really tell you anything about it," Miss Sullivan said when the Inspector (following a surmise, an overheard remark and sheer logic) asked her whether Emily York's imminent bonanza would change things at the settlement house.

"Why not, Miss Sullivan?"

Her voice was sanded only at the margins by the abrasives of time. Yet she was surely in her mid-seventies. She breathed with a difficulty not surprising in view of her bulk, which her birdy-quick skeleton and tiny feet must have found a fearful burden.

Her nose was extraordinary; the Inspector wondered if she knew how fatefully it must have affected her lifelong tenure on the "Miss." Her innocence of glasses was explained by neither contact lenses nor vanity; and this was a great boon, for after the first few moments he conversed only with the warm, shy, joyful little person who dwelt inside her eyes. They were of a clean-bleached blue, with a snapping washline quality, like summer linen of the softest, highest grade laundered and set out to dry daily in the sun over a lifetime.

"You see, I know nothing about it." But Miss Sullivan's remarkable eyes were saying happily, *But I do, I do!* And when the Inspector refused to accept that spoken denial and merely stood waiting quietly for more, it was as if the little person inside darted to the right, to the left, hunting something to hide behind—not at all fearfully, but *Catch me! Catch me!* like a laughing child running off with a present which was not hers at all.

"I mean, Miss York wouldn't want me to say a word," she said; and still the Inspector waited, applying no pressure, the small smile on his lips genuine, evoked by the pleasure of her secret. "And I've promised, Inspector, really I have."

"If you told me," he asked gently, "are you afraid she'd change her mind about whatever it is she intends to do with the money?"

"Oh, dear, no! Not Emily York! It means too much to her."

The Inspector said craftily, "She's a fine woman." They beamed at each other. "I overheard something," he added, "when I came in. In that room to the left of the entrance?" The room to the left of the entrance was a sort of stable for the idle, the beaten, the sodden, the rudderless human hulks of the neighborhood.

"You mean in the reading room?" said Miss Sullivan.

"In the reading room," he nodded. "One of the men wanted to leave and go down to the Seaman's Mission for a meal and a bed, but another one told him to stay put and make himself known to you ladies, because big things were going to happen around here soon and you'd need their help." (This was his freehand translation of the bum who had said, "I'm cuttin' this cave, it gives me the goddamn itch. Let's go Sea-Missy and pray us some slops and a shelf." And of his one-eyed adviser who had pulled him back on the bench and said, "Jest you set and smile and give 'em a good pitch. Git acquainted here. The Vinegar Virgin gone come th'oo thet door one time soon pushin' a buggy full o' gold bars. You best be in line, man, 'cause she gone buy us a hotel in the country. Ev'body knows that.")

"Oh, yes, some of them would do, well, just anything for Emily York," said Miss Sullivan. "I wonder how they heard?"

"It isn't really going to be a hotel, then?"

"Dear me, no!"

"They'll be disappointed," said the Inspector, shaking his head. "That's what the poor fellows think it's going to be."

"Well, it *isn't*," she said firmly, and the one inside said pleadingly with her eyes, *Ask me! Ask me!*

But—"They'll really be disappointed," he said, and half turned toward the door.

"Oh, but they won't. Oh, dear, must you—? Please!" Her little hands fluttered and caught each other and trembled together. He thought: Those hands belong to the eyes. "Please shut the door." He shut it carefully. She said, "I *can* trust you . . . ?" and the eyes said, *Please? Please?*

"Miss York will never know I know," he assured her.

The eyes sparkled. With conspiratorial zest she said, "Turn *that* over!"

He followed her small finger to the wall, grasped the frame of a large yellowed street map of the settlement neighborhood and the nearby waterfront, turned it over and stepped back.

"Sometimes we just sit here and look at it," she half sang, half whispered.

It was a housing-plan elevation. A box in one corner was occupied by an architect's rendering of a cottage. A flagstone path wound around a lawn to a porch whose roof was supported by square fieldstone columns joined by Byzantine arches, and enclosed by a low concrete-capped parapet. What could be seen of the porch floor was brick tile, and Miss Sullivan explained that the interior would be floored with tile also, a satin-finish ceramic which would clean easily, glow with color and last forever. The building itself would seem larger inside than it did outside, with its ells and gables. The small panes of the many windows, as well as the fanlight which repeated the porch arches, would have their occasional stained square, so that inside by day, outside by night, color would brighten the beholder.

"Rambler roses across the front," Miss Sullivan crooned, pointing. "Ivy on the south and west walls, and forsythia on the north side to look winter in the eye when it comes to bloom. Here mountain laurel and dogwood. And here bleeding heart. And all along the edge here babies'-breath. And every year, hollyhocks and sunflowers and zinnias and honeysuckle. You'll see!"

Looking over the larger plan, the Inspector asked, "Where's this going to be built?"

"It's not far from New York—I mustn't say where, because Miss York only has an understanding about the land, and if people found out about the village, why, land values would go just sky-high and use up all the money."

The Inspector suddenly saw the correlation between the cottage and the curving rows of identical inkblots on the large plan. "She's intending to build a whole *village?*"

"Well, how else could we do it?" cried Miss Sullivan. "Forty-two cottages just like that one—it was to be thirty-five, you know, but now that poor Mr. York has passed away, and there's one less to share the estate, we'll be able to manage seven cottages more. And an administration building, and the help's quarters, and so on. Over here, by the way, is a stone outcrop big enough for us to quarry all the stone we'll need for the cottages and other buildings. All this here—eighty acres—is fine farmland. Here in the south quadrant we'll have a modern cow barn; pigs here; geese and ducks and chickens here. Maybe turkeys, too, though we're not sure of that yet—they're said to be *very* hard to raise. And over here we'll have the slaughter shack for the fowl, the smokehouse, the refrigerator rooms—oh, and of course this is going to be a huge hay barn. This section is for the workshops—carpentry, ceramics, a wool shop if we decide to raise sheep . . . Oh, and here! These are our greenhouses. Three for forced truck-gardening—for out-of-season things, you know—and two for flowers."

"I see," murmured Inspector Queen. "Self-supporting, eh? Maybe even showing a profit?"

"Well, of course we'll have a large staff, and they're to be *well paid,*" Miss Sullivan said with sudden severity, as if he had assumed an *ante-bellum* society, "so in the beginning we'll be satisfied to keep our heads above water. But we'll be producing milk and butter and cheese and bacon and hams and dressed fowl and vegetables and flowers, and Miss York said something about perhaps making our own bread and of course country furniture and hand-turned pottery and"—she paused for a long and happy gasp of breath—"and *goodness* knows what else. So we ought to manage most of our expenses even without the guests."

"The guests?" the Inspector echoed, mystified.

"Those gentlemen you saw downstairs."

"Those—" He coughed hurriedly.

"Yes," Miss Sullivan said with asperity, "those—gentlemen!" and he cursed himself for his *lapsus linguae*. The one inside—the one behind the eyes—could shoot bright bolts of indignation. "Dignity, Inspector Queen, *dignity*. Who needs it more than the weary and sick and homeless who never learned a skill or belonged to anyone or anything? Here they'll have the opportunity to grow strong, to be treated with decency, to acquire an individual *meaning*. Every last man of them will be called *Mister*. Each will have his own room, with his own possessions in it, and we'll be there to —yes, to *cater* to him, to find out what he likes and doesn't like, what he's able to do and what he's not. Oh," Miss Sullivan cried, "it will be wonderful!"

Very carefully Inspector Queen said, "I think you might wind up with—well—a gang of long-term freeloaders."

There came into the child-eyes a shimmer of scornful wisdom. "They will be *paying* guests, Inspector!"

"With what will they pay, Miss Sullivan?"

"With *themselves*, don't you see? Each one will be extended credit, depending on his needs. The longer he stays, the greater his debt, true. *But*. For everything he does for the village after we teach him a skill—making a chair, hoeing a row of corn, tending the chicken plucker—his debt is reduced."

"And if he never gets out of the red?"

She smiled. "Do you know, Inspector, most people—even fine people like yourself—have the minds of accountants?" The Inspector blushed, something he had not done for forty years. "Never get out of the red! Won't he have learned a trade? Won't he be rested, well fed? Won't he have discovered the satisfaction of a clean body and the stimulus of a fresh attitude toward life? And if he should find himself wanting to belong to something bigger than our village, he'll go back into the world, but with what a difference! He'll be *new*, self-confident, full of hope." She was so illuminated from within he could have groaned. "Inspector, it will *work*. You'll see!"

I don't have to see, the Inspector thought. I see daily.

He saw Centre Street line-ups—shills, pimps, muggers, gunsels, sharks, sharpies, touts, shiv artists, bums, pushers, addicts, creeps, morons, dips, muscle men, maniacs, and all-around misfits. In a parade, a cascade, that never stopped. He thought piously: Dear God, let this pipe dream of hers stay just that. She's too old to have to take the dirty truth. Or is it possible—I mean, am I such a jaded old crock . . . ?

His ears prickled a warning, alerted by a note in that burble of half song. ". . . just to give them those things, those simple and essential things, like the right to be called 'Mister.' *That's* what Emily York wants her money for. *That's* why she lives the way she does, in just two rooms of that big house, on a social worker's salary, turning practically her whole income over to the settlement house here. And that's why she'd do—oh, anything—to protect the York estate."

"Sorry," said the Inspector, controlling his voice with the discipline of a TV announcer. "I didn't quite get that, Miss Sullivan. Protect the York estate from what?"

"Well . . . from anything that might threaten it." She was suddenly troubled. "I mean, anything that might reduce her share of it . . ." He could almost see the girlish Miss Sullivan deep inside place little palms against an appalled mouth. "I'm afraid I'm talking too much."

"I wouldn't misuse it," he said, quickly and warmly.

"Thank you." She hunted for something in his face and seemed to find it. "Thank you," she said again, and went to the plan and set her frail fingers under the frame. The Inspector hastened to help her. Together they turned it over, and for a moment they stood tandem, looking at the yellowed street map of the blighted neighborhood and the noisome waterfront. Then Miss Sullivan turned her back on it and asked, "Was there anything else you wanted to know, Inspector?"

"Well, I don't mean to pry—"

"Don't you, now!" Miss Sullivan laughed her gasping laugh. "And you a police officer." She stopped laughing, and sighed, and lowered her great mass carefully into the vast chair behind the desk. "Sit down, Inspector Queen. I'm afraid you're no better at deception than I am."

He grinned feebly, drawing up a chair, feeling chagrin and guilt and something else that eluded classification. "I'm taking up too much of your time. You've been to York Square, Miss Sullivan?"

"Goodness, yes. Often."

"Just in Miss Emily York's house?"

"Oh, no, I've been asked to dinner, one time or another, in all but Percival York's. Chiefly at Emily's, of course. Many's the time the two of us have worked through the night on plans for the village." Miss Sullivan said suddenly, "You think we're both impossible dreamers, don't you, Inspector?"

"Oh, no," he said. *Was* it possible?

"Oh, yes," she retorted. "Well, perhaps we are. I remember Emily used to dream of turning the four castles into one neighborhood-house type of community. But that *was* impossible, she said, because her share of the estate simply wouldn't be enough to buy the others out. You see, the village upstate is planned for just men. But with York Square we could have a headquarters building and three houses for women—one a residence club, say, another a clinic, the third a school. It *would* be nice," she said wistfully.

"How about now?" the Inspector asked, and despised himself. "I mean now that Emily's share is going to be a million or so larger?" She looked at him, and he said, "There I go, prying again, right?"

She gasped with laughter again. "Yes, bless you. But that's not a very nice thought, Inspector, is it?"

He thought: You can bet your lavender sachet it's not a very nice thought. But very not-nice thoughts are why I'm here. And he found himself wondering how old was the controversy over the end and the means. Did a perplexing whiff of it pass through the massive skull of some prehuman homunculus the day he hurled his brother into the jaws of a saber-tooth so that he himself might escape?

In this particular balance, lonely on one pan of the scales, stood Myra and Percival York—Myra a mental and physical invalid, Percival unlovable and unmournable; and on the other pan huddled a street swarm of human wreckage—to be reborn, to be grown whole again and (to the Inspector, above all) to be taken off the streets and out of the cluttered courtrooms. For possibly the first time in his life Inspector Richard Queen, the old hound dog of Centre Street, sniffed at the idea of being just a little blind, just a fraction forgetful, just a tiny bit obtuse . . . It was this damned Sullivan woman!

The Inspector shook himself almost visibly, aware of her soft song-voice. "Beg pardon?"

"Are you all right, Inspector?" she asked—was asking—anxiously. "Oh, dear, I've made you angry."

"Not at all," he said gallantly, and grinned. "You couldn't."

"You looked so very stern suddenly."

"I was thinking of how Robert York died," said the Inspector, and told himself aloud with hushed force, "I don't *like* murder, no matter *why* it's done." And felt much better for having said it.

"Poor Emily," murmured Miss Sullivan.

"Would you say she's taking Robert's death hard?"

"Oh, she is. Dreadfully."

"I wouldn't have said so."

"Because you don't know her, Inspector. Dear Emily is very controlled. Threats or violence"—surprisingly, Miss Sullivan chuckled—"are things she simply will not *allow*. Time and again I've seen her stand up to rampaging drunks, raving addicts, the worst hoodlums. She'll walk right into danger without a *thing* showing, though I'm sure she's as afraid as anyone else. She's the same way about grief, I suppose."

"Very controlled," the Inspector repeated thoughtfully.

"Take yesterday, for example. She just worked a bit harder, that was all. You wouldn't have realized anything was disturbing her unless you knew the signs. Like her losing patience. At little things, never the big ones."

"Oh?"

"A door banging somewhere. Mustard on a sandwich when she'd ordered it without mustard—goodness! she never notices what she eats. But how she carried on about that mustard. And then there was that silly card—"

A shooting thrill, much like a little bolt of lightning, almost lifted the old man out of the chair. "Silly card?" he said. "What do you mean, Miss Sullivan?"

"I saved it." Miss Sullivan began opening drawers. "It's here somewhere . . . Why, she'd just come in and taken the mail out of her bag—she always brings her mail from home to the office—and settled down as usual to go through it. All of a sudden she made a kind of *tsst!*—"

"*Tsst?*"

"*Tsst!*" Miss Sullivan corrected him, repeating the exclamation point he had left out. "And she hurled the card and envelope to the floor. *The floor—Emily!* Here it is." She handed the plain white envelope to Inspector Queen, who took from it the five-sided white card bearing the H.

After a while the Inspector looked up. "Did Miss York happen to say why this bothered her so much?"

"Oh, I don't think it bothered her at all. Not the *card*. More the nuisance of it, I'm sure. You see, I know her." Scanning his face, Miss Sullivan apparently read doubt there. "I mean, had it really bothered her—the thing in itself—she'd have called me over to look or made phone calls, or . . . or any number of things. She threw it like that because it *wasn't* important, you see, not because it was." She said again, "I *know* her."

"Did she discuss this with you at all?"

"Well, of course I picked it up and said, 'What on earth, Emily—?' and she"—the young smooth one behind the bleached old eyes puckered with remembered hurt—"and she was sharp, quite sharp, with me. What she said was, 'Let me alone!—please.' And it wasn't a very big 'please,' so I knew she was already sorry for being sharp, that she wasn't troubled about the card, only annoyed with it."

"Then why did you keep it?" he asked, because he had to.

"Oh . . . that's me all over," Miss Sullivan laughed. "Always pick up a glove because one day I might find the mate. That card isn't a thing, Inspector, if you really look at it. It's a *piece* of a thing, strikes me. So the other piece must be around somewhere."

"You ought to meet my son," said the Inspector suddenly, heartily. Then before she could answer he asked, "And so Miss York didn't even attempt to guess what this might be?"

"I mentioned it at lunch," she said, her voice infused with the shyness she had felt at the time, "and all she said was, 'Oh, it's a ridiculous advertising teaser,' and I could see she didn't want to talk about it. It could be a puzzle of some kind, don't you think?"

"Could be," said the Inspector, and he slipped the card into the envelope and the envelope into his pocket, not hurrying, not asking permission. Her eyes followed it, but she made no protest. He rose and said flatly, "I'm coming back."

"Oh, dear, Inspector. Surely you've squeezed out the last possible drop?"

"I mean, Miss Sullivan," said the Inspector, "I'm coming back when this is over."

"Oh! Please do," and the one inside twinkled unabashed in Miss Sullivan's clean-wash eyes. "Please *do*."

12. Divergent Attack

They met in the park at young Nathaniel York's memorial plaque. It was quite dark. Tom Archer, for all that it was a warm night, without a threat of rain, carried a trench coat.

"Hello, guardian angel."

"Tom!" said Ann Drew. They no longer opened their conversations with, "How's yours?"

"Sorry I'm late. I had to go pick up a girl friend."

"Oh?"

"How's Miss Myra?"

"About the same. Sometimes I think she doesn't realize about Robert, even though she went to the funeral. What girl friend?"

Something said *Yeep!* in a high soprano. Unnoticing, Tom said, "I get so *dog*-gone sorry for her."

"Sorry for whom?"

Yeep!

"Miss Myra, of course. I wonder what she was like—before."

"Tom Archer, will you answer my question? What girl friend?"

Yeep! This time it was loud and clear. She clutched his free arm. "What was that?"

"What was what?"

"Didn't you hear it?"

"I didn't hear anything."

"Something went . . . yeep," she said.

"Went what?"

"Yeep!" she repeated angrily.

"Honey," Archer said, "do you feel all right?"

Yeep! Yeep!

"There!" she said triumphantly. Then she said, "Tom Archer, are *you* making that noise?"

"On my honor as a non-philandering philosophic philatelist, *I* am making no noise."

Yeep!

"Then who is?"

"Beelzebub, I presume."

"*Who?*"

"Beelzebub," said Tom Archer, "meet Ann. Ann, meet Beelzebub." So saying, he swept back the coat rolled on his left forearm and extracted a squirming, yeeping German shepherd puppy with unstarched ears and enormous feet.

"Oh, *Tom,* he's *sweet!* Oh, oh, oh!" she cried and crooned, nuzzling the puppy. "Isn't he the softest, funniest—"

"Isn't *she* the softest, funniest," Tom corrected her.

"I thought you said his—its—her name is Beelzebub."

"Quite so. I'm not the first sage to observe that the devil is a female."

"*Most* humorous," Ann sniffed, rubbing her cheek against the puppy's silk coat and making it whimper with pleasure. "Beelzebub! Why did you give the poor little thing a name like *that?*"

At which Tom Archer whispered an explanation in her ear that turned it lobster-shell red.

"So some of those 'gentlemen' are hopelessly loyal to Emily York?" Ellery mused aloud. "Do anything for her? Anything at all?"

"That's what Miss Sullivan said."

"And would it be out of order to hypothesize that some of the aforesaid gentlemen might be equally loyal to Miss Sullivan?"

The Inspector regarded his son with shock and, very nearly, distaste. "If you're hinting that Miss Sullivan is capable of hiring some soup moocher to pull a murder in order to increase Emily York's share in the estate, Ellery, you have an evil mind. Why, that woman could no more do such a thing than—than I could!"

"Don't jump salty, Dad," Ellery grinned. "What's with this old lady? You sound as if you've fallen in love."

"I've talked to her," his father mumbled. "You haven't."

"Exactly. Therefore my judgment remains unimpaired. And besides," Ellery said, holding up a peace-making palm at the glint in his father's eyes, "the kill might have been made without her knowing a thing about it. Just for the sake of argument: Let's suppose somebody's planning big things for that village of theirs. Let's say further that the ladies know nothing about it—and so that we won't be detoured, let's not speculate just now about who's sending the cards. Now then: What do we have?"

"I don't know what we have," said the Inspector irritably, "but I damn well know what we don't have. We don't have an earthly reason—assuming all this is being done to make that dream village come true—for *Emily's* life to be threatened. Because Nathaniel York, Senior's will specifically calls for equal shares or all to survivor. That means that when Robert got his head blotted out, his share went into the family stew. And if Emily should be murdered, *her* share would have to follow Robert's into the pot—*not* into a personal estate which she could will to the building of the village. So Miss Sulliv—I mean, the village project can't possibly be the motive behind Robert's death and Emily's getting the second card."

"Oh, but it can," said the son.

The Inspector shoved his jaw out. "You show me how!"

Ellery began to push the two cards around on the coffee table. "Why," he murmured, "have we been calling the H-card Emily's card?"

"What?" the old man said blankly.

"I said, Why do we assume this H-card is meant for Emily?"

"Because—because"—the Inspector spluttered—"what in time kind of question's that?—because the envelope it came in was *addressed to her!* Because when you set the card with the H right side up—with that off-center crossbar in the high position, the way it's meant to be—it gives you the house due north of Robert's, and that's Emily's."

"You mean like this?"

The Inspector stared down at the way Ellery arranged the cards:

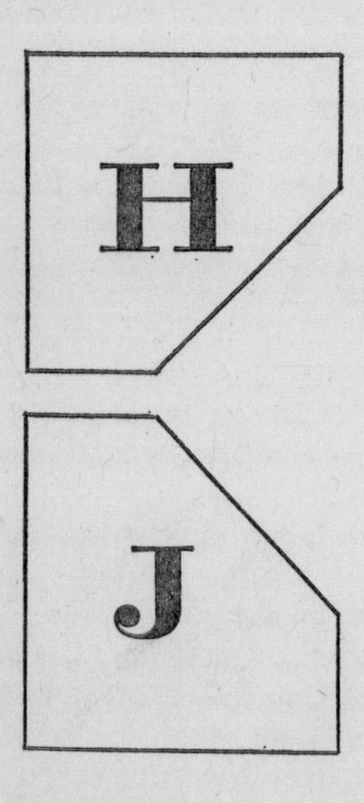

"Certainly!"

"But suppose the sender of the cards," said Ellery, his silvery eyes tarnished no longer but polished to a glitter, "suppose he's one of those very clever coots you read about in detective stories—"

"Especially yours," muttered the old man.

"—especially mine," nodded his son, "and Rex's, and John's, and Miss Christie's, and other practitioners' of the delightfully improbable. And suppose he's playing a game with you—us. And he says to himself: Let's see how good they are. Let's play ducks and drakes and fat red herrings. Let's see if they can figure out—before the event—that I really meant the H-card to be in *this* position."

And, swiftly, Ellery's long fingers turned the H-card upside down and shifted it from the northwest corner of the hypothetical square to the southeast corner:

"My God," breathed the Inspector. But then he shook his head. "No," he said. "When you turn the card upside down this way, it makes the crossbar of the H come below-center instead of above. And that's wrong."

"Usually," agreed Ellery. "But I've seen it below-center. And in some fonts dead-center."

"But the address on the envelope—'Miss *Emily* York'—"

"That's where our opponent gets to laugh. Deliberately throwing a threat at one house when he intends it for another, knowing how we'll hate ourselves in the morning."

"But in that position it's *Myra* York's house!"

"Myra York's house," nodded Ellery; and the silver clouded. "Myra York, who's feeble and of no use to anybody except possibly this Helen of Troy who takes care of her—Myra York, who wouldn't begin to know what to do with all those bushels of money. And with Myra York out of the way, there'll be even more bushels for somebody who does know what to do with 'em. Somebody like Emily York, say—who in this hypothesis would still be alive, remember. Emily York, or, by extension, her—and your—Miss Sullivan, whose motive has to be construed as identical with Emily's. So you see why you can't rule out that unbuilt village as being behind this game, Dad?"

Inspector Queen was thinking doggedly: Not-Miss-Sullivan-I-don't-care-what-you-say. But aloud he muttered, "Maybe Myra

York, hmm? . . . Well, we can't chance it. I'll phone headquarters."

"No riot squads, *please*," Ellery called from the foyer, where he was shrugging into his topcoat. "I'll see to Myra's safety. Dad—this once—let's see if we can't catch our quarry instead of scaring it away?"

"Very funny," snorted his father. "No, no riot squads, just a stake-out of watchful pedestrians. And what's this I-we-our stuff?" The old gentleman grinned suddenly. "I thought you were through with case work."

"Get thee behind me," growled Ellery. "And while I'm in that territory—may the player on the other side be damned! He's crazy, and that puts him way outside the competence of chemistry and the computers."

"What d'ye mean crazy?" shouted the puzzled Inspector. But he had only an eagerly slammed door and happily sprinting footsteps for an answer.

13. Tactics

The blonde (they have surprising sensibilities, some of them) made a little *moue* when her eye fell on the Gideon Bible. She picked it up and slid it into a drawer, out of sight. "But, Poochie," she said, "you're just no *fun* right now."

"Don't take it personal," said Percival York, from the bed. He opened his mouth to its widest with an audible *yawp!*, and with his thumbnail and forefinger he went hunting for a piece of steak caught between a lower left bicuspid and a molar. After a brief struggle he captured it, glared at it redly, then ate it. "I'm living through the longest six months in my whole entire life. The longer it gets, the worse it gets, and the worse it gets, the more time it takes."

"Yes, and that awful thing about your brother, too."

"My *cousin*. And you can't say that is so altogether awful."

"*Poochie!*"

"Oh, God, lemme for once in my life say what I want to say like I want to say it without some bluenose bastid telling me how I should say it!"

"Are you calling me a bluenose bas—"

"No-no-no—not you—no," Percival York said hurriedly. "I just get mad sometimes, is all. You can say anything you want if you say it some special way. Like my cousin's head was *struck* by a stone block—all right; but my cousin's head was *squashed* by a stone block—oh, no. Like you can say lady of the evening to anybody, you can say *prostitute* to a lot of people, but if you say *whore* everybody gets mad."

"*Poochie!*"

"Just a figure of speech, like, baby. Now about my cousin. I got real sick of that Robert sitting on his big fat money—yeah, and on a lot of mine as well!—looking down his nose at me *whatever* I did. Am I a poor relative? Am I old enough to do what I want?"

"You're not *old*, Poochie."

"But all the same, it's like he ain't dead yet. It's worse. Cops hanging around. Old Emily shoving her nose in where Robert's used to be. I can't even bring a chick to my own house, I got to come to a fleabag like this! You don't think I'll even get to sign the bill downstairs without an argument, do you? And besides, that bastid Archer."

"Who?"

"Some bastid college wise kid Robert hired, *he's* still there and, mind you, watching the estate—watching *my* money. It ain't like I didn't talk nice to him, y'understand. Why, I could lower the boom on him so fast!—but I never, and I got more gold coming to me than he ever saw or ever will. 'See it my way, old pal,' I says to him, 'and you'll never regret it.' When I didn't have to ask him a-tall, I could of told him! But you think he could see it my way? Hell, no. 'I'm just as sorry as I can be, Mister York,'" Percival minced and mimicked, "'there isn't a thing in the world I can do. It's up to the Board of Trustees.'"

"But, Poochie, it *is* up to the Board of—"

"He could of been on my side at least, f'evven's sake," Percival whined. "It's bad enough I got to go to some college jerk to try and spring a few grand to pay some bills without I got to walk off with my tail between my legs. He'll be sorry he ever saw the day. What's left in the bottle?"

The blonde handed him the bottle and he looked not at it but into it, as one does into a television screen. "One thing he'll never get the chance to do again is stop my credit. Stop my credit in a store, the bastid. How do you like the nerve?"

"Archer did that?"

"Naaah, not Archer, my squash-head cousin Robert, and it serves him right. Even my bookie." In mounting rage, Percival gripped and shook the bottle like a hated throat. "So much as a pair of socks I got no credit. Right down to the damn liquor store!" he shouted, raising the bottle to hurl it across the room while the girl squeezed her eyes shut and put her hands over her ears. But when after a moment she opened her eyes, he was still sprawled on the bed, the bottle was still raised, and his own eyes were screwed down tight. His high forehead shone with the sweat of rage. Slowly he lowered the bottle and drank hard and set it cautiously on the night table.

"You don't want to get so worked up, Poochie," the blonde said with anxiety.

He opened his eyes and gradually brought her overlapping curves into focus. "Six months to wait for that money and sometimes I don't know if I can make it. Tell you something, long as them two are still breathing, that spooked creep Myra and that Emily"—he spat on the threadbare rug—"I got to wait the whole six months. The hell, I wish they'd get their heads squooshed, too. Like to squoosh 'em myself. Fact, maybe I will."

"Poochie!"

"You think I wouldn't? Old Robert gets his head squished and he can't run down no more of my credit accounts, can he?"

Surprisingly, she said, "Poochie, he never."

"Who never? What are you talking?"

"It wasn't him. Lenny told me."

"Lenny who? Told you what?"

"Lenny Mauchheimer, he's the manager at that cut-rate bottle store of yours. He said it was your sister Emily."

"I know it was my sis—*cousin,* damn it! I woo'n't have the likes of her for a sister, I'd of beat her brains out in her crib. Sure it was Emily. But Robert put her up to it."

"Lenny says no. Lenny says the way she tells him off he gives odds it's her own idea."

"Oh, God, it figures, it figures. That Robert, now, he was a blocker, know what I mean? Try something, he stops you. But he never *started* nothing. Emily, she's a starter, got more goddamn guts than a brass bucket of chitlins. She's all the time scared I might get sued and somebody grabs a lien on the whole estate. Sure, it was Emily from the start. Robert, I apologize."

"You said there's enough to handle *anything.*"

"I told you she's crazy. How do you like that? Stops my accounts. Bluenose ol' frigate wouldn't know how to spend it anyways. Lemme check," he said suddenly.

He reached for the phone, dialed for an outside line, then dialed again. While he waited for the ring his whole being seemed to change. He still sprawled in the bed; he still presented an ungracious view of pigeon shoulders, red eyes, hairy chest and scrawny lower ribs resembling spread hands pressed into risen dough. Yet when he spoke his voice was resonant, his diction perfect, his accent Harvard—somewhere between beginning-senior and postgraduate consistency; such a voice must have behind it entire walls of morocco-bound volumes.

As she watched, the blonde slowly raised her enameled hands to her mouth and covered it with one, with both, and permitted the escape of a single tiny nicker from her Swedish nostrils. Percival York, in the midst of his performance, gave her a broad wink which detracted not, by the shadow of a subjunctive, from it.

Into the phone he said, "Mr. Pierce? Ah. This is Mr. Tomlinson of Swath, Tomlinson, Sweggar and Peach. In a routine survey of the Nathaniel York, Senior accounts, we find here a notation that Mr., ah, Percival York has canceled his credit arrangement with you. He has? Pending, ah, settlement? Very sound—yes, indeed. He sent you an advisory, of course? I beg your—? Oh, a messenger. *Not* a messenger? My goodness. Eh, eh, eh." (It was at this lofty and controlled expression of mirth that the blonde forcibly corked her wide mouth and valved her hilarity down to a nasal susurrus.) "Miss Emily, of course. Eh! Eh! Still very sound. Good day to you, sir, you stoopid bastid."

Percival hung up, and the blonde's squawk of merriment fused with his enraged shout: "How you like that, the stinkin' ol' *bitch?* You know what I'm gonna do to her? Oh, God, I can't think of anything bad enough; I'd like to cut her up some way she could watch herself bleed to death. Wait a minute."

He snatched the phone again, dialed outside, then another number. This time, when he spoke, there descended on him a mien so furtive, so seedy, that even on him it showed. His voice was harsh and quiet and issued from far back in his throat, and his almost nonexistent lips moved for labial sounds only—nothing else. "Freddy Merck here. Yeah, Detroit. Hey, I got a placement, second and third races Goshen. Long distance, that there Percy York. Yeah, Percy York. Why he calls long distance is his business but I hear a word around, don't play him, he's got a cousin Robert York sends a cousin Emily York around telling lay off or else. So I stalls him, he's calling back. Whadda ya know?"

Quite easily audible throughout the dingy room, the receiver answered back with a quiet harshness to match Percival York's mimicking, though its sibilants were cigar-squelched and its intonations archetypical Brooklynese. "Whaddaya mean you hear a word around? I myself phoned you the first one practically about this hatchet-puss Emily York barged in here and lays it on the line. And where'd you get this b.s. about this cousin Robert York sending her? Listen, Merck, *nobody* sends that broad; she makes trouble around here all the time. So what the hell's with you? Hey? Is this Merck? Hey! Who the hell is this?"

"This," said Percival in the episcopal tones of some giant cathedral bell, "is God, and it were well you mended your ways." He hung up with a new roar of indignation at Emily York's duplicity, which clashed in the air with the blonde's screek of laughter.

"The dirty old two-face bluenose *bitch!*"

"Oh, Poochie, you shouldn't talk like that. You never hurt a fly."

"A fly," raged Percival York sententiously, "never hurt me."

14. Strategy

Ellery rang, and waited, and rang again; but he could only bring himself to wait four seconds or so. He had his thumb on the bell for the third time when the door opened and a small straight lady in her early fifties, wearing an impossibly white apron, put out her hand and said, "All *right* already. Don't the bell geschplit," in tones of the hex and the schnitzelbank, of Appelbachsville and Perkasie, land of the noodle and strudel.

"Miss York?" said Ellery. "Miss Myra York?"

"She's not in," said the small lady, "and she is out, besides," and she began to close the door. Ellery deftly blocked her.

"You'll be Mrs. Schriver."

"Ach," she said, "I will, will I?"

"I've got to see her," said Ellery. "It's urgent."

"She nobody never sees and your name I don't care what is."

"My name is Queen."

"No, it ent," Mrs. Schriver said flatly.

There had been times when Ellery had desired to conceal his identity; he had seldom had to assert it. It was a strange experience. "I am so!"

"No, you *ent*," the housekeeper said, and shoved at the door. Ellery shoved back. "Mr. Queen was already here whoever-you-are."

"That was my father!" Ellery cried through the narrowing doorway—she could push very hard. "I'm Ellery—*Ellery* Queen."

She opened the door and leaned close enough to him to scan his hairline and eyes. "By gummitch, it could be. A very nice man your father is. Why he calls you Ellery Ellery?"

Ellery let it go. "Mrs. Schriver, is Miss Myra all right? I think she might be in danger."

Mrs. Schriver bridled. Though her hair was pulled back so hard from her brow that her forehead gleamed with tension, she conveyed the impression of hackles rising. Her blue eyes leveled, and above them appeared two angry eaves. "From *who*, danger?" And this, thought Ellery, is the bodyguard's bodyguard—if she cares about the body in question, and she does.

"I'm not sure," he said candidly. "But I'd rather be careful and not need to, than need to and be careless."

Approvingly she swung the door wide. "Come in."

He entered and in one swoop took in the neat wild miscellaneous character of the place. "Where is she?"

"In her room—" The intonation of the housekeeper's Pennsylvania Dutch voice was such that the three words were incomplete; yet what more there might have been was snipped off and silenced by a firm quick clamping of the lips. "You have her to see, mister, or to see her you want? Which?"

Ellery smiled. "What I must do is make sure that she's all right, and that she stays all right. But I want to see her, too."

"But she is all right." Mrs. Schriver was still weighing the issues carefully.

"You know what happened to Robert York, Mrs. Schriver."

"*Gott*." She flashed a look upward, either at Myra York's bedroom or higher. Suddenly she said, "I will see if you can come up."

"Is Miss Drew with her?"

From the stairs Mrs. Schriver said, "No, Miss Drew is out the dog walking," and went up at an energetic pace.

Ellery grinned and glanced about. To his left he caught a glimpse of the marble head of a laughing girl, and he stepped into the parlor to admire it, which he did whole-heartedly. He was reflecting that there ought to be a law, or at least an artistic convention, demanding that all things as beautiful as this be mounted against such a horrendous background of gimcrackery as was in this room, when he became aware of upstairs voices—one quietly, steadily pleading, the other trembling on the limits of control and, somehow shockingly, even quieter than the other.

"He can't come up. I won't go down. I'll never see him again. I knew he'd come. I won't see him. I said I'd never speak to him again and I won't. Send him away. I won't—" On and on and on, in a smooth terrible cooing, while the Dutch voice soothed and assured: "Shoosh, *Liebchen*, him it is not. You believe me, honest. Shoosh. He is going, he is gone already. And besides, it is not him at all." That the Dutch voice gradually won, Ellery detected by the waning of both voices, until at last they were only troubled breathing and solicitous breath.

He stood in the foyer for a long time listening to what he could hear and then for what he could not hear—so respectful of the silence that he was afraid to creak a floorboard or a toe-joint lest he cause that dreadful whispering hysteria to come to life again.

At last Mrs. Schriver came downstairs, making not a sound. Very close to Ellery she said, "She is all right now, but she is not all right."

Ellery got the message. "As long as she's all right," he nodded. "I obviously came at the wrong time, Mrs. Schriver. Stay with her as much as you can. Take care of her."

"Ach, I will," she muttered, and showed him to the door. At the door, the housekeeper said suddenly, "Miss Myra thinks I say Mallory. You come again back, hear?"

"Mallory?" Ellery said swiftly, but she had shut him out. He shook his head and stepped into York Square.

The last of the day was merging with the first glow of the city's night. Ellery glanced with curiosity at the old-fashioned street lamps, little and low and gleaming yellow, one to each facet of the park's diamond shape, and each precisely opposite the entrance to one of the absurd Disneyland castles. The lamps had been electrified, but whimsically, so that they duplicated their gaseous past, making themselves merely visible without importantly illuminating anything. If Robert's killer were the sniper-from-the-shadows type, Ellery mused, the little park wouldn't be bad for his future operations.

Strolling along the southeast margin of York Park, he wondered what this killer was made of. Am I right in concluding, he thought, that the H-card may be meant for Myra York rather than Emily? Have I really anticipated his strategy? In either case, how will he move? *If at all!*—since it suddenly occurred to Ellery that the Player's first move might have been his last—that threatening the life of Emily . . . *or* Myra . . . was a tactical feint, the prime purpose of the Game, the removal of Robert from the Board having been its only purpose. And is the dropping of two-hundred-pound granite blocks his M.O., or is his earmark versatility? . . .

At this moment a patrol car pulled into the Square and passed

Ellery. Instead of turning off and away at the next corner, it cruised all around the park and suddenly screeched about and rocked to a stop, its headlights exploding in his eyes.

"Oh," said the patrol car. "Excuse me, Mr. Queen." The car shot back and moved on. Through watering eyes Ellery saw it pause at the northwest corner while a man in a light topcoat stepped out of nowhere and exchanged a few words.

And maybe he does mean to try again, Ellery thought, and I'm glad I'm not the only one who thinks so.

At the southern point of York Park stood the person he was (at the moment) looking for. She was staring reflectively at the dark rectangle of a bronze plaque inlaid in the turf. Ellery came silently up behind her and squinted over her shoulder.

IN LIVING MEMORY
OF
NATHANIEL YORK, JR.
BORN APRIL 20, 1924

"Looks like a misprint," he remarked.

"*Oh!*" she shrieked, starting violently; and there came whirling into the yellow light toward Ellery a face so harmoniously proportioned, with such liquidly level great eyes, so sculptured a mouth, such delicately arched nostrils, that his pulse raced off in instant pursuit; in spite of his father's warnings, Ellery had expected anything but this.

"Wow," Ellery said. "I mean, I beg your pardon. I mean, for frightening you half to death. I certainly didn't mean to." There was a ferocious "Yeep!" from the puppy at the other end of the leash she was holding, and Ellery recoiled and said foolishly, "There seem to be two or three 'means' too many."

With indignation already chasing fear, she dropped both to laugh. He had not heard such music in his life. To his own amazement, he felt himself moved to coyness. "And, sir, your pardon, too," he heard his voice say to the puppy. "You must be Miss Drew."

"*I'm* Miss Drew," said the girl (Mozart, he thought, the shimmery movement of the 40th). "*That* is Bub. Short for Beelzebub, my bodyguard."

"Again your pardon, sir," he said to the puppy.

"Miss," she corrected him.

He defended himself—"It *is* dark"—and smiled at her. For sheerest joy, that there could be any face ever quite so pleasing. "My name is Queen."

"*Ellery* Queen." She was not visibly impressed. "I know your father." And she began to speak of the Inspector in the warmest way, as if he were an old dear friend.

Ellery had to chuckle. He was always running into perfect strangers, passersby, who breathed, "*Ellery Queen?* Why, I've read your—" or "Queen! Who solved the Yiffniff Case?" He had even felt it not too unbecoming on occasion, in his books, to refer to that looking-glass version of himself as "the great man." So far none of this was in effect in York Square. It was the paternal Queen who had apparently opened doors and hearts.

"You make my feet feel too small for his footsteps," he said sweepingly. "And my *chapeau* too big for my suddenly shrunken head."

"Oh, I know about you, too," Ann Drew said quickly; and how, in that ochreous light, could he know that she blushed? "What was that you said about a misprint?"

He pointed to the plaque, its Walt-burnished letters shining faintly from the darkness. "*Living* memory," he said. "It's usually *loving*."

"Not with old Nathaniel it wasn't," the girl said promptly. "From what I've heard, he didn't make mistakes—misprints or any other kind. And as for 'loving,' the scuttlebutt is he hadn't much of that in him."

"Nathaniel, Junior was his son?"

"And only child," Ann nodded. "Loving or not, that old monster had an empire to leave Junior and he meant to do just that. Young Nathaniel had other ideas and got out from under. Senior simply wouldn't accept it. So much so that when word came of Junior's death the old man refused to acknowledge it."

"Hence *Living*. Hm!" Ellery studied the plaque. "Hence a birth date only—no date of death. Quaint! Junior *is* dead, I take it?"

"Well, unless you're a hair-splitter. He ran away to sea, jumped ship in a one-burro Central American port, headed for the jungle—and except for some broken camera parts, a sun hat and a belt buckle he was never seen alive again. The hat, by the way, was split in two by some unblunt instrument."

"Where were the things found?"

"About forty miles upstream, in a shallow grave. The native who stumbled over it headed downriver to spread the news and get a reward, if any, and he brought the belt buckle with him in proof of his story. Unfortunately," the girl added, "when the port authorities went back with him they found that he'd left the grave open. You just don't do that in those jungles, not unless you're satisfied with bits and pieces."

Ellery looked at her wonderingly. "A gruesome tale for lips of coral."

"The grue wears off after you've heard the tale twenty times and told it twenty more," she said coolly. "Oh, I can be shocked, Mr. Queen. You should have heard my maidenly shriek when that devil Tom Archer told me why my shepherd's name is Beelzebub."

"Why is it?"

"That," said Ann Drew grimly, "I'll never tell. You or *anybody*."

"Oh," said Ellery, trying not to dislike Tom Archer on such vague grounds. "So old Nathaniel would never admit his son was dead?"

She toed the plaque with the tip of her improbably slim little shoe. "That's the evidence. He backed it up, too, with that will of his."

"Oh, yes, the will," Ellery murmured. "The papers have been full of it since Robert lost his head. They haven't been able to make much out of that first clause after the whereases, the one leaving everything to young Nathaniel if only he'll show up breathing to claim it. And that would be a matter of some concern to the York cousins, of course. Aren't they all nephews and nieces of Nathaniel, Senior?"

"That's right. It's a complicated genealogy, but as I understand it Nathaniel, Senior was the only one in the direct line, so he inherited all the money and York Square and so on. The whole family's dead—and accounted for, incidentally; no belt-buckle business—except the four cousins."

"Three."

"Three," she amended soberly. "Who did it, Mr. Queen?"

"I'll tell you," Ellery promised, "but not now."

"You don't know now."

"Something like that." He regarded her with fixity, and she held it with level eyes. "Have you any ideas?"

Ann made a face, but what she could make, with a lovely face like that, was only another lovely face. He noticed her glance flicker toward the northeast house, and away. "Whatever I think is pure wish," she said, and suddenly performed a tomboy grin Ellery found enchanting. "Don't quote me, or anything. It's only a feeling."

"Percival?" At her guilty start Ellery said, "You glanced at his house. Any more substantial basis for the feeling?"

"Oh . . . the disgusting way he talks—and most of all, I suppose, the way he looks at me. As if . . ." A rather helpless sound came through those astonishing nostrils. "Well, look. I'm afraid to wear a fitted coat. Actually. Just last week I bought something designed by Omar the Tentmaker. I *hate* it," she said between her teeth, turning now to face Percival York's castle resentfully. "I suppose you'll think that's silly, buying something you don't like because of the way a man looks at you?"

Ellery had to brace to keep his arms from offering their manly sympathy. "There are girls who accept that sort of look as a compliment," he said avuncularly.

"To be looked at as if you're stark naked? No, thank you! But it's worse than that. He looks your *skin* off, too. Sees right through to your bones, like an X-ray, drooling all the while. I don't know who did that—that thing to Robert York, Mr. Queen, but any time something like that happens to *him*"—it struck him suddenly that not once had she voiced Percival's name, as if to do so would materialize him like an evil spirit—"you'd better come looking for me."

Poor, lovely, troubled child, Ellery thought, still in the uncle vein. "If I do," he smiled down at her, "it needn't be for committing a murder. So don't. I mean, *please* don't."

It worked. She began to twinkle. "All right, Mr. Queen, I won't."

"And according to the will the four cousins have had to occupy the four houses to be eligible for the jackpot?"

"You change subjects right deftly, sir," Ann Drew murmured.

"Yes, for ten years, which in six months they'll have duly done. I think old Nathaniel hoped they'd all raise little Yorks to live on and on here and create race memory and preserve family tradition and all that. The will permits them to do anything they want with the interiors of the houses, but the Square and York Park have to remain untouched by human hands, except for maintenance."

"But none of the four married?"

"Not once. Robert was afraid, Emily couldn't bear the thought, Myra just wouldn't, and Percival just can't—he's already married to his own sweet self."

"Now, now," Ellery cautioned her, waving her away from the dark subject—and, in a self-betraying moment, finding his hands grasping her upper arms to turn her forcibly away from the northeast castle. Her flesh was soft-not soft, just right for male hands, and he released her and with an effort avoided inspecting his hands which, for a mad moment he was convinced, must now be luminous. "You're probably right about Robert's fear of marriage—his perfectionism and rather defensive sense of fairness would have shied him off. And my father gave me a pretty succinct impression of Emily; you may be right there, too. But why do you say Myra wouldn't?"

"I can't tell you that," she said without hesitation.

"You can't, or you shan't?"

"All right, I shan't."

"Oh, come—" Ellery began, only half teasing; but she said, "No. Please. It isn't my story to tell. It's Myra York's. And will you take my word that it wouldn't affect the case?"

He considered her carefully. He liked her loyalty. He also liked . . . But just now he was working. He said suddenly, "It concerns Mallory, doesn't it?"

"Then you do know!"

Blessing the darkness, Ellery stood still and kept silent.

"He must have been a real stinker," Ann said passionately.

"Mm," agreed Ellery. He tried a wild one. "She expects him back, doesn't she?"

"Every minute. Every living minute. And the older she gets, the worse it gets. It's got so she thinks every knuckle on the door, every passing footstep, is Mallory's."

"She thought I was Mallory, according to Mrs. Schriver."

"Ellery—Mallory—of course! Oh, dear!" Ann cried. "She's so *fuddled.* She's lived so long with the single idea of turning him away if he ever comes back that nothing else exists for her. She's quite sensitive in some ways, you know—about the phone, the doorbell; she's quick as a cat to hear them. And then sometimes she figures things out with remarkable good sense. Like . . . well, I remember thinking, with Robert dead and the big estate coming due—so much more of it now—that would bring Mallory back if anything would. I naturally didn't voice this. You know, the very next day after Robert was killed—when everyone was saying oh poor old Myra York, she doesn't even grasp what's happened—she said to me out of a clear sky, 'Well, Ann, I suppose he'll be back the moment he hears about *this.*' And then she asked me, 'Do I still have that lovely black lace dress, the one with the little collar?' She's actually planning to be all dressed up for the big scene when Mallory shows up and she tells him haughtily to go and never darken her door again! Which, of course, she wouldn't tell him at all," Ann said suddenly, "even if he did show up. She'd go all to pieces, I think beyond mending. But it's all she has, this dream of telling Mallory off for having left her at the church. That, and . . . Well, it's all she has."

Ellery decided to ignore the "and . . ." for the moment. "It's been a long time, hasn't it?"

"Oh, yes, nearly fifteen years. During which the poor thing's been slipping slowly downhill until—" But the girl stopped there.

Ellery made a lightning decision. "Miss Drew, you'd better be aware of this. I'm afraid Myra York may be in considerable danger of sharing Robert's fate."

"*Myra* York?" gasped Ann. "But . . ." And then she spun about. "*Who's that?*"

A male figure was clattering toward them, waving his arms like a Signal Corpsman at the height of a battle. "Ann! Ann, is that you?"

"Tom!"

Tom Archer came panting up out of the gloom, gasping and gulping. "Ann . . ."

"Tom, what's the matter, what's happened?"

"Ann." The young man stared unseeingly at Ellery. "Miss York's been *killed!*"

15. *Attack Resumed*

He had written:

...place yourself at the seventh pillar counting from the downtown end of the station, keeping the pillar between yourself and the downtown entrance.

Be there promptly at 5:20 P.M.

At 5:30 begin to watch carefully the crowds coming into the station.

At approximately 5:42 you will see her enter the station. She will probably stop between the fourth and fifth pillars, facing the express tracks. She will doubtless remove a newspaper from under her arm, refold it, and begin to read: if so, so much the better. If not, you will have to be a little more careful.

When you are sure she will not observe you, stroll to her location and stand near her and behind her.

At 5:49 the uptown express is due into the station. As this train comes in, while it is still traveling at speed, and at the last possible second, you will push her from the platform into its path.

Do not attempt to run. You will find a great press of people toward the spot. Work your way backward until the crowd thins out. There will be a local train waiting with its doors open. Step inside and sit down, and remain there quietly until the train moves off. If by any chance there is no train, wait for one.

You may ignore the presence of guards or police. This is my plan and I shall protect you.

I am with you wherever you go, whatever you do. I know where you are at all times; and I know what you say, and what you see, and what you think. I know, for example, that you know who I am and that you will not bring yourself to speak my name.

Be sure, as always, to dispose of this as you have my other letters.

I know I need no longer advise you as to your conduct during the interesting days and nights ahead. This formula will guard the rightness of all you do, and will protect you against your enemies and mine: Be yourself, be obedient to me, trust in me.

For I possess all powers, My Dear Walt, and I am everywhere.

Y

16. Further Development

It was, Ellery was to reflect later, in the deepest sense kaleidoscopic. "Miss York's been *killed!*"—mere syllables, shaped disturbances of the atmosphere; but in their precise time and place they imparted a rhythmic shifting and reassembling of people and events that was sheerly ever changing and ever beautiful. Bit met bit slowly, perfectly, mingling, passing, permuting, the final pattern unrealized until the very end. And yet each shifting bit was detached and distinct, in its own substance unchanging and unchanged—and had been so (and this was the tantalizing worst of it) from the beginning, seeable and knowable by the discerning eye.

But there had been no discerning eye . . .

"Miss York's been *killed!*"

The motion starting the kaleidoscope on its course, imparted by the four words in Tom Archer's gulp-and-gasp, was at first explosive. It was the instant flight of Ann Drew, bounding across the street, leaping to and through the door of the southeast castle, flying past the housekeeper and up the stairs, to rock Myra York in her soft-not soft young arms and weep at last.

It was Ellery, turning at a sudden hail from the street, wondering with some lesser part of his mind how the car had got there without his hearing it; running to it, exchanging a word with its driver, then calling to young Tom, who, after delivering his fulminating message, had stood drawn and shaken: "Mr. Archer! Go home, please, and wait for the police!"—his voice an uncharacteristic whiplash.

It was Percival York, paying off a taxi at his door, flanked suddenly by two tall men in topcoats, one of whom said, "Get inside, please, Mr. York," with an iron politeness whose urgency communicated itself to Percival's feet.

It was Inspector Queen, in the Queen apartment, banging down the telephone and to his own surprise uttering a word which, when he had heard it from the lips of a raided madam, had shocked even him; then running out clutching hat and coat to meet the squad car he could already hear wailing toward him.

And it was Walt, forty minutes later, blinking at the tall form of the patrolman who opened the door when Walt touched Emily York's bell.

"Who are you?"

"Walt," said Walt. "Miss Emily sent me for these." He extended a package. Inspector Queen charged out, looking wild. "Package for Emily York," said the officer with unvoiced meaning.

"It's the handyman. What is that, Walt?"

"Miss Emily sent me uptown for it."

The Inspector took the package, opened it. "Map pins?"

"A special kind I get her on East Eighty-seventh Street."

"You just got back from getting these?"

Walt nodded.

"Do you know what's happened to Miss Emily?"

"No," said Walt.

"She was killed by a subway train." When the handyman simply stood there, expressionless, the Inspector decided to interpret it as shock, and some of the harshness went out of his voice. "I'll keep these," he said. "You go to your room now and wait for someone to come question you." He looked again at the man. "You understand that?"

"Yes," said Walt.

"Go with him," the Inspector said to the officer. "Then come back here."

The old man stood glumly in the lighted doorway, watching the comings and goings of police cars, marked and unmarked. Soon—damn it all, there, now!—the press. And tomorrow Joe Dokes and his missus, shuffling through York Square and gawking at the four York castles. Why did people do it? Why this herd curiosity about a street, a house, windows, doors? He was a public servant, the Inspector mused, but there were times when he would enjoy loading all rubbernecks onto barges and towing them out to sea to be served, with ceremony, to sharks.

And speaking of sharks. Sure, the press made approving noises about Hero Cop Slays Maniac. But the noises they made over some human fault in a police officer were Niagara's roar by contrast. Oh well, it wasn't a beef he articulated much any more; it was rather a daily low bitter-tasting rumble at the back of his throat. Once you learned that to the press only the noise mattered, you could almost take it.

But you didn't have to like it, and that tall figure hurrying across the park with the seeming-to-lounge distance-eating stride, that would be one of them. By God, just this once he'd blast. Get the newshounds off his tail right at the start and keep 'em off till this confounded thing began to make sense . . . Sure enough the fellow was coming straight for Emily York's . . . sure enough, thought the Inspector as he filled his lungs, he was going to let this one have it!

But it said, "Dad?"

The old man let out the lungful, tipped his head down and sidewise, and glared at his son. The son stopped at the foot of Emily York's steps. "Seems I was wrong," Ellery said.

"Don't start your breast-beating," snapped the Inspector. "Come on in," and he went back into Emily York's bleak foyer, leaving the door open for the penitent.

"You know something?" Ellery muttered when he was inside. "Six families and nine homicidal lunatics could live in this place and hide eighty-seven kid printing sets, and who'd know?" For, along the hallway leading back to the kitchen, every door but one was shut, every transom dark. "Poor Emily."

"Poor anybody's murder," said his father. "And especially this one, because it hurts more people more badly than even what that subway train did to Emily York."

"You're still thinking of Miss Sullivan."

"All right, so I'm still thinking of Miss Sullivan!" Inspector Queen snarled. "Yes, and of all the hundreds of deadbeats who'd've had a catch of breath and maybe a new start, too! And now won't get either."

They fell silent.

Finally Ellery said, "You do call it murder? Positively?"

"I do, and I will. Even when my nose is rubbed in the fact that we don't stand a monkey's chance of proving it." The Inspector shrugged. "Well, at least it clears *her*."

"Does it?"

The old man stared. "What do you mean does it? Emily's dead, remember?"

"She still might have murdered *Robert*. So *her* murder might be an answer of sorts after all."

"You're not serious!"

"And you're so right," Ellery said gloomily. "I'm not. About the only fact that stands out is that Emily's death diverts her hunk of the millions from that drawing-board village to the York estate —and to whoever survives. What do you have there, Dad?"

"Where? Oh, this. Map pins." The old man opened the box. "Made in West Germany. Sold by a specialty shop in Yorkville." He squinted at the sales slip. "Bought by Walt. He just got back from there, didn't even know Emily York was dead. When I told him, he was speechless. But with Walt you never know. From all the expression on his face, I might have told him the time."

"Dad," said Ellery. "Just how dumb is Walt?"

"How dumb is a robot? Ask me something answerable."

They were walking up the hall now, and Ellery said, "Where are we going?"

"Emily's room. Once a maid's room. Just off the kitchen." The Inspector paused outside the one open doorway. Ellery went past him into the room and looked around.

There was an aged roll-top desk with a chair as hard-seated and straight-backed as its late owner. The most prominent thing in the crowded little room was a free-standing clothespress of Georgian vintage, a monstrous piece with immense overhanging gingerbread eaves and a coat of dusty yellow calcimine. What passed for a bed was a narrow slab of three-fourth-inch plywood standing on six gas-pipe legs with crutch ferrules for feet, its mattress a lumpy affair covered in duck and no more than three inches thick. Except for another, smaller chair, that was all.

"Brother," said Ellery with a shiver.

"Well, all she did was sleep here," grunted the Inspector, "and do her paperwork."

"She slept here and worked here and at the settlement house. Where in God's name did she *live?*"

"This was what she called living."

"All this self-denial for a dream that never came true." Ellery popped a cigarette between his lips savagely. "But about Walt," he mumbled as he lit it. "Where is he now, Dad?"

"I sent him to his room with a man to make sure he gets there. Forget Walt, Ellery. He couldn't be behind a thing as carefully planned as this." The Inspector tossed the package of map pins onto the alleged bed.

They both turned at a curious patois of noises. A policeman appeared from the front hall.

"Inspector Queen, he insists—"

"First things first," the Inspector said. "What about the handyman?"

"The dummy? I got him tucked in okay. But then on the way back—"

The officer was overridden, and, from the sound of it and his growl of protest, thrust aside; for there appeared in the doorway the livid specter that was Percival York, eye-whites saffron with rage, tall forehead scored with it. "There you are, Queen! I *demand* to know the meaning of this. Arrested on my own *doorstep*. Get *no* answers to questions. Someone said my cousin Emily's been killed. *I will not be persecuted!* Your job is to *protect* me. I could be in danger. I could be *next!*" The two plainclothesmen were in the foyer, waiting.

The Inspector spoke. He spoke very, very quietly, and Ellery experienced the almost sphincteral reaction of attentive awe which this special quietness had brought about in him from childhood.

Softly, then, the Inspector asked, "*Have* you been arrested, Mr. York?"

Nothing could be funny in the presence of that voice; otherwise Percival York's response would have been ludicrous. It began with one syllable of blustering shout; and with each succeeding one it diminished in volume dwindling down the emotional scale from fury to anger to irritation to perplexity to caution to finally frightened silence. "Well," he shouted; then, "What the hell do you call it when I, I, I . . ." Then he swallowed, and stood sweating.

The old man looked him up and down. "Where have you been during the last hour or so, Mr. York?"

"Out," said York sullenly, but under that frosty lens his defiance was childish and feeble. The Inspector certainly did not acknowledge it; he waited as if the man had merely coughed. Percival York then said, "I was with somebody."

"Who?"

In a repellent combination of wheedle-and-wink, Percival York said, "Now, now, old boy, we wouldn't involve the name of a lady, would we?"

"All right, Mr. York," the soft voice said, "that means we can get right on down to Centre Street. If I have to check the alibis of eleven million people to break this case, I'm prepared to do it. But I'm starting at the top, Mr. York, and that means I'll spend ten weeks or ten years, if necessary, on you."

"Now see here—"

"Now *you* see here!" and the too-quiet voice at last crackled like heavy glass yielding to heat shock. "Your cousin Emily York is dead. You are one of two people who stand to gain the most by it. It's as simple as that. You'd better have one brass-bound beaut of an alibi, Mr. York! Are you ready to answer questions?"

Percival York was pale. "But I didn't—"

"I'm not asking you that," snarled the old man. "I asked you who you were with."

"Whom," murmured Ellery, and bit his tongue.

"Well . . ." Percival York stood stripped—of anger, arrogance, petulance, all pretense. What was left was ugliest self-concern. "All right."

"Thank you," said Inspector Queen. "No, not now." He turned to the policeman. "You take Mr. York home. He's to stay there till we come for his statement. And he's going to think his alibi over until it's just exactly right—aren't you, Mr. York?"

"See here," Percival York muttered. But it was an empty thing, a way of departing; and at the old man's very slight head motion York followed the uniformed man meekly out.

"What was that all about?" asked Ellery, after a moment. "You really think he did it?"

The father folded his arms and gazed out at nothing. "Worse luck," he said, "no," and looked suddenly at the son, sore-eyed. "Ellery, I let that jerk have it *because* he's a jerk. I don't like him. I don't like him so much I've had a tail on him ever since his cousin Robert stopped that stone block with his skull. Don't you think I know where Percival was today? Hell, I even know who he was with—whom!" The Inspector struck his fist, painfully, into open palm. "Don't look at me that way."

"Who, me?" Ellery understood what his father wanted to say and could not: that he had let the job climb on top of him, that personal motivation had crippled a good police officer's performance. "I can hardly afford it. With me it was cleverness, trying to outsmart the player on the other side, seeing a move that wasn't there. So off I tear to make sure my Myra's protected from the foul fiend, and he gives it to Emily as advertised. I'd suggest an immediate back-to-work movement. And for a start, from now until this thing is broken, you ought to put a tail on everyone—everyone, that is, whom you can't lock up or in. If it accomplishes nothing else, it'll at least relieve the pressure on the Morgue."

It seemed to help the old man, for he squared his spare shoulders and raised his head.

"And then," continued Ellery briskly, "problem: how to ferret out this cutie-pie."

"The hard way," sighed Inspector Queen. "We find out everything findable about everybody. Get it all on paper, put the paper in a pile, then start from the top. We'll find him, son." He looked at his son. "Or am I using the wrong pronoun?"

"No," said Ellery. "We is correct."

She stumbled, and young Archer caught her elbow. He did not let it go. "Are you all right?"

"Tired," said Ann Drew wanly. "Wrung out, unplugged, de-starched—*tired*."

"You shouldn't try to do so much."

"I don't do anything. I'm just *there*. Like Mrs. Schriver, bless her heart, and the policewoman. But this has been going on—what is it, eight days now?—since poor Emily was killed, and once in a while one of us has to take a shift off. Which means the other two carry double packs."

"They ought to get someone else, then."

The girl shook her exquisite head. "We all want to do this particular job, Tom. Miss Myra's used to the combination; and another face would make her, well, unpredictable again. I'd rather be haggard than have to go through any more of *that*."

"How's she taking it? I mean, does she really know what it's all about?"

"How can you ever tell, with her? Sometimes she's so, well, brisk, so quick; talks about all sorts of things, laughs a lot . . . Then all of a sudden she'll grab your arm—she's awfully strong—and insist on knowing if that wasn't 'someone at the door.' When that happens, every rational thought seems to go out of her poor head, *whoosh*."

"But does she know she's being guarded?"

"I'm not sure. If she does realize she's in danger, she doesn't seem to care. She'll think of things for us to do that would make us leave her by herself. Once—for heaven's sake, Tom, don't breathe a word of this, especially to Miss Constant, the police-woman, because it happened while she was taking her break—Miss Myra insisted I go look for some peach preserves she said were in the cellar. I told Mrs. Schriver to keep an eye on her—she was in the kitchen preparing lunch—and while I was gone Miss Myra got all dolled up and somehow gave Mrs. Schriver the slip and I just happened by dumb luck to catch a glimpse of her in the street through the little cellar window and how I got to her and brought her back so fast I'll *never* know. I was so nervous it was two hours before I noticed that I was all soot and cobwebs."

"The good old death wish," nodded the erudite Mr. Archer.

"Oh, stuff," said Miss Drew. "It's just a game she plays."

"Or maybe," he said suddenly, "maybe she knows something nobody else does."

"What's *that* supposed to mean?"

"I don't know," he said. "Sometimes my mouth says things without prior consultation."

She looked at him abstractedly. "You worry me."

"I do?" Archer moved closer, and so did his voice. "Glory be for that—"

"Now, Tom, *don't*."

"Don't what? Did I say anything? Make passionate love to you? Propose something? Permanent? Temporary?"

"Tom, *please*."

"How did you know I was about to say something that would make your 'Now, Tom, don't' a logical reply? Maybe I was going to ask you out for pizza pie *à deux*. Maybe I was going to say good-bye. Was that it? Did you think I was going to say good-bye and you couldn't face it, so you stopped me? Oh, Ann, Ann, do you really love me so much?"

She stamped her foot. "Tom, stop it!"

"Stop it? Well, now I know. You don't want to marry me. Or could it be that you just can't stand pizza?"

"Don't, don't, *don't!*" The hysteria in her own voice snapped her out of it. She pulled her chest up like a braced cadet, and then let her breath out deeply. "I'm sorry, Tom. I've had a wretched day."

Tom Archer looked like a nice little boy caught with his hand in the collection plate. "No, Ann, no, I'm the one who's sorry. Please. Worry takes different forms. Some people go around dropping things, some burst into tears at a raised forefinger, some kick dogs and children. Me . . . I talk."

"Then you must be *very* worried," Ann said with a quavery ghost-smile.

"I am." He kicked something in the imaginary half-dark.

"About us? We're not Yorks, Tom."

"We know that," said Archer blackly, "but does this damn killer?"

"What do you mean?" gasped Ann.

"How do I know what I mean? I get the nasty feeling that he knows more about us than we do—"

"Tom." She looked at him, and he could just make out the enormousness of her eyes. "It's someone we *know*. Isn't it?"

The lovely fear-stretched eyes, the horror-touched tone, instantly turned Mr. Archer in the opposite direction again. "Who," he asked airily, "really knows anyone? Let's talk about something else. All right?"

He tilted her little chin, and after a moment she smiled and murmured, "All *right*. What about?"

"You carry the ball this time," he suggested.

"Let me think." She cocked her head, a finger to her lips. "Oh, I know. Do you know what lox is?"

"Certainly, it goes with bagels."

"Not that kind, silly. Lox is liquid oxygen. Did you know that if you dip a rose into lox and then drop it, it will shatter like finest crystal, right down to the *tinkle*? Isn't that lovely?"

"It certainly is," he said doubtfully. "Where—?"

"Or take Roquefort cheese. Did you know that Roquefort was discovered by pure accident, when a goatherd lost a bucket of milk in a cool cave?"

"Wait a minute—"

"Or let me tell you about the Trobriand Islanders . . ."

"Wait—a—minute! Where did you pick up these scraps of wisdom? You've never . . . I mean, this has the smack of very recently acquired useless information. Where did you get it, Ann?"

"I don't believe I care for your tone, Mr. Archer," the girl said coldly. "If you must know, at dinner this evening."

"At dinner?" Young Archer sounded skeptical. "From Mrs. Schriver, no doubt? Or Policewoman Monster?"

"Policewoman *Constant*. And you know perfectly well it was my evening off."

"Ah, then you were out with somebody?"

"I don't know why you assume the right—"

"Who?"

"Tom, I bruise easily—"

"Whom were you out to dinner with tonight?" he cried, fiercely, shaking her.

She dimpled. "Ellery Queen."

His jaw dropped, so far that Ann almost giggled. "Ellery Queen," he breathed, and Ann's giggle impulse vanished. For over Tom Archer's face dropped a mask of great ugliness. "Why did Queen ask you to dinner, Ann?"

"Tom, I don't think I like you tonight—"

"Why did he ask you out?"

This time, although she cried out faintly at the grip of his hands, he did not release her. "I *don't*. I mean, like you tonight. Or maybe any other time! Is this what you're like when you're jealous?"

"Jealous, hell," Archer said, so flatly that she stopped squirming. "All I want to know is why he took you out."

She whimpered, "Why does any man—"

"Don't give me that, Ann," he snapped. "Queen isn't any man. He's a detective on a case. He's working. He works all the time. Including at dinner with a suspect."

"Suspect?" the girl gasped. *"Me?"*

"You can't be that naïve. Certainly you! We're all suspects. Listen, Ann, this may be serious. What did you tell him? What did he worm out of you?"

"Worm out of me? Nothing!"

"What else did you talk about?"

"Oh, the Seebecks—"

"The Seebecks." He stared down at her.

"Is there something wrong with that, too?" she flashed. "Mr. Queen told me all about how Seebeck worked for a banknote company that printed stamps for foreign countries—"

"Don't tell *me* the story—I told you, remember?" Archer was very close to her now, but there was nothing close about his voice; it was as remote as the next galaxy. "What I want to know is: How did the subject of the Seebecks come up?"

"It just came up," she wailed. "Tom, what's got into you?"

"Think!" he all but yelled. "Think! How did it come up?"

She searched his face; in hers were hurt, bewilderment and, nakedly new, fear. "Is it so terribly important?"

"*Yes!*"

"Then you'll have to stop shouting at me," she said firmly. "We were talking about . . . yes, Robert York, and what a queer little man he was. So regular, so starched . . . sort of—oh, you know—like a wind-up toy of a man."

"Well?" Archer said harshly.

"Let me think! . . . Oh, yes. Mr. Queen wanted to know about the exceptions. He said there are always exceptions when people live by rules and clocks. And I said I couldn't recall any except that time Robert called you in about the Seebecks that evening. You remember, Tom. He sent Walt."

"What did you have to tell him that for!"

"Why not?" She looked at him like a scared little girl. "Tom, you've never spoken to me like this before—not *ever*. Oh!" she said suddenly, remembering. "Mr. Queen seemed to know that you and Robert York had a bad quarrel over those Seebecks, so naturally I couldn't deny it."

"It's the way it looks, that's all," Archer muttered. "You shouldn't have told him anything."

"But, Tom, Tom, no matter how it looks . . ." She swallowed and said, too quickly, "I mean . . . Oh, I don't know what I mean!"

"I didn't kill him," Tom Archer growled, "if that's what's at the back of your mind. Or Emily York, either."

She wet her lips. "Tom, I never said . . . What's *happening* to us?" she cried. "This is awful. Tom, let's get back to where we were. You were going to ask me something. What was it?"

He regarded her bleakly. He did not seem the same man at all, the man who had released that tumbling flood of euphoria only minutes before.

"Nothing," he grumbled. "It doesn't matter. *You!*" he shouted to the little park. "You can come out of hiding now and take Miss Drew back!"

And when the somewhat abashed plainclothesman stepped out from behind one of Walt's mathematical box hedges, Tom Archer turned on his heel and stalked back to Robert York's house and, presumably, his own room.

17. Attack Advanced

He was writing:

I hasten to reassure you, My Dear Walt. You have been worried — just a little, am I correct? Yes, indeed. For I know what you said to the Adversary — every word. You did not doubt that, did you? Of course not. It was your knowledge of my presence that has since caused your worry.

Know, then, that you conducted yourself admirably. You did perfectly. You answered with only just as much of the truth as would be of no real value to him. You volunteered nothing. Again I say — Well done!

Do you feel better? I knew you would.

My Dear Walt, trust me. You will be free from harm, for you know I control all things. And trust yourself, too. When in doubt, trust yourself by being yourself.

You cannot speak my name.

You may not speak my name.

Aside from this, say what you will.

Enclosed is a new card. Get your printing set out of its hiding place and ...

18. Counterattacks

Inspector Queen put away his keys and walked like the tired man he was to Ellery's study. He found the sometimes dim light of his life crouched over the desk, blinking sightlessly at the silent ranks of the Encyclopædia Britannica through the old blue smog of unventilated tobacco endlessly smoked.

"Whew," said the Inspector, fighting his way in.

Ellery sprang to his feet, alive and aware on the instant, with no transition. "It's *got* to mean something!" he cried to his father. "Don't you agree?"

"Don't I agree to what?" sighed the Inspector, sitting down in Ellery's good armchair and stretching his aching legs.

"Oh," said Ellery; and he began to pace swiftly back and forth, head bent, torso forward-inclined.

"Aside from the fact that right now you look like Groucho Marx," said his father, "I don't know what you're talking about. Whatever it is, I hope it makes sense." The old man's sigh turned to a growl. "Three times now I've had search warrants for those four cookie-box castles. Today I didn't split the squad up. This time we *all* went to *all* the rooms of *all* the houses. If there's a child's printing set in York Square I'll eat it. What have *you* got?"

"What?"

The Inspector, squinting up, repeated himself.

"Oh!" said Ellery. "Why, Dad, I don't know. I mean I *know*, but not what it means. I've found a lowest common denominator for four people in York Square."

"Oh?" said his father, slowly reaching for one of Ellery's cigarettes; he almost never smoked cigarettes. "Who?—*whom?*"

"Ann Drew. Tom Archer. Mrs. Schriver. Walt."

The Inspector said, "Really?" He lit the cigarette with slightly trembling fingers, puffed, and sat back. "And what would that be? Your whachamacallit—common denominator."

"Every one of those four came to York Square out of, or by way of, your Miss Sullivan's-Emily York's settlement house."

The old man stopped smoking. Finally he resumed. "And what's that supposed to mean, Ellery?"

"Just what I was asking myself," Ellery muttered, "when you came in. Dad . . ." He sat down suddenly on the point of his desk, like a flagellant. "Take Archer. A sort of parchment prodigy. First heard of as runner-up in a Science Search. Disqualified as under age, but given a special certificate. After that, some scholarship award or other every year.

"Archer has a small inheritance," Ellery continued, staring into his father's smoke. "Ten, eleven hundred a year. Two years in the Army interrupted his doctorate. Straight academic Ph.D. No utilitarian specializations. Never went back to school. Wound up hinging stamps in Robert York's albums."

"Where does the settlement house come in?"

"After his Army discharge he walked in there one day and announced to Emily York that he was a displaced person. Strictly a pleasantry, by the way. He wasn't trying to put anything over."

"Never mind that," said the old man impatiently. "What did he say?"

"Well, he wanted some sort of work he'd never done before—said he was tired of being a schoolboy. Said he wanted to dig a ditch or something, and a settlement house seemed a good place to begin. Emily York replied that there were too many people needing ditches to dig who couldn't do anything else, but there was her cousin Robert and his stamps, and she sent Archer over for an interview. Robert hired him."

"How'd you find out all this? Archer talks a blue streak, but I never caught him *saying* anything."

"I got it from Miss Sullivan."

"Did you!" said the Inspector, and he sighed. "And how is she?"

"As remarkable as you implied, Dad. And carrying on in spite of everything."

The Inspector nodded in a pleased way, reaching over to tamp out his cigarette. "What about the Drew girl?"

"The Drew girl." Ellery hesitated. His father glanced up at him sharply, and Ellery said in a casual voice, "She spent most of her motherless young life taking care of a despondent father. He died, and Emily York got hold of her some way or other and passed her along to Myra. Would you hand me the cigarettes, Dad?"

"Sure," said his father. "My," said his father, "you told that one fast. That's it on Ann Drew, hmm?"

"Well, there's more, but nothing that has any bearing on the case." Ellery used two matches. His parent refrained from comment. "Who's next? Oh, Mrs. Schriver. Mrs. Schriver is a widow from Bucks County whose late husband was swindled by some New York sharpie. She came charging up here with fire in her eye—the swindle and the funeral expenses left her almost destitute—and wound up finding neither the con man nor a job. Emily picked her up, put her back together again and got her started at York Square."

"Leaving Walt."

"Leaving Walt. Walt," said Ellery slowly, "is a considerable mystery. He was an amnesiac. His fingerprints are not on file anywhere, for any purpose. No background, then, and—you know him—no foreground, either. I'm interested."

The Inspector shrugged and sighed. "How about making me a drink?"

Ellery went through the living room to the kitchen and busied himself getting ice and glasses; he returned to the living room, to the bar, and poured and mixed, and all the while he was thinking that his lifelong obsession with mysteries could be accounted for by the implacable fact that he hated them for *being* mysteries—which was to say, things without answers. Amnesia concealed a mystery; an amnesiac was someone with something to hide—the fact that he was hiding it from himself was a mere detail. Walt was an unanswered thing.

"Thanks, son," the Inspector said, accepting his drink. He drank, and then he said shrewdly, "You're still on this Walt kick."

"Dad, look," said Ellery. "All Miss Sullivan could tell me about him is that he was brought into the settlement house one January night, one of a bunch of half-frozen skid-row derelicts. He was just as dirty and ragged, but he wasn't drunk; and of course he was younger than most of them. Miss Sullivan doesn't think he drinks at all, and she ought to know. He was starved, lost, he could read and write, and the only name he could give was Walt.

His clothes told nothing, castoffs he'd evidently picked up in some trash heap—"

"And Emily York realized he wasn't the usual bum," nodded the Inspector, "tried him out on an odd job or two, found he was a good worker, and got the York Square board of directors to give him the custodial job. And there he's been for years. I know all that, son. That's all there is."

"All?" echoed Ellery. "There must be some records—military service, income tax reports—"

But Inspector Queen was shaking his head. "No, son. If he ever had a taxable income it was probably under a different name. He's certainly unfit mentally and overage for military service—I mean, since he went into the amnesia—and before that, well, no prints in the service files. Incidentally, Miss Sullivan got in touch with Missing Persons about him at the time he came into the settlement house; they couldn't match him up with anybody on their lists, and there's been no subsequent lead to him. He's just a blank, son. I told you the other day, whoever's behind these murders has a calculating intelligence that's just out of Walt's league. Amnesiac! It's just too . . . too corny."

"Corny it may be," muttered Ellery, "but if I were you I'd have him watched all the same. Or you might find yourself losing another York."

"Don't worry, he's being watched along with the others. But he's not costing me much sleep. As to losing another York," the Inspector took a long swift swallow, "sometimes-by-God I wish we would!"

"What?" said Ellery.

"If we could lose one *without* losing one, so to speak. Because look," the Inspector said. "We have one murder that's certainly a murder, and one death that's probably a murder but couldn't be proved even if somebody confessed on a polygraph. Each of our prime suspects *could* have killed Robert—"

"Or, as in the case of the women, got some sub-prime actually to push the stone—"

"Yes, so that gives us X-number of sub-primes. Emily's death: the number of primes goes down, the number of unknown possibles goes up. We know Myra was home in the Square and that Ann Drew was with her. Archer was out, but he can probably prove where he was. Walt was uptown buying map tacks. Percival York and his whatever-she-is—"

"Odalisque?" Ellery suggested absently.

"Whatever *that* is!—anyway, they were being tailed. Mrs. Schriver was in Myra York's house, cleaning. And there were X-hundreds of your sub-primes on that subway platform—and besides, who's to say Emily didn't just get a dizzy spell and fall off the edge under her own steam as the train came in?"

"So you'd like to lose another York. I'm still not clear why."

"A killer can get away with one kill, but when he tries it again the odds start to mount against him. You know that! Well, he's done two now—let's assume it's two—and he's still riding the odds. But this time they're way up there. So if he'd only pull one more murder we'd have him—I think. All we've got to do is figure out how we can get him to do that without its actually costing us another York."

"Quite a problem," Ellery said dryly. "But maybe we're doing just that by having Percival and Myra under twenty-four-hour surveillance? So he's bound to be caught if he tries again. I don't see how we can miss short of stupidity or criminal carelessness. I know I wouldn't relish the chore of trying to crawl under the fences we've built, Dad. Not if I wanted to crawl out again."

"And meanwhile we sit around sucking our thumbs," grumbled the Inspector. "Damn it all, Ellery! There ought to be some way to pressure this whozit into making his play."

Ellery rolled his cold glass along his forehead therapeutically. Inspector Queen stared across at him. But all Ellery said when he rose to freshen their drinks was: "Maybe there is."

Thought Ellery: The prod, the goad, the phrase that gigs, is; *I know all about it.*

"I know all about it," he said ominously; and Tom Archer, hunched behind the barricade of the late Robert York's desk in the dim specklessness of the late Robert York's study, started violently.

Archer swallowed, his young Adam's apple jumping like an ambushed cat. "All about *what?*" It failed to come out with the scandalized virtue he was aiming for.

"Well, let's see," Ellery said in his most obliging drawl. "When

Robert York sent Walt to fetch you that night, he was a very angry man."

"*What* night?"

"The night," Ellery said sonorously, "of the Seebecks."

And it worked!—for Archer bit his lip, and one hand on the desk kneaded the other hand on the desk until he caught sight of what they were doing and clenched them into silence.

"Well?" Ellery barked, when he estimated that the young man had stewed in his own juice just long enough.

"Oh, damn," muttered Archer, looking up at last; and he gave a wry grin. "What would you have done if I'd told you about it right off?"

"Hauled you downtown," Ellery said promptly. "Want to go now?"

"No, I don't."

"Better give me the whole story, then."

"You said you knew it."

Ellery, who had dropped into the Morris chair across from the desk, climbed to his feet. "Let's go, Archer."

Archer clawed at his scalp. "Oh, hell! I'm sorry, Mr. Queen. I've been out of my mind with worry about this thing. I knew you'd find out sooner or later. But I just couldn't bring myself to come clean. It looks . . . well, I don't have to tell you how it looks."

"Yes, you do."

Blindly Archer took one of Robert York's tissues from the right-hand drawer and dried his face. "I take it you've been to Jenks & Donahue."

Ellery grunted the kind of grunt that universally means whatever worried people are afraid it might mean.

"Robert York said those Seebecks were worthless reprints," Archer muttered, "and I got sore. Because I was equally positive the stamps were *not* reprints. Well, as you now know, I took them down to Jenks & Donahue and had them put through the wringer, everything—black light, horizontal beam, colorimeter, watermark, and gum analysis—and found out what Mr. York had been able to tell with the naked eye! He had a feel for stamps that was uncanny. Of course, he'd been right and I'd been wrong. The stamps *were* Seebeck reprints." He looked at Ellery pleadingly. "What could I do? What on earth else could I do?"

"What did you do?"

"Went out and bought genuine ones, of course. Paid seventy per cent over list for them, too. It took every liquid centavo I had."

Ellery said with dawning understanding, "So then you went back to Jenks & Donahue, this time with the genuine ones, had them run tests on *those,* they gave you expert confirmation in writing, and *that* was the report you showed Robert York. And he never knew a thing about J & D's original report about the reprints. Is that it, Archer?"

"How could I bring myself to tell him?" cried Tom Archer. "I'd got myself into a bind with York when I challenged his philatelic eye, and he'd said that if Jenks & Donahue proved me wrong about the Seebecks he was going to fire me. I couldn't let him do that, Mr. Queen, I just *couldn't.* It wasn't the job; I could always get a better job. The thing is, I didn't *want* a better job."

Ellery understood perfectly, having in the near past dined with Archer's reason. But he said only, "Go on."

"I felt like such a heel," groaned Archer. "Mr. York was so contrite over what he now thought had been *his* mistake that he gave me a raise and a power of attorney to act for him in the management of the four households. He couldn't do enough for me; and the more he did the less I could bring myself to tell him what I'd done."

"He was bound to find out eventually."

Archer wet his lips. "You keep hoping not. And playing it by ear, each thing that happens. And one thing leads to another thing, and you keep getting in deeper . . . I'm so glad he never did find out."

"You'd have done a good deal to keep him from finding out?"

"Oh, God! Anything."

Quietly Ellery let the three words rise in the dim room, ballooning and expanding until they filled the whole breathable space. He watched Archer take note of the silence, then listen to it, then study it, and finally—"Oh, *no!*" Archer cried. "When I said 'anything,' Mr. Queen, I didn't mean *that.* I'm no killer," he said urgently. "Do I look like a killer to you?"

"Few killers do," Ellery remarked sadly.

"But why would I do a thing like that? If Robert had found

out about those Seebecks, the worst that would have happened is that I'd have had to leave."

"So much for not telling *him*. But why, Archer, didn't you tell me?"

"Put yourself in my place, Mr. Queen," Archer pleaded. "Would you tell anybody you'd had a violent quarrel with your employer—shortly before someone dropped a two-hundred-pound stone on his head?"

"A familiar argument," Ellery said. "The fallacy in it is that you're in a far worse position when the quarrel is found out. Did you really think no one would find out?"

"I certainly never dreamed it would come out through Ann."

"Mr. Archer." Ellery rose. "I don't at the moment believe you're our man. But I also don't care for what you did about those Seebecks. It gives you a tricky character, and this is a tricky case. Take my advice: from now on keep your nose very, very well wiped."

"I'll remember that, Mr. Queen," Archer said bitterly.

And I won't tell you, Ellery thought, that you have no credible motive; and that, if you'd been planning Robert's murder, your directly antecedent actions would hardly have included a heated quarrel with him; and, anyway, that your alibi stands up.

Aloud, and gently, he said, "And about Ann Drew—be consoled. She couldn't help telling me. To borrow a phrase, Archer: I have my methods." He added in total afterthought, "And why I should be telling you this I'm blessed if I understand. I could easily fall for Ann Drew myself."

At which Tom Archer had a smile—a small smile, but a smile —for him; and Ellery, departing, smiled a small one back.

"I know all about it," said Ellery coldly. He had encountered the handyman coming down the walk of Myra York's house.

Walt returned a round, mineral gaze and moved his slack full lips in a sort of windup. If he was surprised, startled, angry, fearful —*anything*—it certainly did not show.

What came out of his mouth at last was, "Yes."

All right, pal, he's thrown you the ball. What are you going to do with it? "Mr. Archer and Robert York had a quarrel before Mr. York was killed."

"Yes."

"Mr. York sent you to find Mr. Archer."

"Yes."

"What did Mr. Archer say when you located him?"

The round eyes closed and opened—it was too slow for a blink. "He saw me and he said, 'God.' "

"And you said—?"

"That Mr. Robert sent me to find him, and to say he's got a Seebeck."

"Why didn't you tell that to the police?"

"They did not ask me to."

"Didn't you know it might be important?"

The flat-finished eyeballs were concealed again by another of those slow-motion blinks. "No."

I believe you, Ellery thought. "What were you just doing in there?" He pointed to Myra York's house.

The handyman removed something from his side pocket and extended it. It was a five-and-dime package of screen patches. "The corner was rusted out on the screen porch. I had to fix it."

"Is that all you did in Miss Myra's house?"

"No." The man produced a plastic flask of a patented muriatic solution. "I took a stain off the second-floor bathtub."

Ellery regarded him gravely. Walt stared patiently back. And Ellery knew then that he could ask questions and get answers from now until noon of St. Swithin's Day and learn never a thing.

"Anything might be important to the police, Walt. The smallest thing. You try to remember, won't you?—and if you think of anything you forgot to tell, come right out with it. Do you understand me?"

"I understand."

Namelessly dissatisfied, Ellery went on up to the house and rang the bell; and so preoccupied was he with his dissatisfaction that, when Mrs. Schriver opened the door, he forgot his magic goad and said at once, "What was *he* doing here?"

"A hole in the screen he fixes," said the housekeeper, "and from the bat'room upstairs a stain he takes out." She looked at him reprovingly. "Gut afternoon, Mr. Queen."

"Oh! Good afternoon, Mrs. Schriver. How's everything?"

"Resting," said Mrs. Schriver. "Unless with the bell you are unresting her."

"I'm *sorry*," said Ellery. "Could I see Miss Drew?" He knew that the policewoman was also on duty upstairs.

"She is with Miss Myra sitting." She did not mention the policewoman.

Ellery appealed to the determined little chub-face. "Do you think you could get her down here without disturbing Miss Myra?"

"For what?"

"Something very important, Mrs. Schriver. Honest," he added. She invariably made him feel like an unwanted small boy.

"You better," sniffed the housekeeper; and she went noiselessly up the stairs, managing to leave him with the impression that she was stamping with indignation.

A thousand years later Ann Drew appeared; and it seemed to Ellery that she drifted down to him like Peter Pan's Wendy, the time the Lost Boys shot her out of the sky with an arrow; her hair, undone, was floating hurriedly behind her like a bit of cloud trying to catch up. And when—wafting by him into the cluttered parlor—she touched her lips for silence, he realized on the instant that to touch her lips was something he had wanted to do all his life.

She told him in sign language to shut the sliding doors. He did this, and when he turned back he found her looking at him with half a smile on her amazing mouth, altogether trustful. And he did something then at which he would ever after wince in memory—something which had to be done. He said quietly, "I know all about it."

Once he had seen a convulsed virago strike her child, a little girl; this was the same. At the impact there was no pain, only astonishment; then pleading eyes denied the blow; then, the blow being undeniable, came the search for some explanation: *It was an accident*, or *I'm dreaming this*—anything to make it bearable before the pain closed down and terror blotted everything.

He could only loathe himself, and wonder what was coming next.

Ann Drew whispered to the walls, to the wind: "I was sixteen and my daddy was all—oh, he was coming unglued, his kidneys, his liver, his stomach, most of all his brain—the base; it affected his balance. He worked in a library; he loved books, the things of the mind; he could see himself becoming a mindless blob, and it terrified him. Some of the medicine was no good, and some of it they just tried out on him, and some helped, and all of it cost—oh, terribly. And after a while he had to quit working and stay home, a slowly dying man. I couldn't even finish high school—I had to go to work to support us both. I got a job in a store; the salary wasn't nearly enough, but it was the best I could do, because the store was close to where we lived and I had to be able to run home to tend to Daddy. And I found that I needed more and more money, and I had no way to get more except . . . except—"

"By dipping into the till?"

"For almost two years."

Ellery looked at Ann Drew; this time he looked deeply. Lovely, lovely girl. "Virtue may not always make a face handsome, but vice will certainly make it ugly." Poor Richard had never met an Ann. She was untouched.

"But it never touched me!" she cried, and startled him. "Miss Emily understood that. When she dug into me, she looked me in the eye and said I didn't need saving because I'd never been lost. It sounds like—like soap opera, but the truth is that the money I stole was, first, to save my father's life, and then—when I knew it was a hopeless cause—to pay for the narcotics he needed so that he could die without too much pain."

He had a dozen questions to ask and asked none of them. Instead he said gently, "I take it you were caught."

"In the act." The hardened tone was armor, he knew, against that assault from the past. "I spent almost two days and nights in a cell before Emily York—I don't know how she found out—got me off in her custody. But for just that forty-two hours, when I couldn't get to him, or even communicate, Daddy had to do without the two things he needed to keep living—his morphine and me. He cut his wrists." It was no longer a lovely face she turned up to him; it had no blood in it, almost no bone. "No one's known about this, Mr. Queen. Now, I suppose, it will become public property."

"Ann," Ellery said. "Stop being afraid."

Her head came up in a flash. "I'm *not* afraid!"

"You're scared witless that Tom Archer will find out."

After a moment her head went down. "Well," she said lifelessly, "won't he?"

He cupped her chin, and she was forced to look at him. "Ann, has this back-history of yours anything to do with the York murders? I ask you not to lie to me. Has it? Anything at all? Even remotely?"

"Oh, that." She shook her head almost impatiently. "No. How could it?"

He smiled and let her go. "Well, then."

"I don't understand."

"Of course you do."

"You mean you won't tell him." Her voice was stiff with certainty. For her preoccupation with her past had been so complete that its irrelevance to the York case had not occurred to her; and that his preoccupation with the York case would cause him to shrug off the irrelevance of her past was an outcome she had not even dreamed of.

And so she wept; and Ellery, his back to her, waited her weeping out. The whole thing was soundless.

"No, I won't tell Archer," Ellery said to the unobstructed view. "You will."

That brought sound—a breathy sound of surprise and dismay. He felt her clutch, and he faced about. Ann, Ann, he thought, take your hands off me; and he touched her hands and they fell away. He had lost her. No, he had never had her.

"Tell Tom a thing like that?" the girl cried. "And have him go sick inside?"

"Emily York didn't go sick inside," said Ellery. "And she wasn't even in love with you. If that fellow's feeling for you is so feeble it would collapse under the story you've told me, Ann, don't you think this is a good time to find out?"

But the girl was shaking her head and wailing, "Why, why did you have to rake this up?"

"Because in my sorry business you have to rake up everything. And everything, unfortunately, tends to include a great many things that turn out not to matter. Yet it's the only way. Separate out the things that don't matter, and you're often left with the things that do."

19. Sacrifice

Ellery, in Boston, said, "I know all about it."

He looked at Mallory across the desk, which was glossy as a skating rink and very nearly as large. Mallory's big head, with its ruddy face-tones and ice-blond hair, was set off by the heavy brown velvet drapes behind him. He was one of those men who cannot avoid looking like an Old Master; light is always kind to them, and the eye of the beholder is always seized and slightly awed. And he would greet you without rising, and that would feel right to you.

It had felt right to Ellery, considerably to his surprise.

Ellery had had another session with Miss Sullivan, had flown to Boston and winnowed a great deal through certain files to which he was privy by courtesy of the New York police department; then, failing, he had found what he wanted in the Boston telephone directory. Annoyed, he had made his way to the offices of Mallory & Co., had sternly beaten down the successive blocking plays of a receptionist, a secretary and an assistant, had gained the Presence, and had mentioned the name of Myra York. And, "I know all about it."

"I can almost say," said Mallory, "that I expected you." He had the mellow boom, the oiled diction of an Edward Everett or an Everett Dirksen. "Not you personally, Mr. Queen, nor anyone like you, for of course there is no one like you; but someone concerned in York Square's present difficulties."

Ellery tipped his head politely and wondered what on earth this natural candidate for someone's most unforgettable character was leading up to.

"I knew the Yorks—some of them—of course, or you wouldn't be here. No, don't ask me any questions, Mr. Queen," Mallory said, anticipating the nerve impulse behind the still-unmobilized muscle that was about to activate Ellery's mouth. "I am a man who enjoys putting myself in another man's place. It's a knack that put me in mine." He glanced about his endless office, and smiled. "Let me put myself in yours. You have an important murder on your hands, perhaps two. You are making very little progress. It has consequently become necessary to run down everything about everybody, on the theory that this would elicit the—do you still call them clues?—the clues you need. You inevitably unearthed the clue that at one time, many years ago, I was engaged to marry Myra York. I said, don't ask me any questions!"

Ellery's lips closed with a snap. There was a long silence, during which Mallory kept his eyes shut. When he opened them, the effect on Ellery was much like that of the prowl car's spotlight which had smote him the other night.

"You discovered that my engagement preceded Miss York's good fortune in the matter of old Nathaniel's will. She has remained unmarried, two of the four heirs have been sent to their less material rewards, and Myra's large prospects have accordingly become very large indeed. And since I suspect—no, that's unworthy of both of us—since I *know*, because I have kept myself informed, that Myra retains a warped modification of her original interest in me, you were led to wonder whether I might not be tempted to renew my association with her in consideration of those enlarged prospects. You may even be wondering, Mr. Queen, if I may not have arranged the entire sequence of events. Please do not respond to that."

Ellery's mouth clamped again.

"Mr. Queen," Mallory went on to inquire politely, "do you also know why I broke my engagement to Myra York almost two decades ago?"

It was a relief to be able to say *something*. Ellery said, "No."

Mallory seemed pleased. "Very good. I admire the laconic interviewer. Mr. Queen, I am a man who makes plans and, having made them, follows them. I began this useful practice early in life. In those days I made plans for myself and Myra—who was, by the way, most desirable—at that time. When those plans became impossible—I'll amend that: when I discovered that those plans were impossible with *her*—I had to plan her, so to speak, out of them."

The Old Master reached abruptly. His kingly fingers closed about a tooled morocco twin-picture frame facing him, and turned it around. The fingers then spread with a little wave, in gracious invitation. Ellery accepted and bent forward.

One of the two photographs showed a calm-eyed lady with an impressive bust and hair either blond or white; the facing picture was of three corn-fed teen-agers, two boys and a girl, descending robustly in what was obvious chronological order.

Mallory smiled. "*They* are what would have been impossible with Myra." He reached again, this time to turn the frame away from Ellery's view and back to his. "She told me so," he said, now smiling at the teen-age frame of the two, "herself."

"And on her unsupported word—"

"I never act on anyone's unsupported word. As her fiancé, I consulted her doctor. It was true enough. But I had planned a dynasty, and dynasties are grown only in fertile ground. No children, no Myra York. Could anything be simpler? Comment, Mr. Queen."

Said Mr. Queen: "I hardly know where to begin."

"Certainly you know where to begin. You might say, for example: this was a brutal blow to Myra. Admitted. But it was also a brutal blow to me; I was young, too, and she was *very* desirable, Mr. Queen. I had to comfort myself with the truism that it is in the nature of things for us all to endure brutal blows.

"Or say, for another example, Mr. Queen," continued Mallory, leaning back in his tall and massive chair, "that you nosed your way to Boston seeking a suspect fortune hunter; that, having sniffed me out and discovered that I *had* a fortune, you were compelled to doubt your hypothesis; but that, being a man who examines all sides of everything, you gave me further thought and reinstated your hypothesis, on the ground this time that I might be the kind of affluent man whose acquisitiveness is insatiable. My answer to that is, of course: I have no designs on Myra York's millions. I submit corroboration of this statement to your common sense. Already this year my own millions, my investments, this business, have earned more in profits than the entire fortune Myra York is coming into. I will happily instruct my people to open my books to any firm of reputable accountants you may designate."

"As a matter of fact," murmured Ellery, "I wasn't thinking any of those things, Mr. Mallory. I was thinking instead of such unfashionable, if not obsolete, words as responsibility and conscience.

Since you say that you've kept yourself informed about Myra York, you must therefore be aware of her mental condition. Doesn't it bother you that what she is today may very likely be the direct result of your cold-blooded rejection of her years ago?—a rejection, by the way, for something that was not her fault?"

"Nor mine," smiled Mallory, "a fact you have conveniently left out. But aside from that. People are, by and large, what they want to be. You are what you are, Mr. Queen, and I am what I am, because you and I have so willed it. You and I willed ourselves to be successes, so we are. But the principle applies equally to failures. Of course it bothers me to hear of poor Myra's condition; I pity her with all my heart. But pangs of conscience?" He shook his head. "I cannot, do not, and will not accept responsibility for Myra's decline, for that is manifestly something *she* has willed."

It came to Ellery suddenly that this amazing man might be angry, he kept smiling so.

"I beg your pardon?" Ellery said.

"I said," Mallory repeated, "that you might also inquire what I was doing on the night of so-and-so, et cetera."

"That," said Ellery with his own smile, "—now that we have cleared away the smog—is the hard question I'm here to ask."

Mallory spun about on his revolving throne and swept aside the towering drapes behind him. They uncovered an almost unpleasantly large expanse of glass and, beyond it, far below, a miniature panorama of Boston Harbor. The object of his action, however, was neither the glass nor the view; it was propped against the window.

A crutch.

Mallory grasped it and spun back, still smiling. "The evening Robert York was killed," he said, fondling the crutch, "I was lying in a traction splint in Auburn Hospital—that's in Cambridge, Mr. Queen—with a broken femur. On the afternoon Emily York was killed, I was confined to my home, my mobility rather limited by two crutches. I now manage with this one. Of course you will check this, Mr. Queen, although I assure you I would not bring it up if it were not true." He wagged his ice-crowned head. "I'm afraid I'm not a very profitable suspect."

In the silence that followed—although Ellery was sure that

behind the Mount Rushmore countenance the man was shouting with laughter—the telephone rang. It was a relief, for Ellery had been rather desperately trying to think of an exit speech.

"Excuse me," Mallory said, and picked up the phone. He listened, then covered the transmitter with his muscular hand. "It's for you, Mr. Queen. Are you here?"

"Of course."

Stretching far forward to meet Ellery's hand, Mallory explained, "I like to offer visitors to my office the option of lying to their associates," and, still smiling, settled back.

"This is Queen," Ellery said to the phone. "Oh, yes, put him on. Dad?"

And then Ellery went so still for so long that the smile faded from Mallory's face.

Finally: "When?" Ellery said, and cleared some obstruction from his throat. "All right. All right. As soon as I can."

He leaned over and replaced the instrument precisely on its cradle. Mallory's eyes alertly followed the action; there was the slightest crevice between them.

"Bad news, Mr. Queen?"

And Ellery looked down at Mallory in a sort of blindness and said, "For Myra York, the worst. She was murdered last night."

The muscles that managed the center of Mallory's mouth held up all right, but those at the corners gave out. For a moment the massive face might have posed for Tragedy's mask on some theater proscenium. "Poor Myra," he muttered.

But that was all.

Ellery made for the door without another word.

And Mallory said, "Mr. Queen!" and Ellery stopped and turned. The man had reassumed command; the corners were now lifted back into place. "I mean to have that devil caught," Mallory barked, "whoever it is. I'm prepared to post a reward—"

"So there's conscience on Olympus after all." The Queenian torso inclined toward the tycoon ever so little, as if ready for anything. "But this time, Mr. Mallory, money won't solve it. My father tells me he's had the murderer in a cell since ten o'clock this morning."

Their stares locked across the long dueling ground. Both men were pale.

Then Ellery reversed himself and marched to Mallory's door and opened it and stepped through and shut it behind him as bitterly as he could.

20. Breakthrough

"It was Ann Drew," Inspector Queen said, "who found her dead this morning. With the jug on the night table beside the bed. The girl's had a bad time of it."

The old man had been waiting at La Guardia in a squad car when the Boston plane set down. The only thing he could have done to look older would have been to wear silk knee breeches and a ruff. His face was so gaunt, his eyes were so redly rimmed, that Ellery found himself wishing he could belittle this incredible third York death.

"The poison was put into her drinking water, Dad? I should think even Myra would have tasted—"

"Who said there was water in the jug?" The Inspector showed his dentures.

"The joke escapes me," Ellery said sharply. "What would a water jug hold but water?"

"A fair question, except in Myra's case. *That* water jug held straight gin. Now it comes out she's been a secret lush for years."

"That floating walk, that slow slurry coo of hers," exclaimed Ellery. "Did Ann know?"

"Sure she knew."

"Poor kid."

"She's been throwing ashes on her head like a professional mourner. And you ought to see the shape that policewoman, Constant, is in. I had to order her home on sick leave. And Mrs. Schriver's wandering around in a daze, looking twenty years older."

And so do you, Ellery thought. Aloud he said, "Has a card shown up, Dad?"

"What else?"

The Inspector went fishing. He handed over his catch; and Ellery seized the familiar white card with the five odd sides as if it were the key to Solomon's treasure room.

"Lower starboard. Myra's castle, all right," Ellery said tensely. "W . . . W. H before that, J before H. J, H, W. JHW. What the devil! Or—wait! Could it be"—he turned the card upside down—"an M?"

The Inspector stared at it. "M. That's Myra's initial."

But Ellery scowled and shook his head. "Then why didn't Robert get an R, and Emily an E? Besides, notice that in the M-position the card would have to be assigned to the northwest corner of the Square, and that makes no sense at all—that was Emily's corner." He restored the card to its W-position. "No, Dad, this one's meant to be a W. Now tell me about it."

"I was the one who found it." The old man took back the white card and glared at it. "It was in the usual envelope, addressed in the usual style to Miss Myra York, et cetera, and postmarked night before last at the local station. It was delivered in the regular mail yesterday morning."

"But if you knew about it yesterday morning—" Ellery began, perplexed.

"I didn't know about it yesterday morning."

"You said you were the one who found it!"

"*This* morning," said the Inspector woodenly, "when it was too damn late."

"But how did it slip by everybody?" Ellery cried.

"You won't believe it, it's so ridiculous." Then the Inspector's voice turned policeman. "First of all, the carrier says it was Myra herself who took the mail from him."

"*Myra?*" said Ellery incredulously. "How was she allowed—?"

"If you'll shut up, I'll tell you. Mrs. Schriver was preparing breakfast in the kitchen. Constant was upstairs, picking up after Myra. Ann Drew was downstairs, setting the dining-room table. She called upstairs that breakfast was ready; the policewoman called down that Myra was on her way. In the few seconds after Myra left Constant's line of sight and before she got into the Drew girl's, Myra passed the front door—and that had to be the exact moment the postman came with the mail. A thing like that couldn't have been planned by anybody but Satan, Ellery. The breaks."

"But didn't one of them see Myra take the mail? At least hear the doorbell?"

"Ann heard it and came right out. But by then Myra had the door closed, and the mail—a couple of magazines, some advertising matter, a cheer-up note from Miss Sullivan—in her hand. Ann took it from her and led her to the dining room. But Myra could be almighty quick—apparently she'd spotted the W-envelope and slid it into the side pocket of her suit. And then must have forgotten all about it, because that's where I found it this morning—twenty-four hours later—in her suit pocket, unopened." The Inspector paused. Then he swallowed, making a face. "Don't ask me why Myra latched onto that particular envelope. Don't ask me why she was sly about it—not mentioning it to Ann, or Policewoman Constant, or Mrs. Schriver. And don't ask me why she didn't open it. Don't ask me *anything* about this case!"

They became absorbed in watching the police driver fight his way onto the ramp from the Triborough Bridge to the East River Drive.

When they were speeding down the Drive, Ellery murmured, "So now you've got your killer."

The Inspector retorted, "So now we've got *your* killer," and gave him half a grin, the left half. "Go ahead and say it, Ellery. 'I told you so.'"

"But I didn't. He's just bothered me." Ellery scowled at the back of the driver's neck. "By the way, how did you break him?"

"Who said I broke him? I arrested him, booked him, locked him up. He hasn't said a damn word but his name—I half expected him to add his rank and serial number before he clammed up."

"He hasn't confessed?" Ellery asked slowly.

"He hasn't *anything*, I tell you. Anyway, the evidence confesses for him." The old man closed his eyes and settled down on his tail. "Let me tell it from the top. Ann Drew called the news in, hysterical. When I got there I found Myra dead, and those three females . . ." He shuddered. "Took me half the morning to get coherent stories out of them. Even the policewoman.

"By that time," he continued, "I'd found the envelope with the W-card in it, and I'd also had a preliminary report from Doc Prouty about the poison, because some of it had spilled on the night table and on the floor beside Myra's bed—only a few grains, but enough for a quick analysis. Prouty's done the p.m. since, and his findings check. It's a commercial rat poison—arsenic and Dicumerol compound. The box it came from is still on a shelf in the Robert York garage, half empty. The gin in the jug is loaded with it. The glass she drank from is coated with it. And there was enough in Myra's innards to kill a couple of horses."

Their car raced into the almost-tunnel under the U. N. Building, and Inspector Queen subsided. When they emerged he said, "You know how fast that stuff kills?"

"With a big dose? I'd say five minutes."

"The dose was bigger than that," said the Inspector grimly. "Nearer three minutes, Prouty says. Well, yesterday afternoon Walt showed up to fix a porch screen that was torn and to clean a stained bathtub—"

"I know," Ellery said. "I met him coming out, and he told me about it."

"He was upstairs there almost an hour. While he was fixing the screen, Myra was nipping at her jug. And showed no ill effects, so at that time the gin in the jug had to be all right. Then Walt came in to work on the tub in Myra's bathroom. Myra was higher than a kite, so for propriety's sake Ann and Policewoman Constant hustled her into Ann's room. They didn't take Myra back to her own room until Walt finished and left."

"So during that period Walt was alone in Myra's quarters?"

"That's it. And after the women brought Myra back and until she went to bed last night, the policewoman states, neither Ann Drew nor Mrs. Schriver nor anyone else touched that jug—Constant swears to that. Not even Myra, because they wouldn't let her have any more—the only reason Ann didn't take the jug away altogether, she says, is that Myra would have raised holy hell. Anyway, Constant herself locked the bedroom door after they put Myra to bed, and that room wasn't entered until this morning, when Ann unlocked the door and found her dead. She'd obviously waited till they left her alone, then downed a whole glassful of arsenic-flavored gin. Prouty says she died well before midnight. She was mighty cold turkey this morning."

"So only Walt could have dropped the stuff into the jug." Ellery seemed uneasy. "Yet he didn't confess, you say."

"He didn't deny, either!" said his father, the irritation rubbing through.

"And that's it, Dad?"

"No, that's not it. There's more. After I'd got the women's stories yesterday morning, I sent for Walt. When he was brought in I was mulling over what they'd told me, and the card business and all, so I wasn't really paying him much mind. I actually heard myself say to him, 'What's your full name?' as if he were a suspect in the line-up."

The old man paused, so casually that Ellery jerked to attention. "So?" Ellery said. "What's the point?"

"The point," the Inspector said, "is that he answered my question—in full."

"Answered the question in full? What do you mean?"

"He gave me his name. His full name."

"His full name? He doesn't know his full name!"

"I guess I shocked it out of him," the Inspector said with a faint chuckle. "You can do that sometimes with amnesiacs."

"But what is it? What did he say?"

"Why," said the old man, "he said, 'John Henry Walt.'"

"John Henry Walt? Walt is his *surname?*" Ellery turned the name over on his tongue. "John—Henry—Walt. John Henry Walt!" he exploded. *"The initials of his name!"*

"J, H, and now W," nodded Inspector Queen, waving the white card Myra York had received. "It's not really surprising, son. You know how these birds unconsciously want to be caught. This one was signing his name—in installments."

"He's crazy!" Ellery howled, as if his father had not spoken at all; and then he remembered that he had said something like that about John Henry Walt at the very beginning.

21. *Attack Pressed*

He had concluded his most recent letter of instructions to Walt—specifying and explicating the various matters of screen-mending, Miss Myra's bathtub rust stain, the granular material in the box on the garage shelf, and the alternatives of opportunity open to Walt for the dropping of the material into the jug at Miss Myra's bedside—in this vein:

...therefore we have now come to a situation in which you may have to reveal yourself.

You may not say my name, but in all other ways you may answer their questions. Or, if you choose, you may answer some or none at all.

Remember, you need fear nothing, for in this matter you are I. And you know who I am, My Dear Walt. These men cannot harm me, and through me you are immune. You have my blessing and my protection.

I am proud of you. I trust you. I admire you.

Y

22. *Position Play*

He sat dampishly on the rivulets of the old black leather chair near Inspector Queen's desk, all bulge-eyes and grudging hair, and looking not at all like a coming fortunate man. The Inspector's office door was open, and now and again someone would walk in, drop papers in the Inspector's *IN* basket, glance sluggishly at the incipient millionaire and walk out. When these intruders were in uniform Percival York would sigh a small comforted sigh. When the men who dropped in wore ordinary clothing, he would frankly cower until they left. Throughout, he sweated.

The arrival of the Queens, father and son, aroused his gratitude. Percival said, "Hellohellohello," in a warm tone and actually rose to offer his hand, such as it was. Ellery gave a token wave; the Inspector ignored it.

"What do *you* want?" the Inspector asked absently, sitting down at his desk and poking in the basket. He picked out a file folder and at once became absorbed in its contents.

York put his fingers in his mouth and popped his eyes. Then he took the fingers out and said, "Autopsy report on my cousin Myra?"

"Did you read it, Mr. York?" Ellery asked, reading it himself over the Inspector's shoulder. "Nothing spectacular, Dad," he murmured, "far as I can see. Oh, you *didn't* read it, Mr. York. Well, you haven't missed anything." He was about to add, You're also sitting in my favorite chair; but then he shrugged and perched on the corner of his father's desk instead.

The Inspector uttered an impolite sound and scaled Doc Prouty's opus to one side. "I seem to remember, Mr. York," he said, "asking you a question."

"Fair enough," Percival giggled. "I'll ask you one, Inspector, and we'll be even. Did you know my cousin Myra used to be a fatal female?"

"A what?" said the Inspector.

"A lover-girl. Ashtoreth and Freya and Lorelei. What you'd call a vamp, I suppose. That Myra," mourned Percival, shaking his head. "Too bad."

"What are you talking about?"

"And got through the whole thing *virgo intacta*, or I miss my guess," said Percival, sucking on a thumb thoughtfully.

Ellery asked softly, "Mallory?"

"Mallory and."

"Mallory and?" The old gentleman was becoming nettled. "Mallory and! What kind of sense does that make?"

Percival York smirked.

"Let's have it." Although it is not possible to describe the Inspector's tone, except in terms of quietude, it made Percival York stop smirking and begin to talk almost like a rational human being.

"Maybe I'm clobbering a dead horse," the Sole Survivor conceded, "maybe it was only kid stuff, but hear this: Mallory had a rival. Did you know that?"

"No, I didn't," confessed Ellery with gleaming eyes. "Who was the dead horse, pray?"

"Nathaniel York, Junior, in living memory of," exulted Percival, quoting the bronze plaque in York Square. "Gone but not forgotten. Head split open on a tropical mud-flat, all for love and a world well lost. Though he was breathing plenty hard while he had it."

"Nathaniel, Junior was in love with Myra York?"

"Mad about her. Myra was delicious in her bloom, and I yield to no man in my devotion to *l'amour*, but that boy overdid it. Would go about mumbling things like Myra was his oyster and oh how he'd like to swallow her whole—that sort of tenth-grade hyperbole.

"But Junior's papa," continued Percival, lying back to enjoy his sensation, "—that was my revered uncle, Nathaniel o' the Purse Strings—old Nate threw fits. Very loud ones, too, full of I'll-cut-you-offs and thou-shalt-nots and so on—Uncle Nathaniel was co-author of the Ten Commandments, a sort of post-Victorian Moses crossed with the spirit of Billy Sunday. Because Myra and young Nat were first cousins, you see. But Junior didn't care a fig leaf about that, and anyway Uncle's pride and joy was all set to clasp the blushful maiden to his breast and flee, when along comes this Mallory, and Myra falls in love with *him*. And that's when Junior fleed—flew—oh, hell, you know what I mean—and got himself butchered in the Mato Grosso or somewhere. After which, heh-heh, Mallory dumped *her*. And that, gentlemen, is a little-known chapter in York history."

"I thought," said Ellery, "that Junior's reason for lighting out—"

"Oh, yes," said the York remnant magnanimously, "that was part of it, of course. But I doubt if Junior'd ever have given Papa the flirt of his exhaust except for Myra's fickleness. The two things gave him just enough thrust to escape Senior's orbit."

"Well," murmured Queen the younger.

"Well, what?" grated Queen the elder. "Kicking corpses around! Who cares about Junior's love-life twenty years ago, or whenever it was? Is that what brought you here, York? Because if it is, I'm busy, and thank you."

Percival York shot glances to the right, the left and, otherwise unmoving, gave an all-by-himself impression of huddling. "I had to know something."

The Inspector picked up the Myra York autopsy report again; not looking at York, he said, "What?"

"Did Myra get a card? Like the ones Robert and Emily got?"

The old man looked up at that. "Why do you want to know?"

"I just want to." Percival sat up in the chair and pushed out his narrow chest. He also pushed out his lips.

"You wouldn't be scared, would you?" asked the Inspector softly.

"Who, me?"

"All right," said Ellery. "There was a card for Myra, too."

"God," said York. "Oh, my God."

"I don't get this," said the Inspector. "Why does that bother you so much, Mr. York?"

"Because Myra wasn't—well, you know—well," said Percival earnestly. "Or what you might call happy. I'd been rather—I mean, I think maybe—"

"You thought maybe she wrote her own ticket bye-bye? Well, Mr. York, she didn't. What d'ye think we put Walt in the can for—jaywalking?"

Bull's-eye, Ellery thought, watching Percival York twitch.

"He really did it, then . . ."

"You don't think so?"

"I don't know, Inspector. I don't see *why* . . ." He looked at them beseechingly. "May I ask what was on the card?"

"A W," said Ellery.

"W? Did Walt confess?"

"No," said Ellery.

"Then I don't see that proves it was Walt—"

"Mr. York," said Richard Queen. "Remember what the letters on the other cards were?"

"A J on Robert's, an H on Emily's."

"And d'ye know Walt's full name?"

"I don't think anyone does. Even Walt. Especially Walt."

"It's John Henry Walt," said Ellery.

"John Hen—JHW! Ohhhhh. Ohhhhhhhhh," said Percival, the second sound being the sound of revealed truth. "Then he really did do it," Percival breathed, as if this was the first time he had permitted himself even to hope for such a beautiful thing. "Crazy, man! I suppose he's plain psycho. By God," said Percival York, preening himself, "I'm all right now!"

"In the sense that you're safe," said the Inspector dryly, "I'd say so."

York rose, above the slur, in every dimension seeming to have increased by half. "Well, then, *hell*," he said jovially. "We ought to have a drink and I'm buying!"

"Sorry," said Inspector Queen. "On duty, y'know."

"Off duty," said Ellery. "Thanks just the same."

York shrugged. He picked up his hat and jauntily walked out.

Ellery caught his father's stabbing gesture and jumped off the desk to swing the door shut as the Inspector dived for his phone. "Velie? Percival York's leaving the building and I want somebody to ride on his back and I *don't* want him to know; understand? Who've you got—Johnson, Hesse? Then how about Zilgitt? All right, put Zillie on him, and when Johnson or Hesse checks in tell him to tail Zillie. Anything happens to York, Velie, I'll have Doc Prouty uncork the Black Death around here." He hung up and ground his hard old knuckles into his eye sockets.

"Why?" murmured Ellery. "When you've got your man?"

"Don't start going fancy on me, my son," growled the old man. "I've got the right one, all right. Maybe I can't prove Walt knocked Robert York's head off, and maybe nobody can prove he shoved Emily York onto those subway tracks, but I've sure got him for poisoning Myra. All I need's a few bows to tie up the package, and our boy Percival may be hiding some ribbon ends in his pants pockets, that's all."

"He certainly may," said Ellery. "But not just ends."

His father swallowed. Then he leaned back in an exhausted way. "Spit it out. What's that supposed to mean?"

Ellery reached over and took a scratch pad and a pencil and began to draw. "Look at the three cards the victims received.

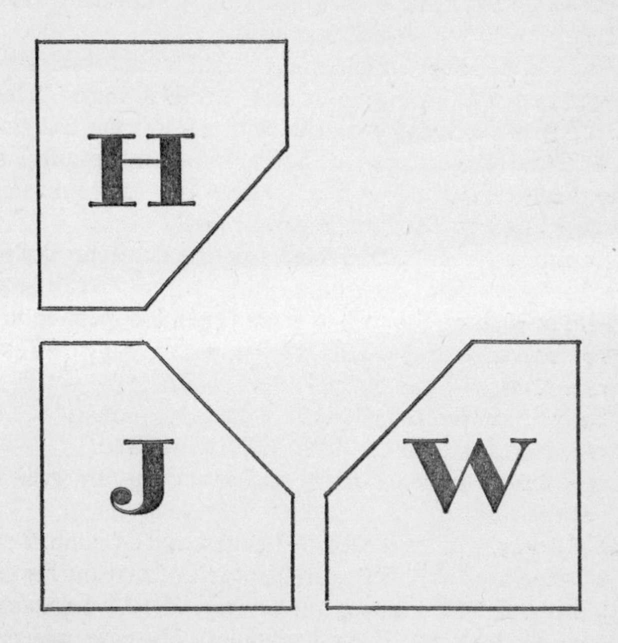

"Arranged like the houses in York Square, granted? They read in order, from lower left, clockwise: Robert's, Emily's, Myra's. Corresponding to the three murders . . . So that leaves Percival."

"So what, for the love of Mike? The three cards have Walt's three initials."

"Yes. But it still leaves Percival, doesn't it? And who profits by the three murders?"

"I don't give a hoot if Percival profits," the Inspector said wearily. "These just aren't murders for profit, that's all. Or even if they are! We know Walt pulled off at least one of them, don't we?—and maybe before we're finished we can prove he pulled off all three, which I'm sold on right now. So what's all the hassle?"

"Well," said Ellery, "suppose Walt's been framed."

"Been *what?*"

"Framed."

"By who?—*whom?*"

"Percival."

The word "framed" had made the old man grip the edge of his desk. The word "Percival" made him let go and lean back, grinning.

"You've avoided the obvious for so long, Ellery, you don't even see it any more. If I understand you, it's not Walt who committed the three murders, but Percival?"

"All I'm asking you to do," said Ellery doggedly, "is to try it on for size."

"Glad to oblige," the old man said dryly. "Robert's kill? Yes, Percy could have pushed that block off. Myra's? A lot less likely, even if we ignore the case against Walt. But for the sake of argument, I'll concede that while Walt was in Myra's bathroom, and the policewoman and Ann Drew were in Ann's room with Myra, Percy could have slipped into the bedroom and dropped the rat-killer into Myra's gin jug. But the middle murder, Emily's, the one practically anybody in New York could have committed—that one Percival did *not* do. Couldn't have. Not possibly."

"His alibi." Ellery was crestfallen. "I'd forgotten that. Although alibis . . ." he began hopefully.

But the Inspector was head-shaking. "Not this one, son. This one is copper-riveted." Ellery was beginning the long, loping pacing that characterized a crisis in his relations with a mystery. "Stop flogging it, Ellery," the Inspector said with kindness. "It was Walt. He planned to wipe out all four Yorks. We stopped him after number three."

Now Ellery was head-shaking as he loped. "I don't buy it," he muttered. "No . . ."

"For Pete's sake, Ellery," exploded the Inspector, "you were the one who was bothered by Walt from the start!"

"And he still bothers me. But, Dad." Ellery stopped loping and faced around. "If it was Walt who did the murders, who sent the cards?"

"The cards? Walt, of course."

"You think Walt has the perception, the creative intelligence to have planned all this? Including those cards?"

"That's a question for the psychiatrists to answer."

"You think that, having conceived the idea of the cards, and executed the idea of the cards, he could also have fooled an old police dog like you, and an experienced squad?"

"Fooled us about *what?*" cried the Inspector, out of temper at last.

"The toy printing outfit he's been using—*if* he's your man. You didn't find it, did you? And you searched, you and your men —how many times did you say?"

They looked at each other, the Inspector no longer angry. *He* had forgotten about *that.*

"Dad," Ellery said suddenly.

"What, Ellery?"

"Your search warrants. Are they still valid?"

"Why?"

Ellery said, "Come on."

23. *Pawn*

"But, Poochie," pouted the blonde, "I never heard you talk like this before."

"I can talk lots of ways," said Percival York. "You said so yourself."

"Did I do something?" she asked plaintively.

Percival looked her over. There was a glitter in his lemuroid eyes, a steadiness of purpose subtly different from the wayward wildness usual to him. For the first time in the blonde's experience he appeared to be a man with a load off his back, and very great plans.

"You did plenty," Percival said with appreciation. "Most of it pretty good. But let us not forget the fact, my maple cream, that you got plenty, too. And had fun, and it hasn't cost you. Out of it you got flowers and candy and clothes and jewelry and you haven't had to worry about rent too much, right?"

"Poochie, I never wanted—"

"And knock off the Poochie bit. This is a public place."

She glanced about. It was a shadowed, discreet, out-of-the-way public place, but a public place nevertheless. "How about that. Why, Poo—I mean honey? We could've gone to the hotel again."

"I didn't feel like it. I felt like coming here. You want to make something of it?"

She slowly sucked in her lower lip, and bit it. It left lipstick on her teeth. "Now you listen to me, Perce. If you think for one minute after all we been through, and I never asked you for a single thing hiding around all the time like I was a I don't know what, and I never did a single thing to you and now you're treating me like dirt, well!" And she picked up her fork and thrust it five times furiously into the heart of her filet mignon. The impact seemed to bring her to a primitive awareness; she took her hand away and stared glumly at the fork handle, sticking up out of her plate like a rocket on its launching pad.

Percival whinnied. "You want me to tell you what to do with it? Cheese!"

She was frowning with puzzlement, anger and hurt, yet she bravely tried to whinny with him. But then she said, as if to herself, "Day before yesterday it was so *nice*."

"Ah, well," said Percival happily. "Things happen."

"*What* happened?"

"A twenty-to-one shot came in, there's hell to pay in the Middle East, and I went down to police headquarters."

"Police head—Perce! What for?"

"They've got the lad who murdered my cousin Myra."

"They did? It wasn't in the papers. Who is it?"

"Walt."

"Who?"

"Walt. Can you imagine that?"

"You mean that bug-eyed creep that walks like on tracks? But *why?*"

"Y is a crooked letter. And so is his head. What difference does it make, O my darlin'? They got him is enough for me."

She sucked in her lip again and bit it again. "Perce. Is this why you're so—so whatever you are?"

"That's it." Percival filled his lungs to the full, which in his case represented an expansion of about three-quarters of an inch. "Sure I'm so whatever I am. 'Cause who do you s'pose was next on his hit parade?"

Intelligence dawned in the blonde's eye. "My poor, poor Poochie! Why, Poochie, you must've been just—"

"You knock that off, you witless itch," Percival said with such sudden and savage fury that she squeaked and fell back in her chair, her beringed hands instinctively raised in self-defense. "Look, Maybelline, this is your last free ride on *my* bus, so you better enjoy it while you can!"

"My name ain't Maybelline, and this is my last *what?*"

Percival shut off his fury and turned his attention daintily to his steak.

"You're kissing me off?"

He pointed a bottle of Tabasco at her gaily. "You're the one said that."

"I don't have to sit here and take this!"

"Right," Percival said in a cheerful tone.

She made an explosive sound, quite dangerous. But then she took refuge in female helplessness, dabbing piteously at her lips and eyes and leaving her napkin a mess of tangerine and silver-gray. "Oh, what's happening to us? What's happening, Percival?"

"What's happening to me," said Percival, chewing briskly, "is I got lots to do from here on out and I can take my pick with who to do it. It's been great, dearie, so don't let's spoil it and you got your western hemisphere in the Russian dressing."

This was a clearly visible untruth. Nonetheless, the blonde sat up straight and patted herself with the napkin. And said with slitted glance, "You can't do this to me, you slug."

"Wrong," said Percival York.

"You wait, mister. You know what I can do to you?"

"You," Percival said, unmoved, "can't do a bloody damn thing, and you want to know why? Because I got too much money, that's why. I got so much money coming to me, why, God couldn't do anything to me."

She jiggled to her feet, death and tears in her eyes, and snatched up her bag and a mink stole made of dyed beaver, and ran blindly toward the door. As she reached it, she screamed over her shoulder, "You'll be sorry the day you laid eyes on me!"

"I already am!" he bellowed joyously, while quiet diners and silent-footed waiters, a hand-polished cashier and a jointed-at-the-waist maître-d' stiffened with shock. "So get lost, you rancid broad! Drop dead!"

The blonde departed and Percival returned to his plate, chuckling. A waiter wrung his hands, then glided up to him. "Everything all right, sir?" he asked, evidently by reflex.

"Everything's just peachy-keen," said Percival, still laughing. He reached across the table with his fork, captured what was left of the blonde's filet and transferred it to his plate. "My compliments to the cow," he gurgled, "and bring me a bottle of Irish stout."

At Ellery's suggestion they stopped first at a toy store. He picked up a toy printing set, like the set established as having been used to print the J, H and W on the cards; then they proceeded to York Square.

Unexpectedly, it was Mrs. Schriver who answered the Inspector's ring at Percival's castle. The housekeeper seemed to have dwindled since Myra York's death—all but her jaw, which was harder set than ever. The red-penciled perimeter of her eyes widened with welcome at sight of the Queens.

"Inspector, Mr. Ellery Ellery—come in, come in."

They stepped inside, conscious of her grief. She stood before them uncertainly, looking from one to the other. "Now what is it?"

"Nothing, Mrs. Schriver," said the Inspector gently. "Is Mr. York home?"

She shook her head. "I am by myself alone, cleaning him."

"Do you know when he'll be back?"

"After the cleaning I am finished and out, I hope it," the doughty little housekeeper said angrily.

"Oh?" said Ellery. "Then you don't like Mr. York?"

"No-no-*no*." Her head vibrated like a plucked string, she shook it so rapidly. "Cleaning he wants, cleaning I do. Only for myself I do it, not for *him*. A *Schwein*, so dirty he is."

"He asked you to clean his house?"

"Yah. 'You clean up my house,' he says, 'while me, I clean up my life,' and he gives me a yoomp."

"A yoomp," said the Inspector uncertainly.

Mrs. Schriver suddenly executed a caper. Neither Queen smiled; there was too much deadly fury in her clumsy imitation. "And he says, 'All now I need is a good woman. How about you, cookie?' And then on the excuse me *Sitzplatz* he *schwumps* me, and he goes away. So mad I am, I got to fight. The *Schwein* I cannot fight, so his *Schweinestall* I fight until better I feel. Ach, the dirt in this house you would not believe!"

"What can you expect from a *Sitzplatz-schwumper?*" murmured Ellery; and, in spite of herself, Mrs. Schriver laughed. He took advantage of her laughter to shuck the paper off his parcel. "Mrs. Schriver, have you ever run across a toy like this one while you were cleaning here?"

The housekeeper peered, frowned, then shook her head. Ellery lifted the lid and showed her the wood-handled rubber stamps and the ink pad. She kept shaking her head.

"You're sure, Mrs. Schriver?"

"When a house I clean," she said emphatically, "I clean. No such thing in this house is."

"We'd like to be absolutely sure. Would you help us look?" said the Inspector; and in the next seventy-five minutes he learned to wish devoutly that he might have the likes of Mrs. Schriver under his command. The little castle concealed no corner, nook, shelf or cranny safe from her probing eye. She even helped them explore the hot-air ducts coming up from the cellar.

At last—dusty, dry, lugubrious—Ellery conceded that the only toy printing set in the house was the one he had brought with him. Mrs. Schriver extorted from them a promise that one day they would allow her to glut them with her strudel, shoofly pie and Dutch beer; and they left her attacking Percival York's dining-room rug as if it were, like its owner, her favorite enemy.

Outside, the old man said almost cheerfully, "So Percival doesn't have it, and that's that. Where do you want to check me next?"

"Walt's room."

"We searched it like Maxwell J. House looking for the last drop. I think three times."

"Robert's house?"

"Inside and out."

"And the garage?"

"We even started to pull the cars apart."

"Let's look there again," said Ellery.

They cut across the park to the garage behind Robert York's castle and indeed looked again. Inspector Queen showed Ellery just where the box of poison had stood; and Ellery demonstrated where Walt said he had been—under the Ryan sports car—when Robert was murdered; and they were about to denude the shelves in order to tap and measure the walls behind them when the son clutched the father's ropy arm with a warning clutch.

And they listened, not breathing, and heard through the closed door footsteps coming stealthily toward the garage.

The Inspector's right hand visited his left armpit and returned with a Police Positive. Ellery squared his shoulders until they crackled, then hunched over and drifted toward the door.

The footsteps came closer, stopped. The Inspector raised his weapon.

The knob turned, very, very slowly. Then—*crash!* the door was kicked open and, "Oh, scheissmonger," said the Inspector disgustedly, and put away his gun.

"You could lose half a head that way, Archer," said Ellery. "Nevertheless, heroic. How are you?"

"You did give me what is known as a turn," said Tom Archer, grinning whitely. "I didn't know who it was."

"And we forgot you'd still be working at Robert's. How's it coming?"

"It's going to be three cuts too high for any but a multimillionaire's private stamp collection. Fantastic." Archer looked around the garage curiously. "Can I help you with anything?"

"No," said Inspector Queen.

"Yes," said Ellery. He reached over to the workbench for his parcel. "We've been looking for . . . *this*." And he snatched away the wrapping.

Father and son were watching the face, eyes, stance, everything. Archer did not turn a hair. "What is it?" he asked, and bent forward to read aloud, "Prints Charming. Oh, I see. This is what those ridiculous cards were stamped with."

"Yes," said Inspector Queen.

"No," said Ellery. "One like it, and we can't find it. Have you seen anything like this around here?"

Young Archer shook his head. "By the way, I hear you arrested Walt. You can't actually think *he* did it?"

"Go on back to your work," sighed Ellery. "We'll be rummaging around for some time."

"Anything I can do to help, sing out." Archer waved and went away.

On their way up the narrow stairs to the upper story of the garage the Inspector grumbled, "I don't know what you expect to find, Ellery. If you think Mrs. Schriver's super-clean and Emily lived like a nun, wait till you see Walt's room. It must be symptomatic of whatever's wrong with him. He couldn't hide a guilty thought in it."

"A man just can't live in a room for years without impressing his personality on it in some way, Dad."

"He *has* no personality. That's Walt's secret weapon." Inspector Queen took out the ring of passkeys he had brought along. "Now which one was it again?"

The second key worked. The old man pushed the door open; it moved as silently as Walt. Ellery stepped inside.

Coming from the dim stairwell, he blinked in the blaze of blankness. The floor was pine, scrubbed white, bleached, waxed; a basic table to match; white curtains simple as pillow slips; an immaculate blanket, white, tucked tight barracks-fashion, on a canvas cot; a plain straight chair, a rectangular table lamp with a base turned from the same white pine, with a tubular white shade. The place was so aching-clean it hurt.

"Might's well live in an aspirin tablet," grunted the Inspector. "Did I exaggerate?"

Ellery stood still in wonderment. "What does he do with himself up here?"

"Reads, I guess." His father pointed.

Betweeen the far side of the bed and the wall beyond stood a small raw bookcase in the inevitable white. Ellery ran over, slid the cot aside—it, too, moved noiselessly—and squatted.

"Talk about one-track minds," he breathed. "*Plywood Projects. Concrete and Masonry Handbook. Woodworker's Manual.* Four books on the care and feeding of lawns. Roses. Pumps. Heating systems. House wiring. And a Bible, the Douay. Wait, here's a paperback *Modern Reader's Bible.* And the *Revised Standard!*" Ellery looked around. "What in God's name would he want with three Bibles?"

"Four," said the Inspector. "There's a King James locked in the table drawer." He unlocked it.

Ellery rose and swooped on the drawer. "The Oxford, with Concordance . . . Dad, this is neat! This figures."

"What figures?"

"Duty. Devotion to Duty—always, always capitalized." Ellery waved at the bookcase. "A couple of shelves full of musts. A must is like a should, explaining the Bibles." He began the long hungry lope, explaining to himself aloud. "He's a zombie, a robot . . . does what he must do . . . should do . . ."

"And nothing he shouldn't?" demanded his father. "Is that your point?"

"Exactly. This room closes the point out, Dad—it isn't even debatable any more. The man who lives in this room could not—repeat, could *not*—have conceived this devious business, as I've held repeatedly. It's too . . . too inventive. Too romantic."

"Romantic!"

"Well, adventuresome," muttered Ellery. "The only way Walt could ever have committed these crimes is by someone telling him to, spelling it all out for him, step by step. And whoever that is, he's not sitting in your jail smiling."

Inspector Queen choked. "There are Walt's clothes."

In one corner of the room, an L-shaped partition segregated the tiny bathroom. White curtains over the doorway. Another across an area where the partition was single wallboard instead of double, with the studs removed. There, on hooks hung in a ruler-straight line, hangers were angled to the narrow space. Two immaculate "good" suits, cheap but cared for: one black, one brown. Dress shoes: one pair black, one pair brown. Work shoes: three pairs, of excellent quality. On shelves, small or wide as needed: stacks of socks, black and brown; underwear; handkerchiefs. Shirts were on hangers, obviously laundered and pressed by hand, for they were not folded. Ironing board hinged from the partition; iron in a cubbyhole. Every possible space in the little partition was used; it was a miniature storage wall, only four inches thick.

"If he hid it here," said Ellery, "he chewed it up fine and painted it on."

"You think that's packed? Look at the kitchen."

Ellery turn around twice before he saw the "kitchen." Stove—a two-burner electric plate—and work surface hinged down from the wall opposite the window. This exposed china—heavy white cafeteria crockery, exactly one service—and a stainless-steel knife, fork, teaspoon and tablespoon upended in the single white china coffee mug. There was no refrigerator: Walt apparently ate from cans and boxes, of which there was a supply on the shelf beside the dishes. No sink: he must use the tiny one in the bathroom.

Ellery closed it all up and walked thoughtfully across to the window, a dormer, which alone broke the boxlike proportions of the room. He could see along the side of Robert York's castle and across the end of the diamond-shaped park to Myra's front door.

Suddenly he threw his forearm across his eyes and stood motionless.

"Son. What's the matter?"

Ellery gave the Inspector an impatient headshake. He flung down his arm and bounded for the door. "I'll be back in a minute," he exclaimed, and raced down the stairs.

His father hopped for the window. He saw Ellery gallop out the side door of the garage, turn and look up while running, stumble, recover and scramble into the building, to race back up the stairs.

"Ellery, what in time—?"

Ellery held up a breathless wait-a-minute palm and dashed to the window, scooping up the chair as he passed the table. He set it before the window, leaped on it and, using his knuckles, pressed upward.

The Inspector gaped. For the dormer ceiling, a mere piece of fiberboard, lifted readily to expose a quite sizable blackness above. Still holding the panel up with his knuckles, Ellery reached over the nearest beam and felt beyond it, shouted, "Dad!" and drew forth a shiny box bearing the legend *Prints Charming.* He jumped down with it, the panel fell back into place with a cushioned *whoosh,* he threw the toy printing set to his father and dropped gasping into the chair.

The old man's face was a sight to behold. For just as all the combined rays of the spectrum reflect to the eye the color white, so all the Inspector's emotions—stupefaction, self-castigation, professional chagrin, anger at subordinates and half a dozen others—produced an expression of total blankness. He proceeded mechanically to set the box on Walt's table, raise the lid, take out his display handkerchief and, with it, lift the letter J from its bed, examine its stamping surface and, shaking his head in a dazed way, replace the J and lift out the H. And then the W. And then all the other letters, and the numbers.

"The only ones showing ink on the stamping surfaces are the J, H and W," the old man mumbled; and, carefully replacing the lid, he turned and looked at his son, who was still breathing hard.

"If I didn't think you might do it," said the Inspector in a sort of croak, "I'd turn around and instruct you to kick me where it'd do the most good. Will you kindly tell me: are you a genius or am I an idiot? A hand-picked squad searched this room, not once but three times. I searched it personally. Yet you walk in here, take one look, point—"

"Oh, come on, Dad," Ellery said irritably. "You just didn't happen to notice one thing, and I just did. This is a dormer window with a pitched roof. Yet inside the window the ceiling is flat. So there had to be a space up there. That's not what's bothering me."

"You're *bothered* about finding this?" snapped the old man. "What's the matter with you, Ellery? This find of yours cinches the case against Walt. It's going to send him to the Chair."

"That's what's bothering me," muttered Ellery. "Because it pins all three murders on him."

"Are you suggesting that the box was planted up there to frame him? That Percival pipe dream again?"

"No, I was wrong about that," said the son wearily. "I don't doubt you'll find Walt's fingerprints all over it. I'm ready to concede that Walt executed the three murders, Dad. What I'm not ready to concede is that he *planned* the three murders."

"What are you doing now?" demanded his father. For Ellery had risen suddenly and stepped back onto the chair.

"Seeing if there's anything else up here."

Again Ellery used his knuckles to raise the ceiling plasterboard. With the other hand he felt around the floor of the hiding place. "Nothing on this side . . ." He changed hands on the ceiling panel and fumbled about in the opposite direction—and then, with almost a surprised look, stopped fumbling. The Inspector, watching him, stiffened.

"What is it, Ellery?"

"Feels like a clipboard," said Ellery slowly; and he withdrew the hand of discovery with care, and the panel came down with a *whoosh;* and it was indeed a clipboard, with a number of sheets of paper held neatly in its jaws.

And as he read the topmost sheet from his elevated position in John Henry Walt's white and sterile room, with Inspector Queen shifting restlessly below him, one hand making futile requests, Ellery sighed a long and satisfied sigh, and some of the hunch went out of his taut shoulders, and even the lines drawn lately on his face underwent erasure.

But when he handed the clipboard to his father, and the Inspector began to read the topmost sheet as Ellery got down from the chair, there was neither satisfaction nor relaxation on the old man's face, only a deepening of its anxieties.

For what the Inspector read was:

Dear Walt:

You know who I am.

You do not know that you know.

You shall.

I write this to let you know that I know who you really are. I know the skill of your hands. I know the quality of your obedience. I know where you come from and what you are doing. I know what you think. I know what you want. I know your great destiny.

I like you.

Y

24. Queen's Countergambit

Ellery Queen was fast asleep when at last he began to understand—really to understand—the rules of the York Square game he was playing.

It did not come to him as a game at first, when he was profoundly dreaming. It began as a series of impressions, whimsical, laughable even; not until then did he find himself locked in combat with a chess piece. But which one? which one?—oh, horrible, it was a bishop, but instead of the miter it had a squashed head . . .

And then he was running, running over the square (squares?), and he was tiny, too tiny to cover that much distance quickly; but he must get there, he must . . . and the squares grew larger as he grew smaller until he could see only one square—York Square, of course, with the four castles at the corners.

And Ellery knew with a great desolation that he was running, had been running, to save a chess piece that was under attack; he saw her standing with her doom descending like a great hand, come to take her away. And take her it did, and then there was the horror of stasis wherein suddenly he must stand where he found himself, helpless, waiting, waiting, and immobile because it was not his turn.

He twisted and moaned in his sleep, and he moved upward from level to dark level—still very dark, very deep, but by a subtle tone less dark than those lightless depths at which the dream (he now knew) had begun.

A pawn went sliding past, dipping to go by diagonally. And as it passed his vision (he was still immobilized, waiting his turn), he knew why it had sidestepped like that: it had taken a piece, one of his best, which screamed as the pawn replaced it on the board.

And the pawn had the face of Walt.

Suddenly he had to make a move (now, *now!*) but there would be no time to think; he must just *move;* and he did; and he knew as he did that it was a terribly wrong move. The shape ahead of him was the shape of Ann Drew, and when she realized what he had done she looked at him with disgust and loathing and began to bleed all over her body; her loathing was infinitely greater than her agony, and he tried to tell her that he'd had to move that way, that there'd been no time to think. But her loathing was greater than his voice, his whole mind; it would never let her understand. And he moaned and twisted, and came up a bit more out of his roiling sleep.

The game was a shooting-gallery kind of chess, with rows of chess pieces moving from left to right, and above them a row of heads moving from right to left. The heads were Emily and Myra and Walt and Percival and his father and himself, and one face that was not a face at all but a blank in the shape of a head. In endless succession they moved, heads to the left, chess pieces to the right, so that from moment to moment Walt was a pawn, his father was a pawn, Tom Archer was a king, Mrs. Schriver a knight. A moment, and it was all changed: Percival was a pawn, Mallory a king, the faceless one a rook . . . a castle.

There was one remarkable instant when all the heads fitted all the chessmen—when everything was as clear to him as if he had always known this curious game and its complex rules. But then the instant blinked away, and he cried out at his inability to remember any of the right heads for the pieces. And he gnashed his teeth and scissored his jaws, because for that short solar moment he had seen the face of the faceless one—the king, the player on the other side.

He groaned aloud, "The player on the other side."

And came higher out of his dream, almost out of sleep.

"Check," someone said. And it echoed, and on each descending pulse a check for $1,000,000 went spinning on the wind.

"And mate!" someone cried. But this was a cry of ecstasy, for a sheet-lightning flash revealed Tom Archer in intimate embrace with Ann Drew. Or did "check" with "mate" mean stop it, stop it? ("Should any man know cause why these twain should not be wed," muttered the bishop, "let him speak now or forever hold his peace.") (Which piece is that? The Queen! Then use the queen, use it, the most powerful piece on the board. Only . . . the queen has forgotten how to move. Who's the player on the other side? Tell me that and I'll remember the moves) . . .

With a wrenching grunt Ellery came finally out of his dream and his sleep. His inhospitable bed angered him, and he lurched up and away from it to stand, weaving, in the dark. His mouth felt like an ant farm, and a faintly luminous rime seemed to salt his eyelids.

He stumped into his study, stubbed his toe, groped for a curse word, fumbled and found the desk-lamp switch, dropped into the chair, lifted the lid of the coffeepot, dropped it back in disgust. And leaned back to gloom owlishly at the bland backs of the Encyclopædia Britannica, Eleventh Edition. A to AND. AND to AUS (Ann to Archer?) . . . He skipped along the attentive row. HAR to HUR (laugh her off!) . . . SHU to SUB and SUB to TOM. (And *that* was clear: kick him in the subway.)

He shook his head and told himself aloud to shut up, which made him glance guiltily toward the other bedroom. And he wondered what his father would say at the sight of him sitting barefoot at his desk in the middle of the night telling himself to shut up. And suddenly, uninvited, inexpressibly welcome, suddenly the dream flashed across his mind, all of it at once; and, father or no father: "Well, sure!" he cried.

For it *was* like a game! There was Walt, the pawn, all but worthless in himself, yet deadly if played with skill—and Walt had been played adroitly indeed. (He and the Inspector had pored over the My Dear Walt letters signed the cryptic Y, letters typewritten with such perfect exactness on the faint blue lines of the cheap ruled paper . . . read them and marveled and discussed, reread and discussed again how clear it now was that to lock up the weapon Walt was merely to lock up a gun or a switchblade and let its user go.)

Yes, Y had played Walt well, with painstaking cruelty. Through his victorious anger at the letters Ellery could have wept at the tragedy of this slow dutiful little blinking man, his past forgotten and his future hopeless, unloving and unloved, a lone cipher in the midst of an involved equation—suddenly receiving those passionless, directing, assuring, omnipotent letters . . . that icy cascade of admiration, those calm promises of greatness: Walt, man of destiny, dispenser of death, the chosen one for that mighty trust . . . loved at last.

Little as Walt knew about himself, he must dimly grasp that

he was less clever than most; yet here he was, outwitting the sharp, outflanking the powerful—even now, silent in a cell, unafraid, for had not his great and awful patron written that no harm would come to him? Of course Walt would not speak! Why should he? He need only wait—rescue was certain, his destiny foreordained. *My Dear Walt.* Safe all along, because anyone, even the great man himself (Ellery winced and writhed) could tell at a glance that he, Walt, hadn't brains enough to be the player on the other side.

Player on the other side . . . Oh, yes, it was a game—a game in which for any piece to be swept off the board meant death, and millions of dollars hung on every move. A game in which York Square was the board, and didn't it have a castle in each corner? Walt the pawn, the castles the rooks. What else?

"Well, sure," Ellery said, again aloud, and again guiltily; but the Inspector slept on in the other bedroom.

For the Queen was there, oh, yes; the queen, the powerful piece—as his dream had had it—uncertain of the moves. (How terrible, the move that left Ann bleeding, loathing.)

What else?

A knight? Do we have a knight? Oh, yes (and Ellery almost smiled)—oh, yes, we have a knight, Percival . . . Sir Percivale, brought to ruin by the dark arts of the Arthurian enchantress . . . Parsifal, "the guileless fool" who at the end became guardian of the Holy Grail; and was that so far gone in its cynical symbolism?

But there's no bishop, no bishop . . . (Only one who is subject to such fantasies of the night can know how very elusive a detail can be, and how desperately desirable.)

But Ellery punched the leather arm of his chair, elated. There was one! For in the olden days of the game didn't they call the bishop an *archer?* He had seen antique sets whose piece in the bishop's square carried a bow. Archer . . .

Pawn, rook, knight, queen, bishop . . . king?

For take the king and the game is over. That's how you know he's the king.

The player on the other side.

The faceless one . . . Immediately Ellery shut his eyes and saw again that mad progression of chessmen changing heads. It was a shock to remember that one miraculous instant when all the right heads were on all the right pieces—even the head of the faceless one. The king, the player on— And now to have forgotten it—

Ellery sprang from his chair. But his left leg had gone to sleep, and he staggered back. The swivel chair swiveled maliciously; he flailed, and the coffeepot jumped off the desk; he lunged and caught it just as it was about to baptize the rug.

Breathing hard, Ellery set the pot carefully back on the desk and started over. (Make haste slowly, aging man. Tell yourself the story of the young bull and the old bull who spotted the herd of heifers in the valley. "Shake a hoof, old-timer," bellowed the youngster. "Let's run down there and smooch us one of those heifers." "No, son," said the old bull with dignity, "let's walk down there and smooch 'em all.")

And Ellery stood on his sensible leg and shook the other until he could all but hear the pins and needles jingle. Then he limped to the bookshelf and fingered out his Bartlett from between Fowler and Roget. And riffled, and squinted, and found what he was looking for; and with his index finger as a bookmark he limped back to the desk chair and the direct lamplight.

> *The chess-board is the world, the pieces are the phenomena of the universe, the rules of the game are what we call the laws of Nature. The player on the other side is hidden from us. We know that his play is always fair, just, and patient . . .*

Ellery arrghed and clapped the book shut. That's what you get when you go bird-dogging for analogies! They strike close enough to make a noise, but then they go ricocheting off into the irrelevant. (What caliber bullet does it take to kill the irrelevant? he thought inexcusably; and: The irrelevant never forgets. He was warned by this that his brain was running too fast for its own good, and he put *Familiar Quotations* and Huxley aside and sat down quietly to think.)

He sat thinking for some time, unmoving except when he crossed his legs the other way. Once he muttered, "But it's my move." After a while his eyes drooped shut. But he had never been further from sleep.

And the move came to him.

Instantly he rejected it. Don't be a fool, he advised himself, you'll lose your knight . . . If only he could recall which head went on which piece! Especially . . . The move came creeping back to him; he stepped on it. He thought of other moves. *The* move, uncrushed, laid its warm head on his ankle and purred and purred. He tried to kick it off. But now it had its claws in him. He sighed in surrender and took it up into his lap. And stroked its unusual carcass, and said, Let's have a look at you . . .

He knew, when he rose, that he had made up his mind long before. He knew the dangers. He knew, also, the infernal nuisance of persuasion and argument he was going to have to go through. None of which mattered.

Ellery shuffled doggedly through the apartment, shot open the door of the Inspector's bedroom so that the knob cannoned into the socket it had dug for itself in the bedroom plaster (a concession which always brought his father up standing, though he might not truly waken for ten minutes or more) and stood patiently waiting while the old man beat the end of blanket away from his ears and snarled "*Wurra, wurra, wurra,*" and similar incantations, ending with, "What in time time is it?"

Then Ellery said, "Dad, we'll have to let Walt go."

Hell broke loose.

PART THREE

End Play

25. Waiting Moves

Mr. J. H. Walt went back to York Square, and a miracle was passed by the fourth estate.

On booking Walt for Myra York's death, Inspector Richard Queen had asked the newsmen to sit on it. He took his oath on a long-term better break if they would go along with him now. Therefore three papers had mentioned Walt's arrest not at all; three had mentioned it, but harmlessly ("held for questioning") in the back pages. The seventh paper, honoring its promise, reported nothing in its news columns; but, alas, from its editorial page crawled That Certain Columnist, who had chewed and spewed as follows:

> *. . . Anyone for a handyman's job? There's one open at a downtown private park surrounded by crackerjack castles. Seems the incumbent can't explain away evidence connecting him with the latest obit in a dead-millionaire epidemic they've been enjoying like on the square. Up to now the police score was 0 for 3, but maybe they're getting the old batting eye back and the Commissioner will be able to point with pride to the Kitty-Korner Killings down at Kosy-Kastle Square.*
>
> *Maybe. Because grim suspicion: Trickling down the left side of this (coff-coff) "liberal" administration could be the sludgy notion that scot-free murder is quicker and neater than taxing the rich to death.*

Now it may be that some of the newspapers went along with Inspector Queen because they respected and trusted him. Or it may be—it may indeed well be—that other columnists had sharply pointed things to say and had them ready to jab, but slipped them back into the scabbard when Brother Rat ratted. And this in turn may have been from contempt for That Certain Columnist's politics (pro-mom, anti-sin, and for anything and everything that promised to incite hatred in the breasts of the masses); or from dislike of his person, which looked, felt and smelled like aging yeast; or from envy of his income, which was counted by computers. Whatever the motivations, the betrayed all worked together to leave T. C. C. high and dry on an uncharted reef, belatedly aware that a scoop is not a scoop unless floated by a tide of like-thinking late-comers. And there he clung until the morning editions swept down on his stranded scoop, with an elemental howl, a typhoon that smashed its hull to the bilge.

For now—said *all* the papers, including the derelict's own—it appeared that Myra was a suicide, consequently John Henry Walt was released from custody; Emily was an accident; and such progress had secretly been made on Robert's case that an arrest could be expected at any hour.

None of this came (officially) from Centre Street.

The Curious Incident of the Embarrassing Moment came about in this way:

Because no man can remain in an immovable state of fear, perplexity or anger and keep his sanity, Ellery swung out into a brief light-heartedness. It was evoked, perhaps, by the sun on Ann Drew's hair. She was walking her little beast in York Square, and Tom Archer was with her; and Ellery was to reflect later that if any one of these entities had been absent he would not have made so erroneous an error.

"Queen!" called Archer. "Do you know what she's going to do?"

"Good morning," said Ellery to Ann Drew; and to the dog, "Good morning, Bud," and to young Archer, "First tell me which of these ladies you're talking about."

"It isn't Bud, it's Bub," said Archer. "She's going to work with me. How do you like those apples! Finishing the collection."

"Bud is? Oh, licking stamps."

"Not Bub! Ann. She's agreed to stay on in the Square and work for me, and the trustees at the bank have okayed a salary for her."

"You actually crave a career of stamp-licking?" Ellery asked the girl, while saying to himself, Would God I were a tender 1869 Gambia 6d. pale blue no-watermark imperf.

"You don't lick these stamps—" Archer began indulgently.

But Ann Drew smiled, an act somehow equivalent to daybreak, which immediately darkened because she also touched Tom Archer's arm. So Ellery sighed and said to the dog, "You and I are in the wrong business, Bud."

"Bub," Archer corrected him again. "It's short for Beelzebub. But don't ask Ann why," he added, fondly teasing. "It shocks her."

"Oh, yes," Ellery recalled. "The thing Miss Drew said she would *never* tell me." And then, perhaps because her hair and her smile had made his head spin, or this sustained whimsy had passed its proper peak, he tossed off words which at once he would gladly have given lifetime first North American serial rights to recall. All he meant was, "Why did you call the dog that?" but what actually emerged from his mouth was, "And just what would shock the likes of you, milady?"

In that split second it came to Ellery in a flood: what she had done as a girl, and how terrified she was lest Tom Archer ever hear of it. Ellery's immediate predicament all but overwhelmed him, for her stricken face was scalding; and "Hey!" cried Tom Archer in swift concern, and stroked her. "Hey, there, it's not as bad as all *that.*"

That was when Ellery said, "Look, I have to run, I'm late for the mumble mumble," and fled.

And there in the sunlight they watched him go; and to Archer's astonishment and delight Ann said to him, "Hold me, Tom, hold me tight . . ." so that he forgot to question what any of it meant.

Living ghosts invaded York Square. Among the strollers and rubbernecks on wheels—among the wiring inspectors, meter readers, inventory men from the estate's bank, postmen, laundrymen and newsmen—a high percentage came from Inspector Queen's and the D.A.'s offices. These ghosts were both seen and invisible. Above and behind, around and under, in manholes with listening bugs and in neighboring buildings with field glasses and cameras, the cordon was thrown around Percival York. He was of necessity informed of what was going on, but he liked it not and he took it dimly. Some of his protection he could see; but a great deal of it was kept secret from him, and therefore Percival never felt that he was getting enough.

Yet it was impossible to rely on him. Not four hours after unreservedly promising the Queens to stay in sight at all times, or to notify the nearest guard when he felt he had to leave York Square, Percival slipped his tails (and was neatly tailed again without his knowledge, thanks to a man on Emily's tower with a handie-talkie and another on a neighboring rooftop with a tight-beam flashlight), and took a taxi to the estate's bank. Here he demanded to know if the terms of his residence in the Square under old Nathaniel's will could be stretched far enough to allow his taking a cruise until the danger was past. The bank official who told him solemnly that, were he to do such a thing, he might forfeit the entire fortune was frankly lying, because Ellery had been there against just such a contingency. Not since that magnificent miser, Jack Benny, was asked by a holdup man, "Your money or your life," had a man seemed in such anguished indecision as Percival York. Living bait, he acted as if he feared the worst by the moment, by the breath, the bite and the swallow (Ellery remarked to his father that York must fear a dozen deaths; no man could be that afraid of only one). The alternative, to flee and lose his pending millions, must have been to him—judging by his behavior—quite as dreadful a prospect as death itself.

Of all things Percival feared, he feared Walt the most.

The handyman had slipped back into his routine without a sign of trauma. He was no trouble to watch; he was thoroughly preoccupied. He had regained his tongue with his freedom; but he had never exercised it lavishly, and he obeyed Inspector Queen's injunction to the letter: to answer no questions about his arrest from anyone, and to refer the persistent questioners to the Inspector.

"Not that he'd spill anything," the old man growled. "You can make Walt answer questions by the yard without learning a blasted thing."

And Ellery nodded, himself preoccupied.

Walt did what he was told. He was told to do little, for he had a sharpshooter's eye for a fleck of plaster, a bald spot on a lawn, a dripping faucet; for the rest, he spent most of his time in his room, since the passing of three of the four Yorks left him largely maintenance duties.

The toy printing set, on which no prints had been found but Walt's, had been returned precisely to its hiding place; so had the letters from Y—after being photostated and microphotographed by the lab. The letters, too, had yielded no fingerprints but Walt's; hence the microphotographs. If they should reveal any sign of latent prints, the originals could always be repossessed for further examination.

"This case, though," said the Inspector sourly, "will hang by no easy threads like that. This is a fall-on-your-face kind of case."

"This case," retorted his son, "is a drop-dead kind of case."

There was little chance that Walt might destroy the letters, both Queens felt. They meant so much to him that, to preserve their wonderful testimony to his worth, he had risked the displeasure of his guardian angel—the only thing in which apparently he had disobeyed Y.

Walt's course and Percival's seldom crossed; but when they did, the result was ludicrous. Small and stocky Walt, with that queer glide-on-tracks gait, the oddly non-reflecting eyeballs, the withdrawn glance—Walt would proceed from here to there like a natural event, a distant flight of birds, or an oncoming winter, unchangeable by anything outside itself. Ambling, shambling, bag-eyed Percival, who ordinarily managed a jaunty step, would—at his first glimpse of Walt—wobble on his feet like a suddenly pierced balloon . . . not so much from weakness as from sheer indecision about which way to go.

At the same time Percival's pressures were not all directed toward escape; he seemed to have a stubborn desire to fluff the whole thing off like a man. If Walt's course seemed to be taking him by at a safe distance, Percival might tremble and flutter, but he would hold his ground; or, if there was a wall or a tree behind him, he backed toward it slowly, never taking his eyes off his enemy, until he stood with his bent-bow spine hard-pressed against solidity . . . breathing noisily, nostrils aflutter, beady eyes peering out over their discolored shelves. So he would stand until Walt was unequivocally past; after which he would slump, and sigh, and straighten up and go about his business. If, of course, the encounter was direct, Percival unhesitatingly ran. It was as if he knew that Walt not only had, but was, some sort of fragmentation bomb.

As for Walt, at a distance or in close, he sidled by at never-changing speed, on a never-changing course, oblivious.

So matters held for almost a week, while the Queens, *pater* and *filius*, waited for the next move.

He was not displeased.

True, there had been delays. But then, the universe itself was created force against force, each modifying the other. The forces seldom balanced; so often there was a flow one way or the other. The hand of God met resistance in the clay it molded, or the molding would have been impossible.

He contemplated the night city through the dirty window of the hotel room. The city's lights danced nervously. He smiled.

He turned, and crossed the dreary little room, and patted the patiently waiting typewriter, and went to the door.

He put out the light.

He locked the door.

He left.

Ann Drew and Tom Archer saw a play in Greenwich Village, took the subway for the short journey home, and a little past midnight found themselves in the dark warmth of York Square. They paused to kiss briefly before the plaque bearing Nathaniel York, Junior's name, because there they had almost quarreled once; and it was from there that they heard the distant sound of weeping.

For a shocked moment they looked toward each other in the gloom. Then Ann hurried off in the direction of the ugly sound, and Archer hurried after her.

The sound drew them halfway around the Square, to Percival York's house; and here they found its source, on the top step, weeping and rocking.

Ann ran up the walk, Tom running after with a warning word. But before she could reach the step, or the word could be spoken, a tall blackness separated itself from a deeper blackness and said sharply, "Hold it, there!" and then said softly, "Oh, Miss Drew, Mr. Archer. Evening."

"*Gosh*," breathed Ann. "I didn't see you at all."

"Inspector Queen's know-how, Miss Drew," said Detective

Zilgitt amiably. "Inspector knows the value of assigning a black detective to a dark night."

Ann smiled a faint smile. Her pupils had adjusted to the darkness by now, and she could just make out the glow of the city detective's answering smile. "Is that . . . Mr. York?"

"Nobody else."

"But he's crying."

"Been crying for close to an hour."

"Can't you do anything for him?"

"I'm just my brother's keeper," said Zillie dryly. "Holding his hand isn't my department."

Ann licked her lip, braced, began the swift movement to kneel by the weeping, rocking Percival. Instantly the detective checked her, with the same gesture taking her purse. Archer, squinting, saw how deftly the man passed it from one hand to the other, weighing it, taking inventory. "Let Mr. Archer hold this for you," said Zilgitt kindly. He handed it over.

"But this *is* your department," said Archer.

"That's right," said the detective, and he drifted in close as Ann sank down before the sobbing man.

"Percival." Ann shook his shoulder gently. "It's me, Ann."

"Didn't want you to—see me—this way," sobbed Percival.

"Ah, now, listen," said Tom Archer. He hauled Ann to her feet from behind. "Let the guy be. Didn't you ever see a crying jag before?"

She shrugged his hands away. "He has *not* been drinking, Tom! Don't you see he's in trouble?" She knelt again. Archer, feeling foolish, stepped back. "Percival?"

"Didn't want you to—see me—like this," wept Percival stubbornly.

"What is it? What's wrong?"

He put down his hands. She reached past to snare his display handkerchief, shook it out and gave it to him. Reflexively he wiped his face. "Annie—I mean, Miss Snff."

"Ann," she said.

Not noisily, Tom Archer spat.

"Don't bother about me. Please."

"Isn't there something we can do for you?"

"Nobody can do anything. I wish I never heard of this place. Or the money."

"You don't have to stay here."

"But I do. You think I've got the moxie to walk away from eleven million bucks? But—"

"Go on," Ann Drew crooned.

Percival slapped his own face angrily with the handkerchief. "But I can't stand it here, either. I've got nobody, nothing."

Tom Archer said, "You'll have eleven million bucks."

"And what's that, all by yourself?" Percival sniffed and blew his nose. "Look at you two, what you've got. Each other. Work you like, that pays your way. And people who like *you*. Know anybody that likes me? In forty-six years I've never had anybody."

"You could still have it," Ann said emotionally.

He shook his head. "I never learned how. You know, Ann," he said, very quietly, "I really did *not* want you to see me like this. This thing's done something to me. You won't believe it, but I've quit drinking—I haven't been near a single horse parlor—I got rid of . . . Well." He made a difficult little laugh. "And here I am, having to *tell* it to people! Where do you start if you want to be like everyone else and you don't know how?"

Tom Archer squatted on a heel beside Ann and looked into Percival's face from a distance of six inches. "You actually mean what you're saying?"

"Tom, he does!" cried Ann. "Percival—Mr. York—look. I know at least three people who'll help. Tom and me—"

"And who else?" It was part leaping hope, part wry disbelief.

"You."

Young Archer rose. "Perce, you be at Robert's house nine o'clock tomorrow morning. I've got a deadline on those stamps, and Ann and I are swamped. I can use your help. Will you come?"

The last known survivor of the Yorks leaned eagerly toward the two young faces, peering in astonishment. Then—"All right!" Percival York said. "All *right!*"

The hardest thing Ellery had had to do was con his father into taking the tails off John Henry Walt after releasing him from custody. The hardest thing Inspector Queen had had to do was con his superiors into looking the other way. By some magic, possibly the alchemy of desperation, both succeeded.

"They're examining my reports," mumbled the Inspector, "when they ought to be examining my head. I've got everybody so dazzled by this thing that no one's opened his eyes wide enough to see that I'm letting an indictable killer run around loose with a completely bare bottom."

"It makes sense," Ellery insisted. "Now that we have positive evidence that Walt's a mere tool, with Mr. Y—why couldn't he have called himself X!—with Y directing his every move, it stands to reason that Y watches Walt closely. When we let Walt go, Y had every right to smell a trap—to expect us to keep Walt under around-the-clock surveillance. We can't afford to scare Y off; we have to force his hand; so no tails on Walt; and maybe Y will think it's on the level—that the Walt make was from hunger, and we saw it couldn't be he. After all, Y doesn't know we're on to those letters of his to Walt. By the way, has the clipboard been checked recently?"

"Yesterday afternoon, by Johnson. He skinned up there while Walt was mixing a little cement to set a loose flagstone behind Emily's house. Nothing's changed."

"You're afraid Y's seen through us?"

"Well, I just said it. Nothing's changed."

"I think we're pulling a successful deception play. Anyway, Dad, it's a chance we've got to take."

The Inspector grunted and poured the breakfast coffee.

"All right, I know how worried you are," said Ellery. ("Who, me?" said the Inspector with a hollow laugh.) "But look, there'd be even less sense to this mishmash if Percival weren't marked for slaughter, too. Well, we have Percival sewed up tight, haven't we? So there's really not much to worry about."

"Maybe we've got Percival sewed up *too* tight." The old man snatched the marmaladed toast out of his mouth and shot a look ceilingward. "Lord forgive me."

"Amen!" muttered Ellery. "More toast, please."

"Maybe that's why this Y hasn't hit."

"Up to now, probably. Percival's led such an unpredictable life—he's ordinarily here, there, yonder and out all night to boot. Y studies his victims' routines and plans accordingly; our Perce hasn't had any routines. But now . . . now, suddenly, he's on time, he's in position."

"And how about that," said the Inspector. "My boys still haven't got over it."

"Maybe there's been another Percival hiding out in that rotten hulk all the time, waiting for a chance to take over."

"Maybe."

"Anyway, the new Perce is bound to tempt Y into a move."

They sat with their thoughts, munching toast and sipping coffee: Ellery thinking painfully of a girl so good she needed no salvation (and why *had* the pooch been named Beelzebub?), and of an evil man, about to be Croesus-rich, who had within him an ordinary and quite decent fellow aching to be born; and the old gentleman recalling the shy, laughing one peeping out from Miss Sullivan's weathered hulk.

"Maybe," repeated the Inspector. "But my innocent-eyed watchdogs are saying—"

"Don't tell me, I know," sighed Ellery. "They're saying it can't last."

The Inspector shrugged.

"It's very possible. Percival's the kind who turns over a new leaf in the way he's always done everything, to excess."

"According to the reports, he's been so damn punctual on that stamp job this week he makes the late Robert look like a slob. Now when Perce says he's going to be somewhere, that's where he is. Except twice."

"Except twice?" Ellery put down his cup. "Except twice what?"

"Except twice this week," said the Inspector with the fretful guilt of the executive who accepts full responsibility for his subordinates' booboos, "when our reborn friend slipped away."

"What!"

"Once," nodded the old man, "he asked Archer for time off to go get his polio shot—his duty, he said, his *civic* duty, for Pete's sake! Archer was up to his ears and forgot to alert the man on duty; the man on duty didn't 'expect' Percival to cut out and was sneaking a coffee break—and where *he* is now," the Inspector interpolated grimly, "he doesn't have much expectation of *anything*. And the other night our boy slipped his leash—don't worry, we've plugged that one—and got back to York Square just as we were pushing the panic button. Apologized, said he went for a walk, didn't mean to cause trouble! It won't," said Inspector Queen through his dentures, "happen again."

"It—had—better—not," said Ellery. The moisture he wiped from his upper lip with his napkin was true fear-sweat. And he picked up a toast crust, looked at it, put it down and began to nibble on his thumb instead.

"Well," said the Inspector, shoving his chair back.

"Dad, before you go." Ellery shut his eyes and flapped his head like a dog drying himself. Then he opened his eyes and said, "Nothing new on the letters, I suppose?"

"You mean from the lab? No, and they blew up those microslides as big as a barn door. Just Walt's prints, period. Why? Did you expect this Y to be careless about a thing like prints?"

"No, but . . ."

"But *what?*"

"I was looking over those print photos yesterday—I mean the original set the lab took. There's something about them that's been bugging me."

His father stared. "Go on."

Ellery shut his eyes again. "I was sitting there, staring at them, trying to visualize Walt reading them, gloating over them—I mean the letters. Judging by the prints the lab brought out, he handled those letters a lot."

"Yes? So?"

"Well, if you really *look* at those prints of his—the way they're distributed"—Ellery opened his eyes suddenly—"you have to see Walt holding the letters by the top corners. As if . . . well, as if he repeatedly held them up to the light, or something."

"If you mean hidden messages," the Inspector said dryly, "forget it. They've been checked for that."

"I *know*. But why would he hold each page by the upper corners? With his thumbs? Because those upper-corner prints are all thumbprints. Why, Dad?"

"If I thought I'd get an answer," said the old man in a voice one part irascibility and one part perplexity, "I'd ask him."

And this time he did get up from the table, because the phone rang.

Inspector Queen came back tautly. "We'd better hop to it. That was the post office."

"Post office?"

"They have a letter down there addressed to Mr. Percival York."

"The same kind as—?" Ellery was twisted about in his chair. "A card-letter?"

"A card-letter."

26. Attack Culminated

He inserted the fresh sheet in the typewriter and, without hesitation in the special silence of the dingy hotel room, began to write with great speed:

My Dear Walt:

Here is your final task, the glorious culmination of all you have done for me and, through me, for yourself.

You will take the enclosed card and, with the usual care to get a clean impression with the rubber stamp and to center it on the card (and remembering that to be correct in this instance the diagonal edge of the card must be at the lower left) imprint the card with the proper stamp so that it looks like this:

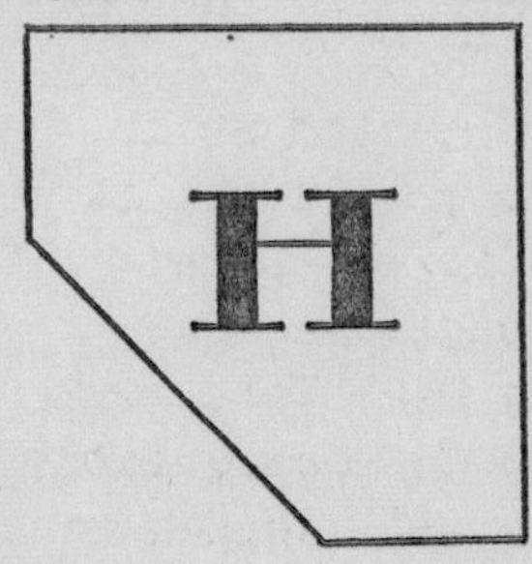

Place it in the envelope, address it to Mr. Percival York at York Square, and mail it at any time before midnight of the day you receive this.

On the following day go about your duties in the ordinary way. Do not worry about Percival York's keeping to his new work schedule. He will almost certainly stick to it.

When you are finished with your work on that day, go to your room. At exactly five minutes past eight o'clock you will step out of your room, ready to discharge your last great work for me.

Just outside your door you keep a foil-lined peach basket which you use for waste paper. Lift the basket. Beneath it you will find a flat package wrapped in white paper. Unwrap it quietly. Drop the paper and string into the basket. Take what is in the package with you.

By this time it will be dark. You will have left the light on in your room and the blind drawn. This is important.

You will then go down the stairs and slip out the side door of the garage. Do not concern yourself about the police; they are not watching you. But be careful not to be seen or heard by anyone.

When you are satisfied that no one is in sight or hearing, go into the rear garden. Stay in the shadows while you step onto the terrace. Move without a sound to the French doors leading from Mr. Robert's study. You will then see Mr. Percival seated at Mr. Robert's desk with his back to you, still at work.

Use what is in the package. You will know exactly how when you see it.

And that, My Dear Walt, will be the end of it. All you need do subsequently is let come what may. Things will happen quickly, but do not be afraid. You will remain unharmed, as befits the lord of all you survey. I, I say this to you.

Dispose of this letter as you have disposed of the others.

I do not say good-bye, as you will soon understand. I remain, My Dear Walt, as ever, and always,

Y

He prepared the white card and folded the letter, and inserted them in an unaddressed envelope and departed from his past procedures in other ways as well.

Among these unprecedented actions:

He strolled over to the street directly west of York Square and, using the apartment-house alley behind Robert York's corner, swiftly climbed the fence between the rear of the apartment building and the York garage.

He slid along the garage wall to the side door, entered the garage, shut the door silently, stood still for a moment listening, then in the darkness crept to the rear of the garage and up the narrow stairway to the landing before Walt's room.

He squatted here, and felt about to the left of Walt's door, and located Walt's peach-basket waste container.

He raised the basket with infinite patience and slipped a flat small package wrapped in white paper under it.

He lowered the basket until it stood squarely on the package, concealing it.

He pushed the unaddressed envelope containing the new card and Walt's latest instructions through the crack between Walt's door and the floor.

He then rose and made a groping, noiseless retreat—down the stairs and out of the garage and along the garage wall and over the fence and through the apartment-house alley, to the street west of York Square.

He slept soundly indeed that night.

27. *Open File*

Ellery had himself let out of the cruiser a block from York Square and—by consuming gobbets of will power—he walked, did not run, to Robert York's house; rang, did not batter; and, when the door was answered, spoke, did not shout. (The Inspector, meanwhile, like a stage manager on the afternoon of Opening Night, slipped anxiously behind the scenes to immerse himself in detail.)

"Good morning, Ann, is Percival York here? Is he all right?" Ellery asked; and only when she frowned did he realize he had said it as if it were a single compound word in German. She rose to the occasion, however, for behind that exquisitely rippled brow was a quick mind; she nodded. "On time and working hard." Quietly she added, "Isn't it wonderful?"

Ellery entered and she took his hat. He could see, down the hallway, the patient bulk of the plainclothesman who waited by the stairs, and through the study doorway Tom Archer leaning over Percival York, who was seated at the desk.

Ellery nodded toward the double doors of the dining room, and Ann caught his meaning instantly. "There's no one there but Bub," she said, and both opened the door and closed it behind them. The shepherd bitch lurched to her feet and padded over to them. She was developing into a splendid animal. Ellery let the puppy sniff his hand and then sought the sleek head, working his fingers around to scratch behind her left ear. Bub issued him a membership card.

"What is it?" Ann asked him; and her trusting face sharply reminded him of another time he had requested an interview with her, and how it had hurt.

"Percival's card is in the mail, Ann. The fourth card."

She went quite pale. "How could you possibly know that?"

"The post office, gentlemanly to the core, refused to let us intercept and examine his mail, but they did agree to watch for just this envelope addressed just this way, and to notify us before delivery. What time does the mailman get here?"

"About ten. Oh, dear. This means someone is still trying . . . What are you going to do?"

"Give him his mail."

She put her hands together. "How awful."

"How awful what?" Ellery demanded. "Letting him get the card when we might spare him the shock? Or do you mean the shock itself is awful? Or this whole devilish business?"

"I was thinking of Percival," Ann said earnestly. "He's come so far. It's been fascinating to watch—how he pushed himself into this, into a work discipline, a hard schedule, regular meals and sleep. And suddenly you could see him light up as if two wires had touched to complete a circuit. Stamps stopped being what he used to call 'nothing.' Now he holds a stamp with his tongs and it isn't colored paper to him any more. It's a messenger of ideas and feelings between people as well as history and geography and politics and so many other things. You know, for a while Perce was *angry*? In a how-long-has-this-been-going-on way? Ellery, I don't want him hurt. It's too soon. He's too—too *new*."

"He won't get hurt," Ellery assured her, "although he's got to get shocked, and scared. There's somebody in the offing who's expecting exactly that, and that somebody mustn't be disappointed."

"What are you intending to do?"

He smiled at her, but not with his eyes. "Restricted information, Ann," and quickly, "Here he comes—and goes. That fellow takes the 'swift completion of his appointed rounds' business seriously, doesn't he?"

Through the dining-room window, diagonally across the little park, they saw the mailman. He was a young one, who leaped up Percival York's front steps, barely paused and was off again. Something in Ellery was whimsically nettled by the speed and casualness. There should have been—at the least—a sting of menacing music. And here, oblivious in his cousin's house, Percival York, instead of releasing a booming laugh (as he did), chased by Archer's comradely cackle (as now happened), should have begun to shrivel under the shadow of a great and featureless foreboding. Mighty poor mood-writing, Ellery told it in his heart.

Ann asked tremulously, "Are you going to let Perce just . . . find it there when he gets home?" He knew she was thinking of how alone he would be at the moment of truth, with no one to turn to.

"Certainly not," Ellery said. "You watch."

And so Ann Drew watched—watched the closed door of the castle oblique to their vantage post, its blind lamps, the grin of its slit-lipped mail slot . . . watched as the door swung inward and the sturdy little figure of Mrs. Schriver appeared, bearing something in two dimensions, a white rectangle.

"She's under orders," said Ellery to the stricken girl. "Complete the delivery," and he left the dining room so abruptly that Beelzebub started and woofed.

Ellery strode to the study, knuckled the door frame to announce himself to Percival York and Tom Archer, and stepped inside.

Because it was uncluttered and otherwise unused, Inspector Queen had set up his field headquarters, as it were, in the little bedroom-workroom of the late Emily York's house directly north of the battle site.

The Inspector and three of his lieutenants were studying a detailed plan of York Square, its four castles and environs, when Sergeant Velie thundered in.

"Jonesy just called, Inspector. He's nosed out a flop joint where some character's been coming in late at night and rattling away on a typewriter in the room he rented."

Quiet settled. The tip of the Inspector's nose had changed color. He stared at the good sergeant as if he had never seen that grizzled enormity before.

"Velie. Tell him to seal that room—"

"Jonesy did that first thing."

"—keep the manager under wraps till I get there—"

"He's got the manager practically hog-tied."

"—get his hooks on the typewriter—"

"That," Sergeant Velie rumbled uneasily, "Jonesy can't do, Inspector. It's gone. The guy checked out."

The old man cursed and jumped up. "What name was he registered under?"

"W-y-e, Jonesy said. Wye."

"Tell Jones to sit on this till I get there!" Velie, for all his bulk, took off like a sparrow. "Piggott, buzz the Robert York house and tell my son to wait outside—now. Then go relieve Hesse—you'll find him in the bushes beside the terrace. Zillie, I'm leaving you in charge of Percival York's skin, and right now it's a hell of a lot more valuable than yours, I don't care what the NAACP says!" Detective Zilgitt grinned. "Now hop."

Sergeant Velie had the cruiser waiting, and he burned rubber down the Square to Robert York's. Ellery made it in one bound, and they headed west.

"What's going on?"

"Somebody leaked," said Inspector Queen through his teeth. "Jones found some fleabag hotel where a man's been staying who used a typewriter at night and calls himself Mr. W-y-e."

Ellery blinked. "Anyone we know?"

"We'll soon find out."

Ellery shifted on his lean rump. "Leaked? How do you mean?"

"He's gone," spat the Inspector. "*And* his typewriter."

"Not necessarily a leak, Dad."

"He's lit out, hasn't he? How else would you figure?"

"Period," said Ellery. "Project accomplished. He's through, that's all."

The Inspector chewed on a thumbnail. "Sure. Of course. This case is getting me . . . Velie!" he howled. "Don't *park* here. Get going!"

"Now he's going to take it out on me," Sergeant Velie said in an aggrieved tone. "What am I supposed to do, Inspector, fly this thing?" They were caught in an intersection jam-up.

"What's bothering me," murmured Ellery, "is—Walt should have received the usual letter of instruction from Y. It ought to be on the clipboard in Walt's ceiling right now. When was it last checked, Dad?"

"About an hour ago, and it wasn't there. Maybe this time the robot destroyed it. What bothers *me*," muttered the Inspector, massaging his rigid neck, "is the post office promised to tip us to any letter addressed to Walt, too, and they didn't. *Why?*"

"Maybe because it didn't go through the mail."

"Then it would have to have been delivered by hand! And the men all swear it wasn't."

"Not this morning. But how about last night?"

"Last *night?*" the old man said blankly.

"Yes. The security force moves as Percival moves. Last night Perce went back to his house, as usual, and the men went back with him. Leaving," Ellery said savagely, "leaving Robert's premises unguarded. Meaning that Y himself, in person, could have slipped up to Walt's, dropped his letter of instructions *in re* Operation Percival, and slipped away. Mr. W-y-e plays a mighty cool game. I'm beginning to feel like an idiot." Then he shouted, "Velie! Can't you get us out of this mess?"

"You, too?" mourned the sergeant; and he once more activated his siren. The traffic tangle slowly unsnarled.

The Inspector began a bitter mumble, "That's what comes—"

"I know," yelled Ellery. "That's what comes of my insistence on taking the tails off Walt! All right, it's my fault! Does that satisfy you?"

His father, startled, subsided. Ellery, ashamed immediately, also subsided. They sat, each man an island, side by side, in silence. Just as Sergeant Velie got in the clear Ellery said, "I'm sorry, Dad," and the Inspector said, "For what, for what?" and they both felt better. But not much.

With surface irrelevance, as the sergeant rocketed them toward their objective, Ellery found himself thinking of Percival York, and how he had taken the arrival of his white card with the second H on it. First Percival had shut his eyes. Then he had opened them. Then he had begun to perspire. Then he had turned yellowish and had seemed about to faint. But when Ellery had reached quickly for the carafe and a glass, Percival had shaken his head and said, "It's all right, Mr. Queen. In a way I'm glad. The waiting, the not knowing, is a lot worse. I'll be fine. Let the devil come. I'm ready." Percival York had rejoined the human race.

Which I'd better do, too, Ellery thought grimly; and he leaned forward, approximately himself again, as the sergeant shot the cruiser up to the curb before the Hotel Altitude.

The word "Hotel" in its title may have had technical justification, but otherwise it was as relative to the conjuration of whispering elevators, cut flowers in spanking rooms all foam and chrome, and noiseless waiters as the one-hoss shay to Cape Canaveral.

The Altitude was an old-law, five-story rattletrap of once-red brick, with flaking fire escapes on its shade-lidded, embarrassed façade, and the mean smell of poverty. Everything about it, outside and in, spoke of dirt and secrets.

The lobby was tiny and so, except for his ears, was the ancient desk clerk. He was bald and unshaven and all but toothless; and he was frightened almost to death by the towering young plainclothesman, Jones.

"This is the manager, Inspector," said Jones smartly. "Doubles as desk clerk."

"You've done a good day's work, Jones," growled Inspector Queen; and, "You," he rapped to the little bald old man, "what's your name?"

The flaccid chin wobbled. Finally, "Gill."

"All right, Gill, let's see your book."

"Book."

"Registry!"

"Oh. Use cards, I do."

"I don't care if you use toilet paper! Let me see the record for this Mr. Wye."

The ancient's hand shook its way through a five-and-dime store tin-box file, located a card.

"No, hold it by the edges! That's right. Now drop it on this." The Inspector had spread his handkerchief on the cigarette-stippled desk.

He stooped over it tautly, Ellery taut by his side. Name: Wye comma dash. Address: New York City. Mr. Wye-comma-dash had checked in seven weeks before, checked out the preceding night. The handwriting on the registration card was as uncertain as a kindergarten exercise.

"Funny handwriting," muttered Ellery; but: "Oh, I wrote this card up," quavered Mr. Gill.

They looked at each other.

"How come?" snapped the Inspector.

"Had to. He made the reservation by phone, said he'd be checking in late, wanted everything ready for him, asked how much the room'd be by the month. Told him, and he said he'd mail it to me. When the money come in, I put the key in Room Three-twelve and left the door unlocked, like he told me to do."

"Did he spell his name for you?" asked Ellery. "This W-y-e?"

"Well, sure. No . . . wait . . . Guess he didn't at that."

"This is your spelling, then?"

"Well, yes."

"Why isn't there a first name on the card?"

"Didn't give me none. I asked him over the phone, and he mumbled something I didn't get. So I put in a dash."

Inspector Queen retrieved his handkerchief in disgust, picked up the card. "When Wye paid the second month's rent in advance—was that by cash, too?"

"Yep." Mr. Gill was losing his fear; his answers came readily now, as if he had suddenly mastered a difficult situation.

"All right," said the Inspector, and leaned toward the ancient across the desk. "Now listen to me very carefully, Mr. Gill. And answer the same way! What did this man look like?"

Mr. Gill retreated into apprehension. "I dunno."

"You don't *know?*"

"He never come by the desk. Left the second month's money on the night table in his room, sticking out of the Gideon."

"Well, you must have seen him—"

"Thought I did once," Mr. Gill said hurriedly. "About three A.M., must have been. Course, it could have been somebody else. I was kind of dozing, like."

Again the Queens looked at each other. Plainclothesman Jones looked on in sympathy.

"All *right*," said the Inspector with iron patience. "You thought you saw him once. What did he look like?"

"I dunno, I tell you. Just saw him—I guess it was him—going out the door. Don't keep much light going, three o'clock and all."

"Well, was he tall, short, big, skinny, blond, brunet, limping? *Anything?*"

Mr. Gill looked helpless. "Dunno. Just a feller going out."

"His voice," said Ellery. "You said—"

"Dunno."

"Wait a second! You *said* you talked to him on the phone when he made the reservation. What kind of voice did he have?"

Mr. Gill seemed about to burst into senile tears. "I tell ye I dun*no!* Voice. Man's voice. Just a man's voice."

"Deep? Medium? High?"

"I dunno," Mr. Gill said, vocally wringing his hands. "I don't hear so good over the phone no more."

Ellery stepped back. "I give up," he said.

"Well, not me!" snarled his father. "Look, Gill! Did this Mr. Wye have any luggage? Do you know *that?*"

"Oh, yes, sir. Little black case, typewriter like. Kept it under the bed. Wasn't here much, just nights every now and then. Some sort of a salesman is my guess," the manager added in an eager-to-please tone. But then he spoiled it. "Though Tillie says he never used the bed."

"Tillie's the maid, I take it?" the Inspector grunted. At the ancient's nod he yapped, "Well, tell her to say out of Three-twelve until further notice!"

Officer Jones inserted a delicate cough. "The maid's been and gone, sir. Sorry about that, Inspector. It was before I got here."

"Tillie cleans real good," said Mr. Gill anxiously.

"Bro-ther," said Inspector Queen. "Okay, Gill—"

"Hold it," said Ellery, returning suddenly from retirement. "If you've had no contact with him, Mr. Gill, how do you know he's checked out? He's paid up through next week, isn't he? Or did he turn in his key?"

"I can answer that, Mr. Queen," said the young plainclothesman. "Seems he dropped it on the desk here last night while the old man was snoozing. That's how Gill knew he checked out—he'd always retained possession of the key before that, or stashed it somewhere outside the room. That, and the fact that the typewriter's gone. He's always kept it here before this. I talked to the maid on the phone."

"Where's the key now?" demanded the Inspector.

"I've snagged it, Inspector, for the print boys."

"Okay, let's go on up."

Sergeant Velie was waiting for them outside a door with 312 nailed to it in rusting tin digits.

"You find anything in here," announced the sergeant, "and I'll eat it."

"Alert the print men, Velie."

"They're already on their way, Inspector. I called in."

The sergeant opened the door and they trooped into Y's room. A chipped enamel bedstead with a hilly mattress; a carpet thin and scabrous as a Biblical leper; a sagging bureau; a chair; a night table and a drunkenly leaning lampstand; a sour-smelling cubby of a bathroom; and that was all.

Nothing.

They waited for the technical men, and watched while the men worked.

Nothing.

"Tillie cleans real good, all right," said the Inspector bitterly; and they left.

In the cruiser, on the way back to York Square, Inspector Queen actually said, "Nothing."

"Something," murmured Ellery. "He's cleared out. He *is* through, except for the minor detail."

"What minor detail?"

"Giving it to Percival. And that's the job of his good, strong, stupid right arm, Walt."

"And that's another thing," muttered the old man. "*When?*"

"Soon, I'd say. Probably tonight."

"I wish I had your crystal ball!"

"Dad," Ellery said, nibbling his thumb, "if there's anything at all we can be sure of, it's that Y knows his victims inside and out. He's got to every one of them by knowing them in the most personal sense—where they'd be, what they'd do, when they'd do it. So Y must be pretty familiar with Percival. I don't think he'd have much confidence in Percival's suddenly getting religion. Y has to figure that Perce is a cracked chalice, likely to lapse into the old unpredictable sinner at any moment. Therefore Y can't afford to wait. He's got to grasp this opportunity, when he knows just where Percival will be and exactly what he'll be doing. Tonight's the night, all right."

"Yeah, you listen to the Maestro, Inspector," said Sergeant Velie. "Did he ever steer you wrong?"

"*Plenty* of times," mumbled the old man; and he sank into the lightless deeps of his misery.

28. Capture

Ann Drew invited them both to dinner. Inspector Queen smiled feebly and excused himself, pleading catch-up work at his office. But Ellery accepted; and, the young couple having persuaded Percival York not to return to his house for a lonely meal, the four made a pleasant occasion of it, with Mrs. Schriver serving and the gargantuan Velie helping out between the kitchen and the dining room, having his own troubles with the housekeeper's sharp tongue and the German shepherd puppy, which growled big-doggishly every time the sergeant came near. The very size of Velie and the proximity of Ellery, not to mention Archer, seemed to stimulate Percival; he exuded friendship and good will, as he had exuded fear at his first sight of the small white card in the shape of his castle plot.

He was pathetically anxious to learn all about stamps, his new-born interest; and Ellery and Archer found themselves taking turns in feeding his philatelic hunger: how to tell the difference between flatbed and rotary-printed postal paper; how it was that a stamp could be immersed in benzine for watermark examination and dry again in minutes with no damage to the ink, the paper or the adhesive—the simplest things. Percival kept asking greedy questions, unappeasable; until it occurred to Ellery that this was his way of keeping his mind off the dreadful situation developing about him.

It grew dark outside.

After dinner they went into the study. Here they chatted for a few minutes, while Percival York seated himself at his late cousin Robert's desk, his back to the terrace doors, and Tom Archer retreated to the library table piled high with albums. Mrs. Schriver finished the dishes and departed; Sergeant Velie disappeared; and, finally, Ann Drew said good night and went upstairs.

Ellery stepped into the hall, retrieved his hat, returned to the study and stood for another moment by the desk. For a long time afterward he was to remember his good-night conversation with Percival York.

"This is so nice," the last of the Yorks said. "I could take a lot of it, Mr. Queen. Sometimes . . ."

"Yes?" Ellery encouraged him, curious.

Percival laughed with embarrassment. "Sometimes I think I have the Sadim touch."

"What's *that*?"

"Midas spelled backwards. It means every bit of gold I touch turns to dlog."

"Gold spelled backwards?" Ellery afterward recalled saying with a smile.

"That's it, and you know what *that* means. I'd explain it, but I don't want to corrupt young Archer there."

But young Archer looked up and defined it precisely; whereupon Ellery shook hands all around, laughing, and left.

On the dot, Walt paused in the black shadow of the garage to peer behind, to the side, and then straight ahead to the illuminated terrace. The only light came streaming through the French doors of the study.

Above him, prone and motionless on the garage roof, Detective Zilgitt touched the *Press to Talk* button on the tiny Citizen's Band transceiver he carried and tapped gently and rapidly on the speaker grille with his thumbnail.

Inside Robert York's house, in the dark hallway, the rasping crackle sounded in the soft rubber earphone in Sergeant Velie's ear. He pulled the pen-sized flashlight out of his breast pocket and flashed it; Ellery Queen, standing in the study, saw it. The same faint crackle sounded in the ears of two detectives concealed at one side of the terrace, a third at the other, in some bushes. None of the three moved.

Clinging to the shadows, Walt oozed from the corner of the garage to a point directly across the rear lawn from the terrace. The black oval of Percival York's sports jacket, its frazzled pale topping of head and hair, were perfectly visible to him.

Walt felt for the flat object in his pocket.

Overhead, a pink thumbnail tapped again. Cars rolled noiselessly across the mouths of the alleys and stopped. A darker shadow, man-shaped, appeared at the garage corner where Walt had first paused. It made no sound at all.

Suddenly Walt melted and hardened, like a flow of lava.

Ellery Queen, hat in hand, had approached the desk in the study and he was talking to Percival York.

Walt waited. Far off, a car rushed by, blatting. Nearer, a boyish voice yelled an obscenity. There was a tinkle somewhere, as if a rock had gone through a window, and the thudding retreat of derisive feet. None of this moved Walt in the slightest. He waited.

Ellery laughed, waved, was gone.

Immediately Walt slid to his left and to the blackly looming bushes. His hand went again to the flat object in his pocket.

And just as he reached the protection of the bushes, the lights went off. Everything blacked out—the study, the terrace, the dim sheen on the lawn.

From the study Walt could hear Percival's hoarse shout: "The lights are out! The lights are out!" and Tom Archer's "Just a fuse, Perce. Hang on a minute. Don't go banging around in the dark—sit still."

Sit still.

Walt leaped across the lawn, its imprint perfectly clear in his brain. He vaulted surely the low margin of the terrace, sprang to the left-hand jamb of the French doors. He waited.

He was crouched there, the little flat cold gun in his hand, when the lights blazed back on like a nova.

Walt fired five shots. Three grouped themselves in the middle of Percival York's sports jacket. The fourth splintered the top right-hand desk drawer. The fifth plowed a long clean furrow along the top of the desk and knocked a stamp album off the table beyond. He managed to squeeze off the fourth shot and the fifth even though his legs were snatched from under him, even though he was struck from above and both sides and grabbed and held and buried under the mass of men diving in over the terrace edges and from the study itself.

Ellery, lunging for breath, stood over the squirming mound.

The detectives slowly disentangled themselves, panting; but even as they separated, at least one hand of each man was tightly pinned to some part of John Henry Walt—flat on his back on the brick-red tiles, smiling like a seraph.

Looking down at that unafraid, relaxed, coldly smiling countenance, Ellery felt his skin crawl.

"For the love of heaven," he said in an unsteady voice, "take it—him—away."

Ellery sat on his shoulder blades and through bloodied eyes stared at the Eleventh Edition. He thought: Suppose they'd climbed Everest and, pulling themselves up on the last crag, had found themselves standing at the bottom? Suppose a man ran what he knew was a three-minute mile and then found they'd forgotten to wind the watches?

He thought: Come on, now, don't wallow in all the things that don't suit you. When feeling low, take an inventory of the good. What have we got that's good?

Our murderer, of course, John Henry Walt in the clink, cheerfully signing a full statement of four premeditated capital crimes. John Henry Walt doesn't defend himself; he denies nothing; he admits everything.

Everything, that is, but the important things.

The why of it all he will not answer.

He still does not know that we have Y's letters. Ask him: "Did you have help?" "Is there anyone else involved?"—and he smiles.

Ellery thought: Oh, that queer little dead-faced man, he has the prettiest smile. Want to see that smile at its prettiest? Ask him what the final H on Perce York's card means. Walt smiles and smiles.

And Ellery thought: The man is crazy, of course. Crazy in the worst way, with a craziness consistent as the law of gravity. With a craziness so consistent as to make him a more reliable tool for Y's mysterious purposes than a sane triggerman would have made.

Ellery brought his fist down on the arm of his chair, jarringly. It was wrong. It was *wrong*. It was like arresting the gun for murder.

The player on the other side . . .

He was brought back by the grate of a key and the thump of a door.

"Dad?"

"Hi," said the old man. He came into Ellery's workroom and dropped his hat on the floor and sank wearily onto the sofa.

"Still working on Walt?"

The Inspector nodded. "I've got what I thought we wanted. And all it's going to get me is that nothing's going to get *him*. He'll be committed. He'll spend the rest of his life on free grub and rent, with movies on Saturdays and no income tax. You know what? I'll bet that's what he keeps smiling about."

"You got nothing out of him."

"Nothing but more smiles." And the Inspector gave such a gruesome imitation of Walt that Ellery winced and said, "*Please.*"

They were silent for a while.

"Anything on the gun?" asked Ellery finally.

"No."

"Did you tell him about the other letters?"

"No, I'm still operating from the one we found on him."

"Prints—?"

"Just Walt's."

They were silent for another while.

Then Ellery muttered, "Did you ask the lab if this latest letter from Y had Walt's thumbprints all over the top corners?"

"No," said the old man, "I looked for myself. They're there, all right."

"Many?" Ellery asked eagerly. "I mean—more than on the other letters, or fewer, or the same?"

"I'd say about the same."

Ellery made a puzzled sound far back in his throat. He reached over and picked up a piece of *Ellery Queen's Mystery Magazine* stationery and held it, dangling, with his thumbs in the upper corners, before his eyes. "Why in the name of Sam Lloyd would Walt—even Walt!—read a letter in this position? I wonder . . . Dad, has he been doing any reading in his cell?"

"Not that way," sighed his father. "Stop badgering me, son. I've had a rough day."

"Wait, Dad. Has anyone said anything to him about Percival?"

"No. He never even asked. By the way, how is our hero today? I haven't had time to call."

"According to Archer, still in mild shock." Ellery found, rather to his chagrin, that he was feeling annoyed with Percival York. Everything had been carefully outlined to him in advance; how the entire evening was a vast trap; how the rear lawn and environs were to be flooded with infra-red light, invisible to Walt, in which a police sharpshooter with a snooperscope on the garage roof beside Detective Zilgitt would have Walt on the crosshairs every second; how the script Ellery and the Inspector had worked out called for a bit of acting on the part of everyone, with the blackout as its climax to provide darkness in which to yank Percival from behind the desk and make a swift substitution in the chair of a bolster wrapped in Percival's jacket, surmounted by a department-store dummy's head. "I guess Perce isn't the new man he thinks he is. Shock! He couldn't have been safer if he'd been locked up for the night in Fort Knox."

"Where's your Christian charity?" jeered the Inspector. "I thought you were pro-Percival now. Look, El, I'm dog-tired and I want a shower—"

"Dad."

"What now?" The Inspector sank back.

"I think we ought to reconsider Percival," said Ellery slowly.

"*Again?*"

"Well, he is the only one who gains from these murders."

"And he planned this last attack—on himself? Hmm?"

"If Percival is Y, why not? If you had planned to get rid of three co-heirs, wouldn't a fourth attack—on yourself—make a good smoke screen?"

"This thought," said the old man, "has crossed my feeble mind, too." He snorted. "Kind of chancy, though, wouldn't it be? If Percival is Y, Walt doesn't know it. And that's one customer, once you give him an order, who can't tell let's-pretend from the real thing."

"It wasn't chancy at all. Percival could count on our not risking his life."

"All the same, those were real bullets, not spitballs."

"And the stakes were real high, if you'll pardon the syntax."

The Inspector rubbed his gray brush of mustache fretfully. "I don't know, son . . . If Perce is behind all this, he ought to apply for an Equity card. Because he sure put on a performance every time Walt got near him. And he knew he was safe then, too."

But Ellery shook his head. "The more you look at it, the more attractive it gets. You can't blink the fact that the deaths of Robert, Emily and Myra York leave Perce York all eleven of the millions.

There just isn't anyone else who benefits by the three murders. Percival certainly knew the habits, characters and routines of his three cousins. He's had an insider's opportunity to watch and evaluate Walt. And to hire that hotel room. And type and mail those letters."

"All of a sudden," remarked his father, "it sounds as if you've got something against Percival."

"No, but . . . Well, I think I've rather resented the concept of Walt as the player on the other side. I'm actually relieved to know now that he can't be. A pigeon!"

"Of courrrrse," said the Inspector wickedly. "Whereas my famous son rates nothing less than an eagle."

"Oh, cut it out, Dad. Anyway, this isn't an eagle-type case. Not if it's Perce York we're hunting. As the criminal—if this were a detective story—he'd be about as satisfying as the butler."

"It's been my experience," sighed the father, "that in the real McCoy you take 'em as and where you find 'em."

"Exactly! So don't give me that eagle stuff." Ellery began to inspect a pipe, sniffing its bole, blowing through the mouthpiece; it had been so long since Ellery had smoked a pipe that the Inspector stared. "The notion's been picking away at me ever since dinner the other night at Robert's. Think of Perce as Mr. Y, Dad. Is he smart enough? Is he weird enough?"

"You've got a point there," said the Inspector, and closed his eyes.

"Look at the offbeat touch—the cards bearing letters of the alphabet. JHW, the patsy's initials. The signed crime. That's always the mark of a certain kind of nut, the kind who likes to pull the strings from out of sight, the god of the machine. But what good are his power and his cleverness if he personally can't take a public bow for them? So—the signature. Sometimes it's a message in lipstick. Sometimes it's a zigzag symbol, like the Mark of Zorro. Sometimes, by God, it's on a global scale and he strews swastikas around. Our boy goes for initials."

"My son the psychiatrist," murmured his father, keeping his eyes closed.

"My point is," Ellery continued doggedly, "that, having tacked Walt's initials onto the evidence—and all the time resenting having to give the credit to the wrong man—our mastermind can't resist adding *his* exalted hallmark to the murders he's manipulated Walt into committing for him."

The old man's eyes flew open at that. "His *hallmark?*"

"Certainly. And it's a very clever hallmark, because it could have two meanings . . . The other day I mourned the fact that the writer of the letters didn't sign his letters 'X.' I forgot that 'Y' is a symbol of unknown quantity, too. So . . . Y, the unknown quantity; and that's to tell us we don't know who he is. But there's a Y in this case who's also a *known* quantity; and when he types that Y at the end of his letters, that's to tell us that we *do* know who he is."

"York," said the Inspector, sitting up straight. "The *initial* Y!"

"And Q and E and D," said Ellery; but he said it glumly, as if he were still not satisfied.

"I'll be damned," said the Inspector. But then he frowned. "Wait a minute, Ellery, you left something out. There were four letters, the first three giving us J, H and W. But the fourth gave us another H—on Perce's letter. Where does that come in?"

"There," confessed Ellery, "you've got me. That extra H is the pain that's been attacking my neck ever since the Percival letter came. I can't seem to fit it in anywhere. J, H, W—and then another H." He shook his head. "Anyway, how does my argument sound to you?—Percival York as Mr. Y?"

"The way I feel right now," said Inspector Richard Queen of police headquarters, "I'd even take *that* mess of non-evidence to the D.A. if I got one more little push."

It would make nice dramatic unity here to report that the telephone rang, bringing Inspector Queen the information that would afford him the one more little push he craved.

Actually, nothing of the sort happened. And when it did happen, there was no fanciness in it about symbols and initials and such.

For the following morning the Inspector received a note, marked *Urgent*, giving him a telephone number to call; and, on calling it, the old workhorse of Centre Street was told by a certain blonde that she was now prepared to sign a statement implicating Percival York in the York Square murders. He went to see her clippety-clop; and very shortly afterward he galloped to York Square and formally arrested Percival York.

It was mid-morning, and Percival was working away at Robert York's—now Percival York's—stamps in concert with Archer and Ann Drew.

When the Inspector intoned the arresting formula, Percival blinked slowly and said to Ann and Archer, "I told Mr. Queen I had the Sadim touch. I *told* him," and, with tears in his eyes, he patted Beelzebub good-bye and went docilely.

29. Discovered Check

When Ellery dropped in at the Robert York house two days later he found Tom Archer sullen, Ann Drew anxious, and both resentful.

"Because if Perce did what they say he did," Archer argued hotly, "he *used* us. As cold-bloodedly and cunningly as he used Walt. It's more than just being shoved around by a greedy megalomaniac. It's that he played on Ann's soft heart. My—my goodfellowism. Our sympathy, forgiveness, generosity. Damn it, Ellery, that's worse than highway robbery!"

Ellery said wryly, "If it pains you to discover that a Nice Man can be a crumbum, Tom, it's life you've got to object to, not Percy in particular."

Ann's anxiety and resentment had a different base. "Ellery," she demanded, "what really happened to make your father decide to arrest him?"

"It's been pretty well covered in the newspapers."

"No, it hasn't," said Ann angrily. "Walt was caught in the act of shooting what he thought was Percival York. Walt's some kind of psycho, and he's confessed to all the crimes. Perce in turn was arrested for having incited Walt to the commission of the murders. Pages and pages of this. But it's all they really say. Why do they leave out so much?"

"In tackling a criminal case," murmured Ellery, his heart not really in it, "you look for motive and opportunity. For the murders themselves Walt had opportunity; his motive was the motive of whoever directed him. Percival's motive is as old as private property; and he had the opportunity to do all the things the writer of the letters had to do. What more do you want?"

"A lot more," retorted Ann. "For one thing, Perce hasn't confessed."

"The law doesn't require a confession for an indictment," said Ellery evasively. "The case against him—"

"If the case against him is good enough," the girl said with equivalent irrelevance, "it doesn't matter how good the *man* is—is that it?"

"The question is," growled Tom Archer, "how good *is* he?"

"Oh, you be quiet!" said Ann Drew, stamping her tiny foot.

"Ann," said Ellery. "In this state a person charged with first-degree murder is given an automatic not-guilty plea. Perce will have his day in court."

"Big deal!" She shook her head, shook it again, Ellery watching the untouchable interplay of highlights in her hair with yearning admiration. "I suppose what really bothers me," Ann said, "is that Perce seemed to be getting so much *better*—"

"For whose benefit?" snapped Tom. "And at whose expense? Look, honey, exercise your female prerogative of deciding guilt or innocence by intuition, but until the courts operate likewise *I* string along with the juridical system."

"You would," said Ann, as if she had suddenly discovered a grave flaw in his character; at which Tom Archer uttered inchoate protest and registered an ocular appeal toward the ceiling. "Ellery, when is Perce to be indicted?"

"The Grand Jury gets the case day after tomorrow. Until then, at least, he's safe enough."

Ann examined him with great thoroughness. "Well, anyway, *you* seem to be sure."

"In my profession and in this life I," said Ellery humbly, "am sure of nothing, ma'am."

Then followed an awkward silence, during which the three looked at one another, and away. Ann said brightly, "Well," and found herself out of words. Tom Archer turned to Robert York's bookshelves, as if inspiration would come to him emblazoned on the spine of some fortuitous volume. Ellery understood perfectly.

The unspoken decision was to drop the subject of Percival York and talk about something else. The trouble was—they made the discovery in simultaneous independence—there was nothing else for them to talk about; they knew nothing of one another aside from York Square and its recent events.

It was Bub, the German shepherd puppy, who saved the day.

She said, "Woof!"

Ellery could have kissed her muzzle. "Got to do something about those ears," he said, frowning critically. The top third of her ears drooped.

"I've been feeding her lots of stiffener," said Archer, in gratitude.

"Bub-baby!" Ann cried, throwing her arms about the puppy's neck. "They're nasty. You're *perfect.*"

"She is not," said Ellery. "Ears have to stand at attention."

"We could send her to the laundry," said Tom. "Medium starch, and so on."

"Monster," said Ann. "Don't think he wouldn't, Ellery. According to him, dogs aren't human."

"They're better than human," said Tom. "Ever know a human puppy to turn a somersault at Bub's age? Or even a shepherd child? One of my talents is to achieve the impossible. Want to see?"

"A man who'd steal the credit from a puppy is a—is a dirty dog."

"Shush, woman, I'm performing. Okay, Bub." Young Archer got down on one knee and held out his hands. The dog came, wagging her hind end furiously. He grasped her overgrown front paws, elevated them, set himself . . . "*Hup!*" he yelped; and rising quickly, he flipped the paws up and back.

The somersault was creditable, although Bub staggered when she landed. She promptly bounded back, to leap on Archer and swab his face with her built-in squeegee.

"Very good," said Tom Archer. "Now I'll do it with both her paws on my forearm. You see, a puppy-dog of this weight . . . What the devil?"

Archer broke off, staring.

"Ellery!" Ann Drew cried. "What's wrong?"

For Ellery stood stiff and still, eyes screwed shut. When she called his name he silenced her with a chopping gesture. The two exchanged apprehensive glances. It was either a stroke or a voice from beyond; and since Inspector Queen's pride and sometimes joy refused to topple, it was evidently the latter.

Suddenly the Queenian eyes opened wide and out of the mouth came a strange, frightful sound—the wordless screek of a man who, having cut himself, sees the gleaming of his own bone.

And then he ran.

Archer and Ann, clutching each other, watched him through the front window. Hatless, the great man dashed out into York Square, glanced frantically north, south, east and west, leaped at sight of a police car, beckoned with furious urgency, spoke imperiously to the driver, then snatched the door open and flung himself into the rear seat.

And the cruiser scorched off, smoking.

30. Interpose

The radio room called Inspector Queen and told him that his son was hellbent for the jail, and would the Inspector meet said son there immediately. The Inspector, who was up to his ears, said no and hung up. The radio room called back. Mr. Queen had asked that this message be relayed verbatim: *I need you.* The Inspector left on the double.

"I've got to see York. *Right now,*" was Ellery's greeting. He had been waiting on the curb when the Inspector's car pulled up; and he had opened the door, lunged halfway in to say these words, then taken his father by the wrist and yanked. Whatever seethed and crackled within the Inspector remained unvented at sight of his son's oyster-toned face.

As he hustled the old man across the pavement and up the steps, Ellery banged his head with the heel of his free hand and babbled hoarsely, "Why don't I see what I'm looking at when I'm looking at it?"

"What?" panted his father; but by then they were inside, and he had to forgo questions in favor of the prescribed amenities.

They hurried down echoing stone steps and along a stark corridor to a short desk and a tall gate. The guard unlocked the gate with a crash, and locked it with a crash. Ellery began to run, the old man stiff-legging it after him.

"What the devil am I running about? Couldn't this wait for tomorrow? Or tonight?"

"No, Dad—"

"You," gasped the Inspector grimly, "had damn well better be right!"

He was right, but too late.

Another gate, another guard, this one accompanying them.

A cell bank.

Percival's cell.

And Percival hanging by his neck from the high window bars.

31. Isolated Pawn

Mr. Ellery Queen, that great man, stood aside to let his father and the guard rush in and cut Percival York down. The great man stood aside, not because he was great, but because he was not. He was simply unable to help, or even to think very much. And after a moment he was unable even to stay there.

He shuffled over to the guard at the cross-corridor. "Where's Walt's cell?"

"Walt who?" said the guard.

"Walt nobody." That's very good, Ellery thought: Walt Nobody. "J. H. Walt. John Henry Walt."

"Oh, the kook." The guard gave directions. Ellery listened. He said thank you. He slogged away.

Mr. Ellery Queen passed a cell immuring a man snoring; a cell containing a man pacing it off; an empty cell; an empty cell;

a turn in the corridor and first-cell-to-the-right. This was indeed occupied by J. H. Walt, Human Murder Weapon.

Mr. Ellery Queen came up close, bilge sloshing, on water-logged legs, with a salty swell trying to share his eye sockets. He clung to the bars—and which is the monkey? he thought—and he looked at J. H. Walt.

J. H. Walt sat like a good little citizen, neatly, cleanly, knees and feet together, reading his Bible. At the corners of his mouth dwelt the shadows of a smile, a serene smile, a smile of peace. ". . . and all's right with the world," the smile said. He did not look up. He was absorbed in his Book.

The bars insisted on trying to slide upward through Ellery's hands. He gripped them, which had the extraordinary effect of squeezing two tears out of his eyes. They scalded; he was glad that they hurt, glad that they turned the prim Bible reader into a blur; glad masochistically, childishly. Pain in any amount would at this moment, he felt, be just. He wished he could be sure that a fit punishment would seal off his bottomless self-scorn; oh, if it would, he would seek out the stern wielder of the nine-tailed cat, whoever he might be, confess his criminal stupidity and be thankfully flogged for it. Fantasy, of course: there would be no escape, ever, from the fury and contempt in which Ellery Queen held the great man.

A hand grasped his shoulder. No matter what policeman this might be, Ellery thought, he can never make a case against me; and this, really, was the core of his despair.

The hand squeezed his shoulder, and the Inspector's voice said, "It's all right, son. We got here in time after all. He did a sloppy job. He's going to be all right."

Ellery felt his hands slip from the bars and his body turn toward the source of the voice. He did not wipe his face or feel embarrassment; in a warm, all-but-forgotten sense, this was his father.

"Hey . . . hey . . ." A soft, drawn-out breath; Ellery recalled its use over barked knees and broken treasures. "Hey, now, son."

Ellery went with his father down the corridor. He could draw a clean breath now, remember his handkerchief, stand six feet tall once more. And it was rue and wry he felt, blowing his nose and trying to grin.

"Want to tell me what happened to you, son?" Inspector Queen asked gently.

"You bet," said Ellery. "I've solved it."

"Solved what?"

"The mystery of Y."

"The what?" cried the old man. "How do you mean, Ellery?"

"I know who it is."

32. Combination

_ _ _ _ _ _ _ _

In the car Ellery subsided into a corner. "Call in," Inspector Queen instructed the driver. "Tell 'em I can be reached at home. And if they reach me at home it had better be important."

After a moment they swung uptown, and Ellery opened his eyes. "Dad, you don't have to make a production of this. You're busy—"

"You've scraped something off the bottom of this case, right?" growled the old man. Ellery nodded. "Well, whose case is it? The quicker you get started, the sooner I'll know what you've got."

"You ought to hang out a shingle," Ellery said. The Inspector kept a knowledgeable silence. After a while Ellery said, "The best way to do this sort of thing is to test every brick as you build. Why don't I ever learn that lesson?" Still silence. Defensively Ellery said to the dome light above him, symbolically unlit, "Yes, sir, I think I go pretty much to the point."

"And *I* think," said his father, "that it would be lovely if you started talking English. Is it all right for me to ask a few questions?"

"Ask away."

"How in the name of Houdini did you know Percival York was going to commit suicide?"

"I didn't. I just saw it as a possibility when I realized that he's innocent. That he isn't Y."

"Whoa!" exploded the Inspector. "What are you giving me, Ellery? He *isn't?* I've never known you to blow so hot and cold about anything—"

"I'm sure," Ellery said; and from the way he said it his father knew that now, at last and forever, the pieces would fit.

"If York's not Y, who is?" demanded the old man.

"I'll be coming to that—"

"Okay, I'll play," said the Inspector with a sigh, and he sank back. "How about this: What made you rush to the jail like that?"

"I wanted to tell Perce York I was sure he was innocent, and not to hang, so to speak, but to hang on." Ellery touched his own neck absently, squinting into some distance. "Dad, I saw this fellow—before his arrest—straightening the kinks out of himself. Working hard. Keeping regular hours. I saw it, I recorded it, but I didn't compute it. Electronic clog, you might call it.

"Here was a man," Ellery frowned at the driver's neck, "taking a good look at himself for the first time in his life. So much so that he could even see past and around a bequest of eleven million dollars, which is a mighty hard trick. He'd faced the ugly fact of what he'd been, and he was doing something about it.

"Now I don't think anybody has liked Perce York since the day he sneered his first word. And at the head of that numerous company you can put Perce York himself. All he really wants is to be like other people, because up to now he's lived with the absolute belief that he's less than other people. The only thing in his whole life he's ever done reasonably well is to mount Robert's stamps in those albums; it was his first, his *first* positive achievement. Know what he said to me, Dad?" Ellery swallowed. "He said, 'I've got the Sadim touch. That's Midas turned backwards.' What he meant was that anything good he touched was bound to turn bad. In a different time he might have said, 'I'm accursed.'"

"Come to think of it," said the Inspector thoughtfully, "when we cut him down and he opened his eyes and found he was still in the land of the living, he looked me square in the kisser and croaked, 'I botched this one, too, Inspector, didn't I?'"

Ellery nodded. "That's it. Now. I think all along he felt he'd never live to get the money, or if he did he wouldn't get to use it. His arrest must have been the end of the world to him and, at the same time, just the sort of thing he expected would happen. In that state he was what a head-candler I know calls 'a psychological emergency,' the result of which is often the victim's destroying himself—either by literal suicide or schizoid withdrawal. The one thing Perce York needed at that crisis was to be told that somebody believed in him, that somebody knew he was innocent. That somebody gave a damn about what happened to him—"

"Ellery Queen, say."

"All right. Now you see why I was in such a rush, Dad. I held the only thing that could help him, and I was the only one who did."

"Well, how about sharing the wealth?" his father goaded him gently. "It's about time, wouldn't you say?"

"Don't jostle me, I'm getting there," scowled Ellery. "Very well. Mr. Y wasn't Percival. Then who?"

"Archer," said the old man suddenly. "Tom Archer. He's smart enough to have seen how to use Walt as his murder weapon. And God knows Archer's been smack in the middle of the premises from the beginning—"

Ellery shook his head. "Not Tom Archer."

"You leading me by the nose really far out?" asked the Inspector sarcastically. "Okay! Let's dress up little Ann in men's clothing and keep trying to believe she was Mr. Wye of the Hotel Altitude."

Ellery faintly smiled. "Let's do no such thing."

"How about Mrs. Schriver?" demanded the Inspector. "She far enough out for you?"

Ellery managed a chuckle at this. "It's not Mrs. Schriver."

"You can bet your sweet asafetida it's not! That would be almost as ridiculous as saying it's Miss Sullivan. Far out . . . Mallory. How about Mallory? He's pretty far out. Boston."

"Not far enough, Dad."

"Look, son, can we stop playing games? There's nobody left!"

"But there is," said Ellery; and he said it in such a peculiar way that the old man's nostrils began to itch. He was rubbing them vigorously when Ellery said, "Here we are."

The Inspector stopped rubbing and saw the familiar 87th Street brownstone façade. He dismissed the driver, and Ellery got out his key, and they trudged up the interior stairs like two very tired men coping with the heavy burden of their unspoken thoughts. When they were in the Queen apartment, Ellery automatically made for the living-room bar, his hands became independently active and he began again.

"What's torn me up so much," he said, "is realizing how plop under my nose it's been, practically from the start. It isn't as if I didn't *notice*. My alleged brain recorded it, all right—it just didn't compute."

The Inspector had long ago learned the lesson of inhuman patience at times like these. There was no point, he now saw, in any further prodding. In the climactic stages Ellery had to be given his head; in his own mysterious time he'd head for home.

"Don't be so hard on yourself, son."

"I couldn't be," said Ellery with profound disgust. He stood a while, then gradually focused on the two glasses he held. He came around the bar, handed his father the highball and retired to the couch with his cocktail.

"The evidence was evident all along the path," Ellery went on. "It was to be seen even in the first murder, Robert's, that this was the work of some species of madman. A madman with a systematized madness."

"But we didn't know then that he was intending to work his way all around the Square, son," Inspector Queen said intently.

"But we did know he'd sort of warned Robert with that kooky J card. Do sane killers—to make a fine distinction—warn their victims of their homicidal intentions?"

The Inspector waved his hand, keeping the wave genial by main force. "All right, that told us—you—that he was crazy."

"Don't give me any premature credit, Dad. I couldn't stand it." Ellery took a swallow. "We—I—should have left that itty-bitty door wide open. But no, I had to keep whittling my sights down to ordinary motivations. Instead of bearing in mind that anything—*anything*—could figure into this man's plans, I—oh, well, it's too late to pick *those* nits."

He emptied his glass and banged it down on the coffee table. "With an open mind I might have guessed the truth by the time we laid eyes on that second card. Because by then we had two letters of the message, J and H. But again . . . I suppose it's because I'm not conditioned to madness. A madman has his logic, but it's not a sane man's logic—and, although I know you sometimes have your doubts, I think I'm more on the sane side than the other way."

"I'll give you that much," said the Inspector. "Skoal."

"Skoal," said Ellery absently. "Where I really fumbled the ball, of course, was in Myra's murder. Even before it *was* a murder. Remember I spoke to Walt not ten minutes after he'd dropped the rat poison into Myra's water jug? He had just left Myra's house, and I stopped him and questioned him."

"So?"

"I'll get to it later," and the old man could have screamed. "Anyway, that was the afternoon I decided to take off and find Mallory."

"Take off is right. We had one dilly of a time finding you."

"I didn't know it would take that long. And my Mallory notion seemed so far-fetched, I thought you'd laugh me off the case. Wait till you see how far-fetched it really was."

"My son," sighed the Inspector, "I reckon I'm just about the best li'l ol' waiter ever."

Ellery ignored this. "I still have the nagging feeling that if I'd picked up my cues and clues, if I hadn't gone to Boston just then, maybe Myra . . . All right, I'll quit being iffy.

"That third case, Myra's. The one with the W. Adding W to J and H and giving us J.H.W.; obviously—what could be more obvious?—the initials of John Henry Walt. Bingo! this so-called mind closes down to any other possibility." Ellery scowled at his empty glass. "Charles Fort, who made a career out of jeering at conventional scientific thinking, wrote somewhere that it takes a special species of idiot—or was it fool?—always to concede that any answer is the *only* answer. All I could see was that JHW were initials, and that the initials stood for Walt's full name. Perfect example of recording and not computing. If I'd remembered that principle I might—I just might—have added insanity to the murder of these particular people, plus J and H and W, and summed up accurately. I had the opportunity to do the simple arithmetic again, when we found the typewritten letters signed with a Y—

those do-my-bidding, I-own-the-universe letters. I could have applied Fort's dictum *then*. And I'd have known. I'd even have been able to prophesy that the next card would have another H on it."

"Do tell," murmured the Inspector, his pulse at last beginning to accelerate. This must be it! "How does that figure?"

Ellery frowned at his father. "The letters JHWH have no meaning for you?"

"Not a glimmer."

"Coupled with someone who calls himself Y?"

"Y? 'York' satisfies me there. Or," added the Inspector wryly, "did."

"You insist on joining Fort's special-species-of-fool club along with me, don't you? No, it isn't York."

"Here we go again," muttered the old man. "Okay. Yoicks. Yehudi. Yuk-yuk. Will you stop diddling, son, and get to it?"

"JHWH," said Ellery, "makes up the Tetragrammaton."

"JHWH," said Inspector Queen, "makes up the Tetragrammaton. What in God's name is *that* supposed to mean?"

"You," and Ellery, to his father's consternation, burst into frenetic laughter, "you have said it!"

"What have I said?"

"God's name—that's what Yod Ho Waw Ho—JHWH—represents. The Name of Names. In Old Testament times it was forbidden to speak the true name of the Lord. JHWH—in its ancient Hebrew, Greek and other equivalents—was the Hebrew way of writing down what could not be uttered. They used the consonants, and substituted the vowels from the words Adonai or Elohim—both scriptural terms for 'God' or 'the Lord'—so that JHWH became *Jehovah*. Or *Yahweh*, the other of the two best-known versions. Yahweh, with a Y."

"JHWH, Jehovah, on the cards—Yahweh, the Y, on the letters . . . Jehovah, Yahweh . . ." Inspector Queen glanced suspiciously at his son. "What are you trying to hand me? That Walt actually thought he was getting mail from *God?*"

"Before sheer merriment overcomes you," said Ellery, "I advise you to reread Y's letters with that thought in mind. 'You know who I am.' 'Have faith in me and I shall guard you and keep you.' 'There is no thing I cannot do.' 'I am with you wherever you go.' 'For I possess all powers, and I am everywhere.' 'You may not speak my name.' And so on. That constant, soothing, reassuring, intimate, *omnipotent* refrain."

Over the old man's face came a look that was very like terror. He actually, in the flesh, shivered.

"Think of poor little lonely, boxed-in, blank-past Walt," said Ellery with the same wincing frown. "No one notices him. No one is concerned about him. No one cares enough about him to like him or even to dislike him as far as he can tell. Erased as he is, he still contains within himself the faint impression of the human matrix.

"And suddenly," said Ellery, "suddenly he's noticed, he's liked, he's admired—he's even asked for *favors!*—by none other than the Lord God Himself. Do you wonder that Walt did as the letters told him to do? Do you wonder that he's never been frightened, has never felt worried, by what might happen to him? That he's refused with the greatest of ease, happily, consistently, to be trapped or cajoled or browbeaten into saying that Name? How could mere mortals touch him? Walt's had it made. In the very biggest way."

"Four Bibles in his room," murmured the Inspector. "*Four.*"

"Yes, and they mean something rather different now, Dad, don't they? Now that we know what fits in. That time I bumped into him outside Myra's, for instance. I questioned him about Tom Archer's saying Walt had crept up on him and Ann. I asked Walt what Archer had said, and Walt said simply, 'He saw me and he said, "God."' It wasn't exclamatory the way Walt said it; it was quite matter-of-fact. God *is* a fact to Walt; they're on the most personal terms . . . And then those initials of his. Coincidence? Miracle? Whatever it was in reality, in Walt's book—or maybe I ought to capitalize it—it was just another manifestation of Him Who was the Author of the letters . . . Meaningless in themselves, these things. But in context, a giveaway. And there I was, day after day, in the thick of it, recording and not computing."

"God!" said the Inspector; and it was impossible to judge how he used the word. "What put you onto this finally, son?"

"Ann's dog, Beelzebub. Familiarly—Bub."

"Ann's *dog?*" His father gaped.

"Yes. After Perce was arrested. When I went over to see Archer. We were kidding around about the dog, and Archer was showing Ann and me how he was teaching it to do a somersault."

"Hold it, hold it," said the Inspector faintly. "A few seconds ago we were talking about the Old Testament."

"Exactly. That's it. Don't you see? I watched Archer show the dog off—lift up its front paws and flip it over backwards. *Backwards.* Something in my brain went—*snick!* clean as can be—and dropped into place. Talk about divine intervention. Something's been begging me for days to look—just look—and I'd see it. But I didn't, I didn't. Till Archer flipped the dog."

"Simmer down, Ellery," muttered the old man. "Try to make sense, for my sake. What's with this backwards-dog business?"

"Dog," said Ellery. "Backwards."

"Dog, backwards," repeated the Inspector. "Dog, backwards. D-o-g . . . g-o-d. G-o-d." And, suddenly, his lips clamped shut.

"God," said Ellery, nodding. He rose and took his father's empty glass and his own over to the bar. "That was it. It made me think, 'God.' And the next thing I knew, I was in the Old Testament, thinking 'Jehovah,' 'Yahweh.' Thinking JHWH. Thinking Y."

The Inspector was silent.

Fumbling with the ice, Ellery said, "Now Jehovah, Yahweh, was a member of no Trinity, was represented by no lambs, suffered no little children. He was an almighty vindictive deity. He meddled in individual lives. And He was always right because He *was.* In Genesis. Exodus. Remember Job. Think of what He did to Onan, to Lot's wife, to everybody in Noah's time.

"And now," said Ellery grimly, "imagine His intrusion into the here and now, into York Square. And let's say that you're Walt. Couldn't He have done these things as far as you, Walt, are concerned? Isn't it perfectly reasonable that He chose to choose you, Walt, as his instrument simply because He felt like it?"

Ellery handed his father the freshened highball, but the old man shook his head and set the glass down. "I'm still foggy on this, Ellery. I mean, what kind of mentality would conceive of pretending to be God Almighty, just to get that poor little slob Walt to do his dirty work?"

"Dad, you haven't been following." Ellery's eyes were quite bright. "No one *pretended* to be Yahweh. The writer of those letters *is* Yahweh."

"Oh, come on, now!" shouted the Inspector.

"In his own mind, to the best of his own devoutest belief and conviction, Y is exactly what he says he is. Walt has no monopoly on unshakable faith."

The old man thrashed about. "That's as wild a theory—"

"It is not," said Ellery with slow and chilling emphasis, "a theory, Dad. I can prove it. I'll go further. I'll take you to Him."

"Gosh," said the Inspector, but the sneer had an undernote of brute anger. "Meet Yahweh in person. I better change into my best suit."

"*He's* satisfied that he's Yahweh," said Ellery, unmoved. "Whether *you* think so or not is, I assure you, a matter of complete unconcern to him."

"I've had enough of this," snarled his father, jumping up. "I don't know what's got into you, Ellery, but I'm not going to sit here all day listening to a lot of mystical—mystical *boloney* mish-mash! Just tell me one thing: Who is he?"

"I've told you," said Ellery, positively luminous. "He's Yahweh."

"All *right!*" howled the old man. "There's some crazy thing you want to do—want *me* to do—I can tell by your eyes. We're going to have a fight about it. We'll wind up doing it. And you'll scare the devil into me!"

Ellery did not deny it. He folded his arms and waited.

Inspector Queen inhaled hugely. Then, in a patient—a more than patient—voice, he asked, "Ellery—son—what is it you want me to do?"

"Turn Walt loose again."

At which hell really broke loose.

There were four of them, crouched on the grimy fire escape outside Room 312 of the Hotel Altitude. Two of them were named Queen. Each of the others represented a round of the wild battle they had fought all afternoon and evening and up to this midnight moment, and which they were still fighting. The third man's presence was the result of the Inspector's last-ditch refusal to go on with any such harebrained and dangerous and disastrous scheme, because the Police Commissioner would never agree.

"Then invite him along," Ellery had said.

The fourth man was here as a result of the Commissioner's total objection that the D.A. wouldn't allow it. "Then let's invite him, too," the Queens had said, in one voice. To enlist co-workers of such substance had proved sound strategy; it handled every human obstacle of lesser weight, like jail wardens. Weightier obstacles were simply not informed; they could be presented with the *fait accompli* "that you've proved your point," the District Attorney had put it grimly, "or that somebody else can figure out three murders and a flubbed suicide on a fire escape." And besides, Ellery had pointed out, there was just not room enough on the fire escape for the Mayor, too. His Honor ran to bulk.

Ellery was inspired, exalted. He planned like a Metternich, he drove like a Legree.

Walt had been released. Someone had said something to him about "insufficient evidence," but he had hardly listened; release was no more than his expectation and due. He was taken to the prison hospital, given his clothes (in which $200 had been planted) and abruptly marched into a private room containing a bed containing Percival York.

Reports on this encounter could describe nothing of interest but a moment of suspended-animation stillness, Walt's specialty. Then they had led him out and turned him loose.

"That's why it has to work," Ellery had expounded in setting up the encounter. "Since we jumped him on the terrace he's been cooped up in a cell with only a Bible to read. Nobody's ever told him he failed to kill Percival York. Seeing Percival alive, his antlike mentality will perceive the unalterable necessity to finish the unfinished job. Still, he's Walt; and he won't know how to go about it. Unless and until he gets another letter. He has to have another letter. He'll get it."

Gill, the gnomelike manager of the Hotel Altitude, had been scooped up. His false teeth chittered and his big ears jerked. He didn't want trouble. Room 312 hadn't been cleaned, it was the maid's night off. Or no, there was a paying guest in 312. Or was there? And anyway, who's going to pay for the room? Faithfully promised the personal vendetta of Inspector Richard Queen and the vacuum-cleaner scrutiny of the Department of Fire Inspection, the Board of Health, the Commissioner of Licenses and the Morals Squad, Manager Gill was suddenly anxious to co-operate.

Walt was not followed. There was no need. He was watched. He was watched in ways that would have been the envy of the city, state, federal and international security forces which had once been assigned the nerve-twitching task of providing protection to Nikita Khrushchev and Fidel Castro during their simultaneous stay in New York City.

From the jail steps Walt had only two directions to choose between; both routes were congested with pedestrians, loungers holding up buildings, watchers from windows and watchers from cars, both parked and on the move.

Walt chose to go north. The men who had been deployed to the south were instantly redeployed, to intercept all possible random developments. Around the little handyman, as he oozed along, there was observably nothing out of the ordinary. But by his movements he unknowingly commanded the shifting and shuttling of a small army of men.

The equipment for Operation Walt was a policeman's delight. Ellery had urged the Commissioner to use a logistical maximum, cunningly justifying the whole, mad, awesome operation as not only the pursuit and capture of a vengeful deity but the equivalent of a high-level, top-secret emergency drill of the first importance. The Commissioner was charmed, and the police and citizens' radio bands soon set up an elbowing clamor of calls. Minute transistor sets relayed messages from one pedestrian to another, from the second pedestrian to a parked or moving car, from car to radio dispatch to Morse flasher and then back to pedestrian again.

Everything was collated and filtered and passed to the Commissioner's earplugs; checked and monitored and refiltered and cross-checked. Sets were pulled off emergency racks and found to contain dead batteries, or no batteries at all. Channel control crystals turned out to be mislabeled; and so on. There was not too much of this, however; and when all was in readiness everyone concerned granted that these equipment delinquencies might not have been discovered for years if not for Ellery Queen's Operation Walt. (Officially, of course, it was known as the Commissioner's Operation Walt.)

The Commissioner's dearest joy was the transistorized squealer, broadcasting on 27.215 megacycles (Band 21), fixed automatically by direction-finders on a whole echelon of mobile stations, and mounted—batteries and all, and all unbeknownst—in the heel of Walt's left shoe.

No, it could be said with confidence that they weren't about to lose John Henry Walt.

33. Checkmate

At first it seemed like much ado about very little, for Walt made no attempt to get lost; in the manner of the ant, he forged ahead as if activated by instinctive forces, without a backward or sidelong glance.

But at one point Walt turned a corner; and when the nearest watchers re-established visual contact they sensed a wariness in him, as if something had suddenly happened to alert his mechanic faculties. Now he occasionally glanced over his shoulder; he re-adjusted his carriage and his stride lengthened, as if to disguise himself. Had the robot become suspicious? It certainly seemed so; and the word, in various inflections, flashed hither and about, new orders were rapped, the lines tightened, reserve forces slipped in to take over from men whose recurrent faces might have caused Walt's sudden caution. The measures apparently had their effect; Walt became preoccupied, he began to hurry, his movements turned purposeful.

He went first to a chain drug store, where he purchased a cheap tablet of lined paper and some plain white envelopes.

He went next to a pawnshop (hair-raisingly, within four minutes of its closing) and came out with a second-hand portable typewriter.

He then stepped into a second drug store and put a coin into the slot of a stamp-dispensing machine.

And at twenty minutes past the eleventh night hour he came to rest on the dissolute sidewalk in front of the Hotel Altitude.

And, of all things, lit a cigarette.

He had bought a pack in the second drug store; they had

wondered about that. Walt did not smoke—at least, the Queens had never seen him smoke; the detectives on the case had never noted his smoking in their reports; no one in York Square had ever mentioned his smoking; and there was no evidence in his room above the garage that he was addicted to the habit.

Still, here he was on the sidewalk before the entrance to the Hotel Altitude, smoking with large, unhurried puffs; smoking, and watching through the plate-glass door the tiny desk with the tiny desk clerk behind it visible at the tiny end of his line of sight, like Alice looking down the rabbit-hole.

A signal was passed.

Gill, the manager, came round the end of the desk to stand in full view of the entrance; he stretched; he yawned; then he shuffled over to a door marked MEN and opened it and disappeared, the door closing behind him.

Walt immediately stopped smoking. He did not toss the cigarette into the gutter; he did not drop it and step on it. He did a rather curious thing: he crushed out its burning end between thumb and forefinger, not quickly, with no evidence of pain, but deliberately and thoroughly; and then, when he was satisfied that the cigarette was out, he tossed the butt over his shoulder with the oddest gesture of contempt and stepped forward and entered the Altitude.

This was the anxious time. Ellery had not been at all sure what Walt would do. Mr. Wye at his last departure had left the passkey to 312 at the desk; Walt had no key.

Eyes watched, ears listened, from everywhere.

He did not go to the desk and behind it, where in the cubicle plainly labeled 312 the tagged key lay in plain sight for his convenience. He did not even glance beyond, or even at, the desk. He strode smoothly and quietly and directly to the stairs.

Between the second and third floors he met a man coming down. At once Walt set the typewriter on the stair and stooped over his left shoe. When the man was gone Walt rose, picked up the machine and resumed his ascent.

At the third floor he made unhesitatingly for Room 312.

Here Ellery's reserve plan proved its efficacy. Before the door tin-figured 312, Walt set the typewriter down again and put his right hand in his pocket. When his hand emerged empty, he frowned. But then the frown cleared and he turned the knob and pushed, and the door swung inward into darkness, and he picked up the typewriter and walked into the darkness as if he had expected nothing less; and he shut the door and touched the light switch, evoking a low thin illumination from a little gooseneck lamp corded to the socket in the ceiling—it left the upper part of him in tantalizing gloom. The duplicate key they had inserted in the keyhole on the room side of the door Walt immediately turned, locking himself in. The miraculous appearance of the key he accepted with utter calmness.

On the fire escape outside 312's window Ellery gave a nervous cluck, and nodded. "Yes," he muttered. "Of course."

Room 312 was at the rear of the Hotel Altitude, so that its fire escape faced nothing but the grimy backs of loft and other business buildings, all untenanted and dark at this hour. They had nothing to fear from curious eyes.

Ellery crouched against the dirty brick wall, eye glued to the eyepiece of a magnifying periscope. His father, the District Attorney, the Commissioner were listening to reports in their earplugs; but now all sounds ceased, and as one man they turned to Ellery.

He nodded. "It's Walt."

"You sure this Y is meeting him here?" whispered the D.A.

"I'm sure."

"That's all right, then," said the Commissioner with satisfaction. The room was bugged; the tapes of recorders in adjacent and opposite rooms were winding.

"Get away!" said the Inspector swiftly. He had a periscopic device, too. Walt had laid down his typewriter and was approaching the window. The four men glued themselves to the wall, two to each side of the window.

Walt tried the window; it was stuck fast. After a moment he turned back. And this was a small triumph for Inspector Queen; it had been his notion to grease the window carefully with a silicone compound and install a quick-release lock, invisible from the room, on the fire-escape side.

"Watch this," said Ellery softly. He had his periscope back in place. The Inspector followed suit.

They had arranged the small night table at the foot of the

bed; the gooseneck lamp was standing on one corner of it. The position of the night lamp and the chair at which Y had sat had been predetermined by examination of impressions on the carpeting.

Walt set the typewriter on the little table and removed its cover. He placed the cover, the envelopes and the cheap tablet on the bed. Then he sat down at the table, his left profile to the window, and reached over to adjust the angle of the lamp. The light sprang strongly to his face.

Inspector Queen made a throaty noise. He straightened up, knuckled his eyes, then peered into the eyepiece once more. Finally he sat back on his heels and looked up at the others in the dim glow from the window.

And he whispered, "*That's not Walt.*"

The Commissioner stooped, and looked, and his tough cop's face rippled with shock.

"My God, Burt," he said to the District Attorney. "Look!"

The D.A.'s lips parted audibly; his jaw dropped; and when he shifted from the eyepiece he glanced at Ellery as if he had never seen Inspector Queen's son before. But Ellery merely bit down on his own teeth and kept watching the man in the room.

The man was reaching over now to the bed. He flipped the cover of the tablet open and removed the top sheet of paper. The Queens hastily adjusted the knurled brass rings of their eyepieces, got the field onto the blur that represented the sheet of paper and focused until they could see it sharply.

"The pale blue lines," muttered the Inspector. "The identical paper!"

The man in the chair slipped the sheet into the carriage of the portable and began adjusting it, apparently for exact alignment with the blue lines.

Choked the Inspector: "I'll be damned . . ."

"What, Dick, what?" asked the Commissioner excitedly.

But the old man's response was to his son. "So that's how you knew. A somersaulting dog, and thumbprints at the top corners of the Y letters!"

"It had to be that," nodded Ellery, without looking away. "From adjusting the paper on the machine so that it typed precisely on the blue lines. From doing it on line after line, because the spacing between the paper's blue line-spacing obviously didn't conform to the machine's line-spacing. The conclusion had to be: Whoever left all those thumbprints at the top corners of the letters typed the letters. Simple." And Ellery added in so bitterly low a tone that only his father heard him, "*Very* simple. It took me a mere three murders and an almost-fourth to figure it out."

And now the man who had been Walt was launched on his letter. He was typing with two fingers; steadily, evenly, rapidly unrolling a stream of words. At each succeeding line he stopped to realign the paper, as Ellery had predicted.

"What's he typing?" moaned the Inspector. "I can't make it out—"

"I can." And Ellery read off the words as they appeared on the blue-lined sheet:

"My Dear Walt:

"You have been all I asked you to be. You have done all I asked you to do. But, because of developments beyond your understanding, our last task remains uncompleted.

"I assure you out of the depths of my admiration and approval of you, My Dear Walt, that this temporary failure is not of your making, and I absolve you of blame.

"There must come now a time of waiting.

"All things in their season.

"Be observant, My Dear Walt.

"Be patient, and be yourself.

"He's stopped typing," Ellery mumbled.

"I think," said the Commissioner, "that's enough. Don't you, Burt?"

The District Attorney's lips were set in a long thin line. "Plenty enough."

"Okay," said the Inspector, "let's take him."

The Commissioner spoke a word into the grille of his little transceiver.

Ellery put a thumb on the window-lock and the other fingers at the bottom edge of the sash, and he gathered his legs under him.

Out in the hall a man drifted, like smoke in a draft, from the room directly opposite to the door of 312, placed his fingers on the jamb and yanked. The entire doctored jamb swung outward, bringing the strike-plate and lock-bolt with it.

The door swung open at the exact second that the window slammed up and Ellery dived into the room.

Electrically quick, the typist's face flashed toward Ellery; the man half rose.

"Hold it," said the detective in the doorway. The face in the light turned toward the detective slowly, slowly and phlegmatically glanced at the revolver in his hand and seemed amused. The man got to his feet and deliberately faced Ellery.

"If I raise my hand, of course," he said in a voice so deeply and surely unlike Walt's that Ellery's scalp crept, "you will cease to exist."

There was a long silence. At the window behind Ellery the faces of Inspector Queen, the Police Commissioner and the D.A. were plaster masks. The detective in the doorway, now joined by two others, began a movement; Ellery checked it with the slightest gesture.

And in the silence they all took in the strange man's imperial stance; his bright, sharp eyes; his almost lipless mouth.

"Please be good enough to tell me," Ellery said with the softest courtesy, "why the Yorks had to die?"

"For the sins of the father," intoned the man at the table.

"Not the fath*ers*?" Ellery stressed the sibilant.

"I have said it."

Ellery bowed his head. "Thank you," he said. At the slight sound of the Inspector preparing to put his leg over the window sill, Ellery casually put a hand behind his back and with it made a peremptory gesture. "We will meet again," he said with deference.

"If I . . . will . . . iiiii . . ."

The *it* dribbled off into silence. And the bright, sharp eyes dulled and blunted and opened wide and opened wider until they were quite round. And the almost lipless mouth began to materialize, to inflate, to become fleshy and wet. And the imperial set of the shoulders wilted, rounding them. And the corded demarcations of jawbone and cheek muscles and neck tendons all softened and sagged and ran together.

And there was Walt.

"Hello, Walt," said Ellery.

"Mr. Queen." And there was Walt's flat, unencumbered voice. The round eyes blinked past Ellery to the window, took in the Commissioner, the District Attorney, Inspector Queen, returned to Ellery.

"Walt, we'd like you to come back with us," said Ellery.

A smile spread the slack lips. A gentle, happy, I-have-secrets-I-am-loved smile.

"Yes," said Walt.

"Dr. Morton Prince," said Ellery a century later. "He pioneered in this thing. But it didn't become general knowledge until those two psychiatrists, Doctors Thigpen and Cleckley, published their remarkable report in *The Three Faces of Eve*, and Evelyn Lancaster herself followed it up, with the help of James Poling, in *The Final Face of EVE*. So I suppose there's hardly anyone who hasn't heard of multiple personality."

Inspector Queen was still incapable of coherent speech.

"I imagine," Ellery chuckled, "that the Commissioner and the D.A. would still be debating whether to put me under psychiatric observation at Bellevue if they hadn't seen with their own eyes how Walt slipped from his second personality back into his first. I don't know why two disassociated personality manifestations in the same body should be so tough to credit. Evelyn Lancaster had three before developing her final one. Dr. Prince documents as many as five in one body, none of them knowing the existence of the others."

The Inspector cleared his throat and found his voice at last. "Poor devil. How do you handle a thing like this? I mean legally?"

"The psychiatrists and the lawyers will have to battle this one out, Dad. I don't think there's any doubt that in the end Walt will be 'protected,' as his *alter ego* Y promised. He'll be studied and treated and taken care of for the rest of his life. And who knows? Maybe he'll develop a third personality, as socially responsible as Walt and Mr. Y can never be."

The Inspector shook his head. "I guess I'll never really *believe* it. It's too much like black magic. That little schmo Walt and that egomaniac Y in the same body!"

"Well, Dr. Prince and others have pointed out that alternate personalities are most often extremely opposite expressions of the bottled-up ego. In one kind of dual personality the ultra-prim, teetotaling spinster will abruptly produce a gin-loving party girl. Robert Louis Stevenson instinctively made Dr. Jekyll the embodiment of goodness, and Mr. Hyde just about as evil as a man could be.

"So here's Walt. It wouldn't be easy to locate another human being who scores nearer zero in looks, intelligence, wit, social and economic standing and what-have-you. It's no surprise, really, that he produces an alternate personality who's very close to infinity."

His father shuddered and was silent again. But then he looked up and asked, "And you really think Walt didn't know he was writing those letters to himself?"

"The head boys will probably have an answer for that. It's happened before, Dad. As I understand it, down deep at the heart of such cases is a demanding hunger, a kind of dictatorial want. Walt *wanted* God to like him and send him messages, therefore he *didn't want* to know who wrote them. Or rather, he'd want not to know."

"And why the Yorks, son? Why did Walt—I mean Y!—pick on the Yorks?"

Ellery twisted his nose thoughtfully. "I really had no idea until the other night—until 'Y,' before he reverted to Walt, gave me that curious answer when I asked him the same question."

"He said something about the sins of the fathers."

"No," Ellery said, "what he said was 'of the father.' Singular. When you stop to think of it, that's a singularly revealing statement. The only father in this game was Nathaniel York, Senior—whose son became so fed up with old Nat's dictatorial ways that he threw up everything, lit out and never came back.

"Dad, I think Walt-Y made an identification in a weird sort of way with young York, Nathaniel Junior, whose jungle death Nathaniel Senior could never get himself to believe. Remember that the old man's will left everything to Junior if he should turn up alive. Walt-Y, I think, took upon himself not only young Nat's grievances but also his right to the inheritance. In a sense, Walt-Y took upon himself young Nat."

"Could be," the Inspector grumbled. "Far as I'm concerned, son, in this case anything could be."

"Including the possibility that Walt actually knew young Nathaniel."

The old man stared.

"It might pay, in fact, to do some backtracking along the trail that ended with Junior's death. You might find that his path crossed Walt's somewhere, that the two might even have been friends. This would have to have been, of course, before Walt broke into two personality pieces. It would clear up a lot, Dad. Why Walt gravitated to this vicinity. Why he drifted—if he did—into the Walt-young Nat syndrome. Who Walt really is, for that matter—or, rather, who he originally was—and where he came from and so on. But I'm pretty sure that somehow, somewhere, Walt knew Nathaniel York, Junior."

Ellery shrugged. "For no reason at all, by the way, I once looked up that birth date chiseled into Junior's plaque in York Park. April 20, 1924. Know when that fell, Dad? On Easter.

"So meek Walt gradually talked himself into inheriting the earth—began to feel it was his due—then began to be outraged that the York cousins were getting it instead.

"What may well have tipped him overside was the discovery, one time when he was poring over his Bibles, that JHW—his own initials—constituted part of the Tetragrammaton. For Walt it was quite logical for 'part' of the Tetragrammaton to become 'most' of it, and finally 'all' of it. That may well have been the exact point in time when Mr. Y made his bow. JHWH. Jehovah. Yahweh. Y.

"And then," said Ellery, squinting through his cigarette smoke at his silent father, "and then Yahweh went to work with a vengeance, as you might say."

Ellery got up to refill his coffee cup, and the Inspector's. Neither had drunk anything stronger than strong coffee since the phantasmagoria in Room 312 of the Altitude.

"So now we have God-and-Nat-identified-Walt brooding over the Yorks of York Square," Ellery resumed. "They had, or would have, so much; and what they would have was rightfully his. Or maybe Yahweh's sense of justice was outraged. A lot of quite sane monopersonality people wouldn't hesitate to charge that not one of the Yorks deserved the treasure. Myra and Percival in particular. Even Robert and Emily, on the at least arguable ground that neither had the slightest notion of the right way to spend that kind of loot. That used to be Percival's point about Robert and Emily, remember? By the way, Dad, is he suing the city?"

"Nah," said the Inspector. "Percival is saintly now. An honest mistake, he calls it; he's ready to forgive and forget."

"Forgive," murmured Ellery, "and ye shall receive?"

"I'll admit," said his father dryly, "that the thought has occurred to me. Retaliatory forgiveness. Perce may have turned over a whole set of new leaves, but there's a lot still in print on the flip side."

"What do you mean?"

"He's forgiven his blonde, too."

"No!"

"Yes. And a sickening sight it was, too. After she read in the papers about his attempted suicide, she camped at the jail until they let her in just to get rid of her. She cried salty tears all over the prison infirmary, and Perce patted her shoulder in a sad and fatherly way and told her it was okay, he understood." The old man grimaced. "Ellery, I wanted to set her down on her fat rump for coming to me the way she did with that out-and-out lie about Percy 'confiding' in her how he'd talked Walt into doing his dirty work. But there's nothing I can do—her statement wasn't made in court or under oath."

"How did she know anybody persuaded Walt to do anything? We sat on that pretty hard."

"A shrewd guess. There's some sort of brain under that mop of hair dye. She lay awake nights thinking it up, to get even with Perce for giving her the boot."

"So now they'll live happily ever after?"

"Guess again," chuckled the Inspector.

"Don't tell me," said Ellery, his cup in midair, "Perce has another doll already!"

"Yump. I was the one brought 'em together. Suggested they could help each other."

"*Miss Sullivan?*"

"That's my boy," nodded the old man, grinning. "I'll bet you didn't know there's going to be—actually going to be—a rehabilitation center near the city that'll be the biggest thing since Father Damien invented leprosy."

"And I'll bet," Ellery grinned back, "that Miss Sullivan gets York Square, too."

"No takers—she does. With Mrs. Schriver thrown in, who's so smitten by the new Percival York she's ready to follow him to hell and back."

To hell and back . . .

Even aside from esoteric terrors like multiple personality, the human mind was an awesome thing. There were apparently key words in key situations, a chance encounter of all the right ingredients.

Ellery sat in silence and thought how, throughout this mad case, while the answer eluded him and he chased it like a cat after a moth, a hidden power had been trying to call it to his attention.

How early had it been that Ann Drew refused to tell him why the puppy-dog was named Beelzebub? How close had he been then, and how much closer that later time when he had turned whimsy into a whip? At any stage in the game Tom Archer could have—would have—told him, had Ellery had the wit to ask.

To hell and back . . .

Beelzebub: the Devil. Archer had wickedly named the dog for the Devil because the Devil is God's opposite . . . and "dog" is "God" spelled backwards.

Well, Ellery thought (and he smiled), perhaps it was too much to expect, even from himself.

"What, Dad?" he said. "I wasn't listening."

"I said, so that ends your game. The one you weren't going to play."

"Yes."

It seemed so long ago. And all of it seemed to have happened to a driveling stranger with a pure bone head. A stranger who had felt he must go on to something else because technology had deprived him of opponents. Such nonsense. Madness, or aberrance—or, for that matter, "that rare disorder" from which John Henry Walt suffered—were outside the jurisdiction of the mechanical equalizers. Someone had to be standing by for such times as the Devil possessed the Player on the Other Side.

"Dad," he said out of his reverie. "Do you remember the Huxley quotation? 'The chess-board is the world, the pieces are the phenomena of the universe, the rules of the game are what we call the laws of Nature. The player on the other side—' "

"What?" said the Inspector, roused from a reverie of his own.

" 'The player on the other side is hidden from us. We know that his play is always fair, just, and patient.' When I first read that," Ellery frowned, "I couldn't buy the 'fair, just, and patient' part. Now . . . Well, I mean, who's to judge fairness, justice? Fairness and justice really aren't absolute, are they? They're conditioned by time and place. They emerge as a function of the rules; what *he* thinks they mean has to affect what *I* think they mean. So . . . I've been standing myself in a corner and memorizing the rest of what Huxley said."

"What was that?" asked his father.

" 'But also we know, to our cost, that he never overlooks a mistake, or makes the smallest allowance for ignorance.' "

"To our cost," said the Inspector thoughtfully.

"It reminds me," Ellery went on, "of something Rimbaud, the French poet, once wrote to a friend: '*Je est un autre.*' Not *je suis*, you'll note. '*Je* est *un autre*'—'I *is* someone else.' Sounds like something out of Joel Chandler Harris. Until you start mouthing it. Then, all of a sudden, it becomes: 'I . . . is-someone-else.' "

But it was too much for the old man, and he stopped listening.

"It's a tough one," Ellery reflected aloud. "It calls on the head. I is someone else . . . Then I ran across Archibald MacLeish's interpretation of Rimbaud's line. MacLeish interprets it as meaning: 'One is played *upon*, not player.' One is played upon, not player," he repeated, savoring it. "Tasty, isn't it?"

But—*to our cost*, thought the Inspector; and he let his eyelids droop, the better to see the board, and the taken pieces lying, discards, in the margins: the bronze plaque to the living memory of Nathaniel York, Junior, kept loving-bright by the machines of Walt's hands; the demolished head that had belonged to Robert York; the country dreams of Emily York, thrown into the mandibles of the great steel underground worm; the little presleep nip of juniper juice in Myra York's little pink mouth, and the instant quiet flash of agony; and, off by itself, in a strange terrain, a place of distortions seen through another dimension . . . off by itself the checkmated king, writhing with hideous life. And, in some hideous way, happy. All for the lack of a bit of regard here, a warming hand there, a spoonful of loving concern in a critical hour.

"To our cost," Inspector Queen sighed.

About the Author

The team of Frederic Dannay and Manfred B. Lee—who, as everyone knows, are Ellery Queen—has written fifty-two books, including those first published under the pseudo-pseudonym of Barnaby Ross, and has edited forty-seven more. A conservative estimate has placed their total sales in various editions at more than 50,000,000 copies. And millions of listeners agreed when *TV Guide* awarded the Ellery Queen program its National Award as the best mystery show of 1950. Ellery Queen has won five annual "Edgars" (the national Mystery Writers of America awards similar to the "Oscars" of Hollywood), including the Grand Master award of 1960, and both the silver and gold "Gertrudes" awarded by Pocket Books.

Ellery Queen's most recent successes are *The Finishing Stroke* and *The Player on the Other Side.* He is internationally known as an editor—*Ellery Queen's Mystery Magazine* celebrated its twenty-second anniversary in 1963—and his library of first editions contained the finest collection of books of detective short stories in existence.

These facts about Queen may account for the remark by Anthony Boucher, in his profile of Manfred B. Lee and Frederic Dannay, that "Ellery Queen *is* the American detective story."